He knelt before her chair

"You do take care of yourself when you're flying, don't you?" Dan pleaded softly for reassurance.

Kellie smiled. "Of course I do. I've got better ways to spend my time than filling out accident reports."

Her lighthearted retort didn't rid him of the dread he felt knowing that Kellie wouldn't be the one filing the report if her chopper went down. But he knew it was all the relief he was going to get right now.

"Can I have your solemn oath?"

"Solemn oath," She traced an X over her heart.

"I was looking for a more—" he hesitated pointedly "—adult way to seal the bargain." He leaned closer, sliding his hands up her thighs.

"Any way you want to seal it," she answered breathlessly.

ABOUT THE AUTHOR

Writing has always been in Peg Sutherland's blood. She wrote her first novel in the third grade, "a cute love story that was completely unpublishable!" she says. Peg went on to become a newspaper reporter and editor before trying her hand at romance fiction. *Behind Every Cloud* is her first Superromance and she's been flying high ever since!

Behind Every Cloud

PEG SUTHERLAND

Harlequin Books

TORONTO • NEW YORK • LONDON
AMSTERDAM • PARIS • SYDNEY • HAMBURG
STOCKHOLM • ATHENS • TOKYO • MILAN

Published April 1990

ISBN 0-373-70398-8

Thanks to Brenda English,
communications manager at Fairfax Hospital
in Falls Church, Virginia,
and the members of the helicopter ambulance service
at Charlotte Memorial Hospital
for sharing their time and knowledge.

CHAPTER ONE

FIGHTING TO SHUT OUT the sounds of feverish activity that had filled the cockpit for most of the fifteen-minute flight, Kellie zeroed in on the landing pad.

A smooth landing. That's all she had to worry about now. The semiconscious child wasn't her concern.

Knowing that didn't ease the knot in her stomach.

The stark concrete and white of the inner-city campus and the older brick buildings that made up Birmingham's medical district faded from focus. Kellie Adams's only concern now was lowering the helicopter onto the cement square in the middle of one of the grassy patches that had survived the rapid-fire expansion near the University of Alabama in Birmingham.

Kellie battled the urge to pick up speed and get the chopper on the ground. *Smooth,* she coached herself, her eyes darting quickly in all directions to spot any last-minute obstacles. *Take it smooth and easy.*

"We'll take the kid inside as soon as you kill the engine," Margo shouted through the crackling headset.

The words confirmed Kellie's fears that the youngster, whose crumpled body had been left on the side of a rural road by a hit-and-run driver, was close to death. Only when every second counted would flight nurse Margo Browning rush to unload a patient before the helicopter blades stopped whirring dangerously.

This was one of those times.

"We're gonna need more than speed with this one," interrupted another, deeper voice.

Kellie's upper lip prickled with nervous perspiration at the words of Chip West, the other nurse in the back of the chopper. Her fist choked the control stick. Damn these last few seconds!

"Can it, Chip!" Margo snapped as the gentle bump signaled they were on the ground. "The trauma team's waiting at the door."

"Oh, no, they're not!" Kellie's mouth went dry when she spotted four workers pushing a gurney toward the landing pad. Terrific! Now all she had to worry about was whether these overeager heroes would get too close to a chopper blade and need stretchers of their own.

Hearing Margo swear impatiently, Kellie turned to catch sight of the dark, sturdily built nurse hitting the concrete without waiting the interminable two minutes necessary for the engine to cool before it could be shut off. Chip was right behind her.

Kellie's blood pounded as she listened to the steady thump of the engine, punctuated by the child's incoherent babbling. The child had moved in and out of convulsive consciousness throughout the flight, never quite able to escape her pain.

As trying as the flight had been, Kellie was even more on edge now, with the trauma team scurrying around the chopper—a dangerous practice that was strictly forbidden.

Blotting the perspiration from her upper lip with the back of her hand, Kellie watched through her Plexiglas bubble, fearful for the young child whose hold on life was so precarious.

Stooping in the forty-mile-an-hour wind created by the chopper blades, the emergency workers scrambled to secure the thrashing child on the stretcher so she could be wheeled to the building without exacerbating her injuries or dislodging the intravenous tube Margo had inserted during the flight.

By the time the trauma crew was rushing the stretcher inside, Kellie was ready to kill the engine.

She was also ready to kill whoever had ignored regulations and permitted emergency-room personnel on the landing pad.

Lowering her head to avoid the blades that spun erratically out of control as they eased to a stop, Kellie dashed after the stretcher. As soon as the child was safely on her way to the operating room, Kellie wanted an answer.

As she neared the gurney and kept pace one stride behind, Kellie's anger over the broken rule faded to the back of her mind. One of the workers, a tall, sandy-haired man whose brow furrowed anxiously, leaned close to the child as the others pushed her stretcher and frantically exchanged information about the extent of her injuries. While Kellie watched, the broad-shouldered attendant used the few precious moments on the way to surgery to calm the child.

"It's going to be all right, sweetheart," he whispered, his voice a soft, deep murmur. Kellie trembled, almost feeling the soothing strength of his fingers brushing the girl's damp cheek.

When the child mumbled something, he leaned closer still, and Kellie listened with him. For the first time, one of the child's cries made sense.

"Mommy?" The limp, feverish mumble tore at something vulnerable in Kellie's heart.

"She'll be here soon, sweetheart."

Kellie saw the child's almost instant response to his reassuring words. For the first time since Chip and Margo had loaded her into the chopper, the child no longer whimpered, no longer writhed feverishly. Even in her semiconscious state, she craved reassurance.

When the attendant spoke again, Kellie wondered if she imagined the tremble in his voice. "First, these people are going to make you feel better."

As the child's moans quieted, the fair-haired man turned to the others, a trim mustache barely hiding the stiff set of his lips. Anger turned his square jaw to granite as he interrupted their exchange of information. Kellie's heart lurched to a halt at the change in him.

"Let's move this parade a little faster," he hissed, lowering his voice so the half-conscious girl couldn't hear. "And see if you can avoid scaring the hell out of her while you're at it!"

Margo bristled for a fraction of a second, then shifted into high gear. "He's right. Let's haul it!"

Kellie wheeled and rushed back outside to the helicopter. Later would be plenty of time to find out who had given the trauma crew its bonehead orders. Right now, she had no desire to tangle with them. Better to wait until the stress level had dipped below the justifiable homicide range.

Pulling her short leather flight jacket tighter around her, Kellie shivered in the late-afternoon sunshine of the first crisp day of fall. The slight chill in the air should have felt good after summer's oppressive heat. Today, it felt bleak.

Kellie's pulse still pounded furiously as she wondered if the girl, who looked no more than five or six, would make it.

Grabbing the canvas covers used to tie down the ends of the helicopter blades, Kellie felt her knees weaken as she recalled the intensity in the attendant's touch, as if he were willing the child to take comfort from his ministrations. A whisper of a breeze ruffled the short, tawny curls at the back of Kellie's neck. She shivered again, despite the nervous perspiration still dotting her upper lip.

In a heart-stopping moment of irrational fear, Kellie thought about another little girl, this one a gawky six-year-old with unruly curls the color of sand—her own Carrie.

Carrie was safe at her dad's house now, another day of school behind her. Nevertheless, the irrational fear tightened its grip on Kellie. It could just as easily have been Carrie lying there on a stretcher, broken and afraid, crying for her mother.

Kellie grappled for control of her shaky insides as she finished tying down the blades and walked to the rear of the craft for a routine check of the oil level.

"Cool your jets, girl." Her voice, deceptively lighthearted, helped check her emotions.

Getting caught up in the stories of the critically ill or injured patients she helped transport to the hospital's trauma center wasn't on her agenda, today or any day. As a matter of fact, the day she started crying every time a heart stopped en route to the hospital was the day she went back to working "eye-in-the-sky" traffic reports and transporting busy executives across the Southeast.

You may have forgotten what a drag that was, she chided herself, recalling the days of rising before dawn and working long past dark. She hadn't minded the work as much as she had minded the days when she saw her daughter only long enough to fix her breakfast or kiss her good-night.

Kellie knew when she started this job that if she let her emotions gain control, it would jeopardize her ability to function in an emergency. Flying choppers was dangerous enough, as her ex-husband never failed to remind her, in a city where air traffic grew heavier every day. But mistakes were easier in tense situations. And there was no room for mistakes in a chopper cockpit.

When Kellie had come on board almost a year ago to help Birmingham Memorial plan its air-ambulance service, she had been grateful she no longer answered to Brian Adams. It sometimes seemed as if her ex-husband had been playing big brother all her life, telling her what to do and when to do it. Even after their marriage had dissolved, almost four years earlier, he hadn't stopped trying to tell her what kind of mother to be and what their daughter needed.

He had really hit the roof when she took the job at Birmingham Memorial.

"How in hell do you expect to take care of our daughter?" Brian had asked, his icy blue eyes and his biting tone clear indications that he thought her decision to take the job was another example of her childish fascination with flying. "You've got to grow up someday, Kellie, and stop playing air cowboy."

"I'll take care of Carrie the same way I always have," she had countered, the familiar tightening in her jaws giving fair warning that her temper was slipping out of control.

"Maybe joint custody makes it too hard for you to play at being a pilot," he said in the same voice he used when he explained to Carrie why she couldn't eat dessert before her vegetables. Kellie didn't like the tone any better when he used it on their daughter. "We could always ask the courts to give me permanent custody. Then you'd have plenty of time for flying."

That was when she lost her temper....

Kellie shook off the galling memories as she hoisted the canvas bags of medical supplies to be replenished, then roped off the helicopter pad.

Chip was already slumped in one of the swivel chairs in the air-ambulance office, his head flung back, eyes closed, arms dangling at his sides. She tossed the medical bags into his lap, but he didn't budge.

"We made it with the patient, but I think we lost one of our crew," Kellie quipped as she searched for her coffee mug among the clutter of folders and newspapers on the counter. When she found the bright red World's Greatest Mom mug, she poured coffee from the large, stainless steel pot that kept her fueled during her shift.

An exaggerated groan from Chip followed her to a cushioned bench. Propping her long, well-muscled legs on the counter directly across from her and resting her head against an oversize county wall map, Kellie took a cautious sip of the coffee. Ugh! Only lukewarm. She wrinkled her nose in distaste, then turned back to Chip, whose only movement had been to sink his lean frame even deeper into the chair.

Kellie massaged the stiff muscles in her neck with a free hand. Chip was a chronic complainer, but his reputation for having a cool head in a crisis had earned him one of the eight nursing slots on the helicopter crew. And most of Chip's grousing was good-natured.

Kellie had grown close to him, and the other ten crew members, in the short six months since the air-ambulance service took its first flight. The intensity of their work, which forced them to face life-and-death situations together every day, brought them closer more quickly than most co-workers.

It also made that closeness essential—they had to perform well as a group because their work held more danger than most other jobs. To build on that team spirit, Kellie had intentionally established four teams, each with two nurses and one pilot, making substitutions only when illness or vacation interfered.

"Not ready for another flight, I take it?" Kellie took another sip of tepid coffee, wondering why she always seemed to be the one who ended up making a fresh pot.

"No more," Chip mumbled. "I'll be old before my time."

"Too late. It's already your time, old man."

Chip grunted at the gibe, one of many he suffered as the oldest staffer on the flight crew.

"That's what they said when I asked for this assignment. Too much stress for someone my age." Chip snorted his derision, but he continued to take deep, calming breaths. "Forty-five is a great age, babycakes. Besides, yours is coming. When you're my age, you'll be planning Carrie's wedding and wondering where all the gray hair came from."

"If I'm planning Carrie's wedding in fourteen years, I'll know exactly where the gray hair came from. I hope she's safely in college at that age." Kellie jumped up and reached over to rumple Chip's mop of thick, graying hair. "So what's your excuse, old man?"

"Kids like you who won't give me time to recuperate." Eyes still closed as he tried to calm his nerves, Chip grinned weakly.

"So recuperate already. I'm going upstairs to log in this flight. Tell Margo to holler when she wants to go refuel. We've got plenty of time before second shift takes over at seven."

At the door, Kellie turned back. "Who was that attendant helping with the little girl? He's new."

"I don't know him, but what a grouch!" Knowing Kellie's notorious lack of interest in men, Chip opened one eye suspiciously. "Why? I didn't think you went for the type who barked orders and expected everyone else to snap to."

"No reason. Tell Margo to give a yell."

Kellie took the steps two at a time, promising herself to look up the new man on the trauma team soon. Maybe he could tell her who'd issued the orders for them to wheel out to the helicopter while the engine was still running; she had to put a quick stop to that kind of risk taking. No emergency room hotshot was going to cause a disaster around her chopper if she had anything to say about it.

Besides, she also wanted to tell him she wished they all had the courage to give as much warmth to the people who came in on stretchers as he had to that little girl.

And it would definitely take courage, she acknowledged as she entered the small apartment where the pilots catnapped on their twelve-hour shifts. *Coming face-to-face with so much emotion takes more courage than I have,* she thought, blaming her brief marriage to Brian for her bad habit of hiding her feelings.

A quick quip and a ready smile were much better ways to handle life's little ulcers, she told herself, catching sight of her daughter's laughing face in the framed photo on the apartment desk where she sometimes did her paperwork. It was wedged between the hospital bowling-league trophy Andy had won the month before and a photo of Jack's smiling young family.

Kellie shivered again, wishing her six months with Carrie didn't always rush by so quickly. Now, for the next six months, she would spend only every other weekend with her daughter. The days until spring, she knew, would be long and cold and lonely.

CHIP'S HEART continued to race long after Kellie disappeared upstairs. Long after the deep breathing and the darkness behind his closed lids should have helped him calm the thundering in his chest, Chip continued to feel as if he'd just finished the last agonizing steps in a marathon road race.

Knowing what he had to do next did nothing to help him slow the furious pace of his pulse.

When the pharmacy technician took a break at five-fifteen, Chip should be able to slip into the pharmacy without being seen. That was only ten minutes away.

He forced himself to sit still for eight minutes.

He forced himself once again to remember what it had been like when he came home from his job bagging groceries after high school. He would toss his books onto the kitchen table, then walk quietly past the living room, where his father dozed in front of the TV, his robe rumpled, his pills within easy reach. The smell of sickness had settled over the house, a scent that had eventually seeped into every corner of the small Virginia home where Chip grew up.

Slowly opening his eyes, Chip dragged himself out of his chair and headed out the door.

His father's gray, sunken face was the only incentive he needed to get him past his fear of discovery as he slipped into the pharmacy.

"LIFT-OFF!" The laughter in Kellie's voice at her ritualistic start to every flight was infectious. Margo chuckled from her seat behind the pilot as they took off for the airport to refuel.

Kellie knew their spirits were soaring in reaction to the tough flight with the hit-and-run victim. Emergency-room work was gut wrenching, Margo had told her many times, even when you weren't cooped up in a four-by-five compartment with a patient who could die any minute. Being in the air offered no escape from the trauma. But they all had to keep the pressure capped or risk blowing the job—which meant losing a life.

"Let's keep it in this solar system, Captain." The dry humor in Margo's voice was the perfect match for her square shoulders, slim hips, no-nonsense cap of short black ringlets and russet skin. She was the quintessential head nurse—as knowledgeable as any doctor, level-headed, but with plenty of compassion lurking just below the surface.

Kellie was one of the few people besides Chip who knew that Margo's sharp tongue had been earned the hard way, in one of Birmingham's housing projects near the heart of downtown during the violent, volatile sixties. As a child, Margo had been a front-row spectator to the racial struggle that had brought the city to national notoriety.

Nursing had been Margo's way out, and now she was driving her own seventeen-year-old daughter hard to earn a college scholarship so she could take yet another step away from the ghetto.

"It's been a rough day." Kellie joked as they passed over an older neighborhood that had declined as the nearby airport grew. "What say we head for the lake? Mom'll fix us some lemonade."

"No way, gal. Not without Chip. He'd have our hides if we played hooky without him. Besides, he needs the R and R worse than we do."

Kellie nodded her agreement, forgetting for the moment that Margo was behind her, barricaded from view. The helicopter had been specially modified, not only to make room for thousands of dollars' worth of lifesaving equipment, but to isolate the pilot from the activity in the small craft. Even the copilot's seat, which would have been to Kellie's left, had been removed to make room for the stretcher.

"How about if we buzz the campus and see if any guys are catching some rays?" Kellie mimicked Jack, the second-shift pilot, whose favorite summer pastime had been scouting for women sunbathing on rooftops at the city's universities.

"Headlights are the only rays they'll be catching this hour of the day." They peered down at the late-afternoon traffic, now bumper-to-bumper on the freeway. A few cars had already turned on their lights in the gray gloom of approaching dusk. "How about if we just refuel this crate and take her home before the new headhunter gets us for joyriding on company time?"

"Spoilsport." Kellie spent a few minutes on the radio, getting clearance from the tower at the airport, then checking in with hospital dispatch. "What headhunter?"

"Where have you been, girl? They've hired somebody new for the executive suite." Margo couldn't disguise her disdain for hospital administrators who called the shots from the comfort of their offices.

"How do you always get the inside skinny about what's going on, and I'm always the last to know?"

"I keep telling you, drop by the Medicine Chest for a little after-hours board meeting. That's where you find out what's really going on at Memorial."

"And all the other hospitals, from what I hear," Kellie added.

She seldom stopped at the neighborhood tavern that had become the favorite watering hole for the thousands who worked in Birmingham's medical district, although she had found it refreshingly friendly and unlike most lounges. Doctors, nurses, technicians and other medical workers mingled in an atmosphere that was free not only of the professional differences that separated them during their working hours, but also of the hunt-and-be-hunted atmosphere that made most bars unappealing to Kellie.

"Maybe now that Carrie's with her dad for a while, I'll have more time." Kellie's lackluster tone revealed that she wasn't looking forward to the time on her hands for the next six months. Abruptly she changed the subject. "What do you know about our new big shot?"

"He's cleaned house at hospitals all over the country. At least, that's the story. Ruthless with a capital *R*."

"He ought to start with the clown who sent the trauma team out to meet us today," Kellie shot back. "By the way, Margo, who was the new guy? The one with the mustache?"

"Oh, him. He really lit into us, didn't he?" Like most people who worked under extreme pressure, Margo wasn't offended when that pressure erupted into gruffness from time to time. "His name is Don. Or Dan. I saw it on his name tag but can't remember. I haven't met him yet." Then, as Chip had, Margo suddenly turned suspicious. "Why so interested?"

"Purely professional. He was so good with the kid, I admired his style."

"Since when are you so interested in bedside manners?" Margo delivered her sly innuendo as the chopper started its gradual drop to the refueling station at the airport.

"Not in your lifetime, Margo."

KELLIE STARED at the ceiling and shifted once again—about the fiftieth time in the past quarter hour that she had wriggled into yet another uncomfortable position on the twin-size cot they tried to pass off as a bed in the hospital apartment.

As head pilot, Kellie insisted that Jack, Andy and Frank rest during their twelve-hour shifts. Usually she hated even trying to follow that regulation herself. But tonight she was working a half shift for Jack, so she was attempting to grab some rest.

Keeping still was often more exhausting for Kellie than letting her hyperactive body run at top speed. Without the paperwork she always had as head pilot and the time she was putting into helping with the hospital's charity carnival, waiting for the flights would have been maddening.

Fidgeting into another position on the too-short bed, she thought of the trip to the grocery store she needed to make before the weekend. Carrie would spend the two days with her, so a refrigerator well stocked with frozen fruit pops, fresh grapes and orange juice was a must.

And Oscar needed a bath. Except that the oversize mongrel must have buried the hose with his bones after the last fiasco. She hadn't seen the hose since the day she tried to bathe the eight-month-old Lab with the help of her sister and daughter. Everyone had ended up wet—except Oscar.

Kellie closed her eyes tightly, willing her racing mind to slow down so she could relax. Instead the weekend ahead popped in to fill the void. Picnicking at her parents' cabin at the lake was as close as she came to allowing herself a lazy day. Although with a six-year-old to keep tabs on, a family outing was often anything but lazy.

Her sister, Rachael, had pointed out that it might be the last good weekend for sailing and sunning. Today's cool, crisp weather meant that football would soon dominate Saturday afternoons in Alabama, where the college game was the ruling passion. Kellie only hoped the chill in the air didn't mean that her Saturday at the lake would be spoiled by dreary weather.

Unable to stand her self-imposed inactivity any longer, Kellie jumped up to flip on the overhead light. Looking around the room for something to occupy her attention, she caught a glimpse of herself in the mirror over the sink.

Running a hand through short, golden curls that were always tousled anyway, she splashed water on her face and looked down in disdain at the tan-and-green jumpsuit that was her flight uniform. The soft cotton blend clung to every generous inch. Even if she didn't have to weigh in at the beginning of every shift to make sure the flight was under weight capacity, she could hide only so many extra pounds in the jumpsuit.

She pondered the merits of a diet soda versus an ice-cream sandwich as she eyed her unruly hair in the mirror. A fear of gaining so much weight that she would lose her job was her best inducement to count calories.

Even that fear couldn't have saved her voluptuousness from crossing the line into plumpness if it wasn't for the fact that she couldn't sit still more than two minutes at a time. Rachael swore that her sister burned a million calories a day simply because she was always on the move.

Bounding down the stairs, Kellie ran headlong into Margo as she burst through the door into the hallway outside the air-ambulance office.

"I thought you were sleeping." Margo looked up to level the friendly accusation, ignoring the fact that being half a head shorter than Kellie might diminish the mock authority in her tone.

"Silly girl." Kellie flashed one of her irresistible grins. "You know I can't stay cooped up in that cubbyhole for more than ten minutes."

Margo shrugged, feigning frustration. "Where do you get the energy of a ten-year-old?"

"Clean living, Margo. You should try it. Want anything from the snack bar?" she called back as she headed down the hall.

"French fries. With extra catsup."

Kellie turned to point a finger. "See what I mean? Junk food. Saps all your energy."

"And what are you having, Miss Nature's Best?"

"Diet soda. With extra caffeine."

Margo hooted.

Kellie raised her eyebrows in mock indignation. "It's practically health food."

After all these months, Kellie still wasn't accustomed to the hospital smell of antiseptics and medications. Or to the steady stream of people pouring into the emergency room in need of help. They reminded her of the unending ribbons of drive-time traffic she had reported on for one of Birmingham's top country-music radio stations.

As Kellie turned the corner into the dingy snack bar, the hospital smell gave way to the aroma of microwaved hot dogs served with canned chili. A booth full of chattering student nurses drowned out the piped-in music. At the table in the farthest corner of the room sat the new man from the emergency room, tilting his chair onto its back legs and clasping his hands behind his head.

He was better looking than Kellie had noticed before. She had been too caught up in his caring manner with the little girl to pay much attention to the rakish sweep of thick blond hair that fell over his forehead and brushed the collar of his white hospital jacket. Her thoughts had been on things other than his square jaw and the rugged chin that made his outburst no surprise. She couldn't be blamed for having missed the deep chest that went with his broad shoulders and impressive height. And he hadn't been smiling, so how could she have noticed the way his smile cocked to one side under his neatly trimmed mustache?

She hadn't noticed before, but those things were impossible to overlook now. No wonder both Chip and Margo had been so amused by her interest in him. He was certifiably gorgeous. And that, she knew from ample experience during her last four unattached years, must mean he was either taken or just as certifiably obnoxious.

Unavailable or undesirable. That was the operative phrase.

Dropping her coins into the machine, Kellie pressed the button for diet soda and let a long swallow of the cold carbonation ease down her throat before she walked over to his table.

Kellie extended her hand. "Hi. Kellie Adams with air ambulance. Have you heard anything about the little girl yet?"

His lopsided grin deepened as he lowered his chair to the scuffed tile floor and took her hand in his. His grip was gentle but firm, his palm slightly rough. The impersonal touch left behind a gentle awareness that was anything but impersonal.

"Dan Brennan, Kellie. Nice to meet you—under less trying circumstances."

Kellie perched on the edge of the molded plastic chair across the table from him, hoping he wouldn't think she was flirting. That must happen to him a lot, she thought.

"Amy's still in surgery. I thought I'd hang around until I see how she comes through it." His voice was slow and deep, as hypnotic as it had been when his murmurs had comforted the young patient.

"I was impressed with the way you worked with her." Kellie tried a sedate smile to let him know she meant her words only in the most businesslike way. But her lips defied control and broke into the broad grin that was her trademark. "I could see her calm down right away when you started talking to her."

Dan looked disconcerted at the unexpected praise. "That's nice of you to say, especially after the way I jumped down everybody's throats."

"Not nice, just true." Why, she wondered, did she suddenly feel so giddy? Surely caffeine couldn't account for her skittering heart. She felt almost the same blood-rushing high she experienced every time the chopper lifted off the ground and she left the earth behind. Maybe she'd had more coffee than she realized. "Besides, tension's an occupational hazard in the emergency room."

He shrugged, his soft brown eyes alight with pleasure. "If I did anything to help, that's only what I'm here for. I'm sorry, but I don't remember you out there. Are you one of the nurses?"

"No, the pilot." He didn't even remember her. Her giddiness fizzled like a leaky balloon. Guys like this one might not be in her league, but it would still be nice to think she didn't fade into the woodwork.

His eyebrows shot up. "Is it as dangerous as I've heard?"

Kellie frowned slightly, wondering if people would ever stop overreacting to news coverage of air-ambulance flights that had ended in disaster at hospitals across the country. Anything new, especially something as colorful as this way of rapidly transporting patients who had no time to lose, received plenty of attention. So a few bad incidents took on much more significance.

"It can be," she answered stiffly. "That's why we have rules. Rules like only flight crew are allowed on the landing pad while the engine's running. Who gave the order to ignore that rule?"

"I did."

"*You* did?" An angry flush colored her cheeks.

"Sorry, but no one spoke up when I said, 'Let's go.' So we went," Dan answered matter-of-factly, ignoring the challenge in her voice. "Hope it didn't cause any problems."

"It wasn't a problem this time, but don't let it happen again." The sting went out of her voice when she realized he seemed to be taking her admonition seriously. "When I kill the engine, those blades go haywire. You could come away with a pretty close shave if you don't know what you're doing."

"So it's dangerous on the ground as well as in the air." His jaw squared speculatively.

"I'll take my chances in the air any day over my chances on Birmingham's freeways," she said pointedly, satisfied that this new trauma team member wouldn't make the same mistake again. But it miffed her to be put in the position of defending the work she did. That happened far too often to please Kellie.

"You could be right," Dan admitted, though he didn't sound too convinced. "And it's certainly good public relations for the hospital, racing people like Amy through the sky toward medical help."

"Public opinion is the last thing on my mind." Kellie tried not to go on the defensive again. "I just do the flying. And the nurses aren't playing hero, either. All we do is try to give people like Amy a fair shake at survival."

"The Golden Hour Theory." Dan lowered his eyes to his now-empty juice carton. "If a life is at stake, the first hour is crucial. Is that how you decide whether to send an ambulance or a helicopter? How badly the patient is hurt? How sick the patient is?''

She could read nothing in his brown eyes, although his forehead was furrowed in what looked almost like a permanent frown. ''That's part of it. Did a patient have a heart attack sixty miles away in the middle of nowhere? Can the patient survive a forty-five minute crawl through rush-hour traffic? Hospital dispatch answers those questions. Then I decide if conditions are okay to fly.''

'' 'Conditions'?''

''No thunderstorms. No fog. An acceptable landing site. That kind of thing.''

Kellie watched him nod as he digested her message, but she knew a few words from her weren't likely to change Dan Brennan's mind if he thought her work was nothing more than grandstanding.

''How did you get into this? Most chopper pilots learned it in Vietnam, but I'm betting that's not your story.''

Kellie had hoped for a change of subject, but his mention of the fighting in Southeast Asia was not what she had in mind. That period of history had intruded on her life far too much already. ''Not directly. I used to fly for a local radio station. Traffic reports. And I free-lanced— hauled executives and government types, mostly from here to Montgomery or Atlanta on business.

''Anyway, that's a long story and I'm on a mission for fries and extra catsup.'' Her broad grin transformed her face once again. ''So I'd better hustle or the head flight nurse will strip me of my wings.''

Dan glanced down at the copper wings pinned over the swell of her breast. ''I wouldn't want that on my conscience.''

Kellie stood reluctantly, sorry to end the conversation, even though his skepticism about her work had peeved her and his too-good-for-his-own-good looks had placed him smack in the category of men she avoided like dessert during a diet.

She almost believed he looked reluctant, too, as she headed for the grill to order Margo's fries.

She gave him a quick wave with the paper tray of slightly greasy, barely warm fries when she left the snack bar. With all the disdain she could muster, she told herself his way with little girls was probably a minor accomplishment compared to his bedside manner with big girls. With eyes like that, how could he fail?

Her smugness faded as she admitted that Dan Brennan would doubtless never bother to discover that Kellie Adams would be absolutely immune to his soft brown eyes. Absolutely immune, she repeated silently, absently nibbling one of Margo's fries.

CHAPTER TWO

THE NEWS wasn't exactly something to shout about, but Dan jabbed the air with his fist in a subdued salute to victory. Then, his silent celebration ended almost instantly as he realized he had no one with whom to share the news.

He hadn't been at Memorial long enough to have any real friends and probably wouldn't for quite a while—especially if he had to initiate the kind of shake-ups he had started in Iowa City.

No one waited at home, either, to share the story of the child who had flown to Birmingham for four hours of surgery following a hit-and-run. And intruding on the family's privacy wouldn't be right, either, no matter how much a part of their tragedy Dan felt.

Amy's parents, who had just talked with the doctor while Dan listened from a discreet distance, were emotionally exhausted and understandably dismayed that their daughter faced an uphill battle if she was ever to walk again.

Dan's heart went out to the young couple sitting in stunned silence and clinging to each other's hands for support after the doctor left. The grime from one of the coal mines north of Birmingham was ground into the father's clothes. And the young mother looked barely old enough to have a child Amy's age. Unlike Dan, they had no clear notion how close Amy had come to dying. Or how much slimmer her chances would have been just a few years ago. Dan had to admit that fact, even if he had other reservations about the spate of helicopter ambulances springing up around the country.

Unobtrusively retrieving his hospital jacket from the back of the waiting-room chair, Dan slung it over his shoulder and headed down the hall toward the exit stairs.

He knew he should be glad to head home. It was late. He still faced unpacked boxes, and it would be another early day tomorrow. But right now the ninth-floor condominium had as little appeal as sitting up in the hospital waiting room all night.

It was a nice enough condo, with all the right amenities. Fireplace, dishwasher, microwave, decorator miniblinds. A roomy balcony overlooked one of Birmingham's most scenic, tree-covered mountainsides, where the fabled iron statue of the god of the forge, Vulcan, held his torch high.

Once all his belongings were in place, it would be as picture perfect as the brick bungalow in Iowa City had been. And before that, the two-story town house in Lincoln, Nebraska, and the glass-and-brass apartment in Lima, Ohio.

But it lacked all the things Dan thought a home *really* needed. All the things the other places had lacked, too. A yard and a dog and a front porch for rocking on summer evenings when the smell of fresh-mown grass lingered in the air. And someone to share it with. Someone to share triumphs—such as knowing a fragile child with extensive injuries just might beat the odds.

As he passed the hallway that led to the air-ambulance headquarters, Dan remembered the glowing smile of the young woman who had flown Amy to safety. Kellie. Kellie Adams. She would care. And he could watch her heart-shaped face blossom into that dazzling smile when he told her the news.

Unless she'd thought of something else to take him to task over in the hours since they'd met. She had been right to jump on his case for presuming to know the rules that governed air-ambulance operations, unlike the physician with the trauma team who had chewed him out for comforting the young patient.

"I may have to put up with you pencil pushers hanging around while I'm trying to save lives," the serious-faced young doctor had snapped after the emergency was over. "But I don't have to put up with you getting in the way. You're here to watch, not play doctor."

Dan shook his head as he rounded the corner into flight headquarters. He had a lot to learn about Birmingham Memorial. And Birmingham Memorial had a lot to learn about him, too. He didn't stand by when he saw something that needed doing. And that little girl had needed comforting. He knew enough to know he hadn't interfered with her treatment. All he had interfered with was the young doctor's sacred territory.

A nurse in a tan-and-green flight suit looked up from the newspaper spread on her lap when Dan stuck his head in the door of the air-ambulance office.

"Is Kellie still around?" He suddenly realized the bright-faced pilot might already be gone for the night.

The woman turned back to her paper as she spoke. "Upstairs."

Mumbles greeted Dan's knock on the door at the top of the stairs. After long seconds, Kellie's sleepy face peered around the door at him.

"It's you." The last word was a yawn as she motioned him in and flicked on the harsh overhead light.

"I'm sorry. I didn't know you were sleeping." He felt like a snake for waking her. He remembered hearing that the air-ambulance people worked twelve-hour shifts and they sometimes napped between flights to stay alert.

But he was pleased to find her as appealing half-asleep as she had been when she'd bubbled her way into his reverie in the snack bar a few hours earlier. Her short hair was in soft disarray. The bewitching tilt of her eyes was as dramatic when they were heavy with sleep as when they had gleamed in passionate defense of the helicopter ambulance service. And if her ring finger was any indication, pilot Kellie Adams was as free as the birds she flew with.

"I'm not sleeping." She ran a hand through her hair and tugged her rumpled flight suit into place. "Just resting my eyes a little."

Dan suppressed a grin. "I only wanted to stop by for a minute to let you know Amy came through the surgery okay."

"Amy?" Kellie's thoughts were still fuzzy. "Oh! The hit-and-run. She's going to be okay?"

"She's got a fight ahead of her if she's going to walk again. But she's won the first battle."

"I'm so glad!"

He heard the smile in her voice before it made its way to her slowly awakening face. For the first time, it struck him that she spoke minus the colorful drawl that still had him turning his head all over town. He wondered if she, too, was a Sunbelt transplant.

"Thank you for coming to tell me."

"I thought you'd want to know."

Dan didn't want to go but could think of no legitimate reason to stay. Glancing around the cramped, featureless room, he caught sight of a framed photo on a small table beside the cot. Kellie was sitting in the bleachers of a football stadium with a little girl about four or five and another woman who looked enough like Kellie to be a sister. A striped cap perched backward on her tawny curls, Kellie was trying to feed a hot dog to the giggling youngster.

Dan smiled wistfully, thinking of his nephews, who were now half a continent away. He gestured to the picture. "Your little girl?"

Kellie nodded drowsily. "Yeah."

"Big job, being a mother. Especially a working mother."

He couldn't be sure, but Dan thought her expression turned wistful. "She's with her dad for six months right now. That's supposed to make it easier."

Something in her voice told him it didn't make things a bit easier. Dan felt almost guilty to be so grateful to learn that she and her daughter's father weren't together.

"I'd better get home and let you get some more rest."

Kellie was now completely awake, as animated as he remembered. And, yes, as stunningly well-rounded as he had remembered. Her lush body—like something out of every man's most adolescent fantasy—was in stark contrast to the girl-next-door ingenuousness she wore so captivatingly.

Thank goodness, Dan thought, for someone who didn't diet herself down to planes and angles.

"Let me walk out with you," Kellie said, stifling a final yawn. "The night air will get the last of these cobwebs out of my head."

Walking beside her down the stairs and out the side door to the parking deck, Dan felt the strongest urge to slip closer and risk brushing his shoulder against hers. But he kept his distance, taking the time to give her the details of the surgeon's report to Amy's family.

"Thanks again for coming by," she said when they reached the small sports car he had driven since a temporary aberration overcame him in a used-car lot two years earlier.

"Thank you. I needed to share the good news with somebody. And I thought of you."

Kellie warmed to hear he thought of her that way. She surprised herself by suddenly wondering if he would hit it off with Carrie. He seemed to like children.

"Guess I should get back and let you be on your way home," she forced herself to say, again reluctant to end their conversation. The cool night air was so invigorating after being cooped up in the flight apartment that Kellie hated to go in. And she hated to see him go, she decided, because she was anticipating her own empty house, so quiet these days without Carrie.

"You shouldn't go back alone in the dark," Dan realized. "I'll walk with you."

Her lyrical laughter floated on the breeze. "Thanks, but that's not necessary. I'll be coming out here alone again when it's time to knock off, anyway."

"You will? Don't you get security to walk out with you?" His brow furrowed in concern.

She laughed again. "They tell me I'm tougher than they are. Thanks again, Dan. See you around."

Unconvinced of her toughness, Dan waited at the deck exit until she safely reached the door to the emergency room before he cruised out onto the street. Watching the gentle sway of her curves as she walked, Dan wondered with regret if he would find out just how tough she was.

Because if he had his way—and there was no reason to suppose he wouldn't—the air-ambulance service would be one of the first things to come under his careful scrutiny.

GRABBING HER OVERSIZE straw bag from the top of the pile of clothes that still needed sorting for washing machine versus dry cleaner, Kellie paused guiltily over the jumble of teal blue and bright orange and sunshine yellow cottons and silks. Ugh! Dirty clothes.

"Mom would die," she muttered, turning to dash out the bedroom door. *This afternoon,* she promised herself. *As soon as we get back. I swear on my mother's ironing board. This afternoon, I wash clothes.*

Kellie braked halfway down the stairs and wheeled around to head back to her bedroom.

"Let's get this show on the road!" Her sister's patient prod drifted up the stairs. "We're gonna be late."

"Again?" Kellie called back, now standing in front of her mirror, holding a cluster of bright, dangling seashells to one ear and a silver-dollar-size copper disk to the other.

Being a little late wouldn't matter, she thought as she compared the effects of the earrings. Brian never had Carrie ready to leave, anyway. Probably too busy nuzzling his new bride, she thought, glad that Brian at last had someone else to boss around. Maybe, for a change, he would lay off trying to tell her how to live her life.

Shells, she decided, dropping the copper disks onto the dresser top and shoving the seashell earrings into the roomy pocket of her cotton gauze skirt.

"On to the lake," she announced as she reached the bottom of the stairs. "What time are we supposed to be there?"

"Right about now." Rachael's feet were propped on the refurbished trunk that served as Kellie's coffee table.

Thumbing through the morning paper, Rachael made no move to stand until she was certain Kellie was finished with the haphazard preparation that always accompanied leaving the house. "Does this mean you're ready?"

Kellie's dramatic looks were toned down to a subtle sophistication in twenty-eight-year-old Rachael. Kellie's golden brown curls were tamed into a shoulder-length page boy. Kellie's love-the-world smile was more manageable but just as endearing. And Rachael dieted her curves to more fashionable slimness.

"Practically ready." Kellie slipped her tangerine-tipped feet into the sandals she had left beside the wicker papasan chair the night before. "What about the picnic basket?"

"In the car."

"And the drinks?"

"Ditto."

"What about Oscar? Has he been . . . ?"

"Fed and watered." Rachael nodded calmly, folding the paper and swinging her feet off the trunk.

"Then, I guess we're— Oh, rats. I've got to take the paint to the hospital. What time is it?"

"Ten. What paint?"

"For the carnival." Kellie frowned at her forgetfulness. "I bought it on the way home yesterday, and I'm supposed to take it by this morning. It's in the back of the car. We've got a group coming in this afternoon to paint props for the fund-raiser."

"The hospital's on the way. We can stop after we pick up Carrie." Rachael picked up her purse, then took her sister by the shoulders and pointed her toward the back door. "Now get your buns in gear, and let's get out of here. Mom's going to be pitching a fit."

"No, she won't," Kellie said as she locked the door behind them. "She'll know I'm just running late. Again."

Kellie leaned over the back porch railing to give Oscar a good-morning pat on the head before they jumped into the station wagon.

Three years separated the sisters, and because they were temperamentally worlds apart, Kellie and Rachael usually masked their strong attachment with teasing and bickering.

"Try to calm yourself before we get there," Rachael coached her sister as they drove the few miles to pick up Carrie. "It's time to play Mommy now, remember? And Carrie shouldn't have to contend with a hyperactive mommy. She's already rehearsing for a school program next month. And she has a new stepmother. So she has enough stress in her life right now."

"Who hasn't?" Kellie intended the remark to come out lightheartedly, but she knew from Rachael's appraising gaze that she hadn't succeeded.

"Still feeling a little insecure about the competition?"

"I'm going to ignore that remark." Kellie kept her eyes straight ahead, knowing Rachael was right. Her head told her it would be good for Carrie to see her father in a stable relationship. But her heart told her that she couldn't stand the thought of someone else mothering her daughter. Of someone else eventually giving her daughter the little brother or sister Kellie couldn't give her yet.

"You can't ignore it forever, big sister."

"I'm willing to try." Kellie sometimes chafed at the way her organized, levelheaded younger sister took on the role of resident adviser. Rachael even mothered their own mom—from whom Kellie had inherited her breezy bent for the unconventional—at every chance. Kellie hoped this new fellow Rachael had started dating loved to be mothered.

"Edgar?" she asked, pulling the seashells out of her pocket to slip the hooks through her pierced earlobes while she waited out the red light.

"What?" Rachael, as she often did, missed the wild leap her sister had taken with the conversation.

"The new guy you've been spending every available minute with since you met him at the meat market. Edgar?"

Rachael frowned. "Elliott. Elliott Franklin. And I met him at the deli, not a meat market. They're two very different things, sis."

Kellie grinned as she took off with the green light, pleased that her pestering had needled her all-business sister, whose life as a loan officer for one of Birmingham's major banks struck her as far too dull for words.

"And we've only been out a half-dozen times. Hardly what I'd call 'every available minute.'" Rachael adjusted her seat belt to straighten an imagined wrinkle in her cotton sweater, pretending to be unperturbed. Kellie knew better.

"I just wanted to make sure I'm not losing a baby-sitter."

"Don't worry. Elliott loves children."

"He does?" Kellie's grin widened. "You've learned a lot about him in a half-dozen dates."

"Just watch the traffic," Rachael instructed, a self-satisfied smile crossing her face. "Living right next door to your big sister can be a real pain. No privacy at all."

"Such a deal you get, and all I hear are complaints." Kellie zipped through a yellow light, not wanting to get caught again and make them even later. By now, she knew, Brian would be pacing impatiently even if her mother remained unconcerned.

"Such a deal *I* get!" Rachael continued the good-natured banter. "Such a deal *you* get, you mean. I pay half your mortgage payment and don't even get to park in the driveway!"

"That reminds me, I'm ready to start stripping the woodwork. Wanna help?"

Rachael groaned, remembering the weekend she had lost to helping her sister put up ceiling fans. "I can hardly wait."

When Kellie had started looking for an older house to renovate in the neighborhood near the hospital, she could find nothing affordable, even with her much-improved salary. The popularity and the property values in the older neighborhood had soared in recent years, as young professionals with plenty of money to spend moved in to salvage sixty- and seventy-year-old houses that had deteriorated.

So when Kellie discovered the brick two-story that had been converted into two apartments and used as rental property, she snapped it up. The house needed tons of work, but she knew she could live in the more spacious two-bedroom part of the house while she renovated, and she could make part of her mortgage payment by renting out the one-bedroom apartment. It had seemed the perfect solution for a single mom on a tight budget.

Her parents, who had long since retreated to their lakefront cabin outside of town, had urged her not to move into the heart of the city. But Rachael, who worked just blocks away, fell in love with the charm of the smaller apartment and offered to help with the renovation in exchange for a break on the rent.

Brian hadn't understood Kellie's attraction for the rambling old house, either. His ice-blue eyes spoke volumes the first time he picked up Carrie at the new address. But then, Kellie didn't care much for the sprawling ranch-style house he bought when he remarried.

As Kellie pulled the wagon to a halt in front of the house and headed toward the door, Carrie rushed outside and ran halfway down the sidewalk to meet her.

"Mommy! Guess what, Mommy?"

Grabbing her daughter for a hug that couldn't make up for the hugs she had missed the past two weeks, Kellie squeezed Carrie close. "I guess you've got rocks in your pockets, that's what. You weigh a ton."

Carrie giggled as she wiggled out of Kellie's arms to bounce excitedly on the sidewalk, her silver-blond ponytail wagging wildly. "Nooo. Daddy said I could take ballet lessons!"

"He did?" Kellie glanced toward the house, hoping her irritation didn't show. Brian lounged against the door frame, dressed for a Saturday afternoon at the golf course. She wondered how many clients of his father's accounting firm Brian had entertained on the golf course through the years.

"If what?" Brian interjected, coming off the porch to meet them. "I said you could take ballet if what?"

Carrie's smile didn't fade. "If Mommy said it was okay, too. Heather took ballet when she was a little girl. It's okay, isn't it, Mommy? Isn't it?"

Carrie's obvious desire to emulate her new stepmother twisted at Kellie's heart. "Your dad and I will have to sit down and talk about it first."

Now the smile faded.

"Okay, sport, why don't you run in and get your bag and kiss Heather goodbye?" Brian gave Carrie a playful swat on the seat as she dashed past him.

"What the hell's wrong with letting the kid take dancing?" he demanded when Carrie slammed the door behind her.

"Why does it have to be dancing? What's wrong with something less..." Kellie struggled for another word besides traditional, grateful that her sister couldn't overhear their wrangling from the car at the curb. Brian had never understood, much less approved, of her desire to teach Carrie that she wasn't locked into only those things little girls traditionally did.

"Less feminine?" Brian's words were a stiff accusation.

"Can we talk about this some other time?" Kellie wasn't up for spoiling her Saturday by arguing with Brian. Usually there was only awkwardness between them, but today she could tell they were prime for the same argument they'd had for years.

Their divorce had come after Brian brought Kellie the news that he had fallen in love with someone else. But the problems had started long before Brian developed a wandering eye....

When they first met, Kellie was attracted to the experience and maturity in Brian, who was seven years older. He introduced her to dry martinis and live theater and making love. And it wasn't long before he was making good money in his father's accounting firm—money that had made him seem glamorous and powerful.

But during their first years together, Kellie grew from a nineteen-year-old college student into a young woman who knew exactly what she wanted out of life.

What she wanted out of life was to fly.

And a wife who wanted to fly was exactly what Brian did not want out of life.

Kellie's fascination for helicopters had seemed cute to him at first, a few years after he had returned from flying rescue missions in Vietnam. Teaching her to fly had fed his ego and established him as her guardian, a position he relished. But when her love for flying became more than a college girl's obsession, Brian's patience ran out. Her two months of formal flight lessons had been bad enough. But her insistence on earning her pilot's license had been the catalyst for their first full-fledged fight.

It wasn't so much her flying he had minded, Kellie realized now, as it was the fact that she was wresting control of her life away from him.

The honeymoon ended the day she flew her check flight with a Federal Aviation Administration rep.

What Brian wanted, Kellie soon discovered, was his little girl back. He wanted someone to follow him like a puppy, awed and eager to learn more. What Brian wanted was a conventional young wife to raise his children and work, if she must, at a sedate, steady desk job.

Kellie tried a desk job for more than a year, working as a receptionist for a country radio station. But when the station's traffic pilot left for a better job in Atlanta, Kellie hopped at the chance to prove to Brian that she could put her skills as a pilot to work.

The job was the first major wedge. Carrie's birth and Kellie's refusal to give up her job and stay home with the baby merely drove the wedge deeper. It wasn't long before Brian found a more pliant playmate.

Swallowing her bitterness hadn't been easy for Kellie, but she had been determined to keep the divorce civilized for Carrie's sake. Brian's new love had lasted only long enough to ensure that he and Kellie had no marriage left to salvage.

Brian played the field with a vengeance for years, worrying Kellie with what kind of impressions Carrie must be forming of relationships between men and women.

When he did at last remarry, the tension between Kellie and Brian increased again. And that, Kellie knew, was due mostly to her own ambivalence about Carrie's stepmother. It was tough coming to grips with the fact that Carrie might come to love Heather as a mother, too.

Kellie fingered the silver-and-garnet ring that had replaced her wedding band. "Has she been good?"

"As good as any six-year-old who thinks the only way to do anything is ninety miles an hour."

At thirty-eight, Brian was growing better looking with the years, Kellie thought, if a little fuller around the middle. His crisp, close-cropped brown hair was still untouched by gray, and the few lines around his eyes gave dignity to a face that bordered on boyish.

Even at that, he was certainly no Dan Brennan.

The comparison brought Kellie's thoughts to a halt. What in the world, she wondered, had made her compare her ex-husband to a man she'd just met?

Besides, you're no Heather, either, she reminded herself, calling to mind the pencil-thin redhead.

"How's the job? I guess it's a relief not having to juggle Carrie and those long hours."

Looking up sharply, Kellie was suspicious of the studied casualness in his remark.

Before she could answer, Carrie flew out of the house again, overloaded with a pink backpack, a pair of roller skates and a disreputable rag doll. She brushed a quick kiss over Brian's cheek and continued her mad dash to the car.

"Guess I'd better run before she drives away without me," Kellie said, wondering what he had been hinting at with his crack about juggling Carrie and her job.

On the way to the lake, via Birmingham Memorial to drop off the paint, Carrie regaled them with her new word for the past two weeks—despicable—and the story of a boy in her class who pulled her ponytail every time they rehearsed their musical program, and her fascination with the new VCR her daddy'd bought for Heather's birthday.

"She's the only one I know who talks more than you, Kellie," Rachael joked as the faded station wagon pulled into the hospital's parking deck.

Carrie hopped out of the car, dragging her rag doll for the trip. "Can Sissy go, too?"

Nodding her agreement, Kellie opened the back of the wagon. She passed two gallons of paint to Rachael and grabbed the other two herself.

Fifteen minutes later, Carrie contentedly followed Kellie and Rachael through the emergency room toward the exit, swinging her rag doll while she absorbed the activity going on around her. Suddenly a loud wail from behind them stopped Kellie and Rachael in their tracks.

The energetic swinging had finally taken its toll on Carrie's aging doll, and Sissy's ragged body went flying against a wall. Carrie held the sundered arm before her in horror, her face dissolving into a childlike mask of tragedy. Kellie retrieved Sissy and knelt beside Carrie to hold her close.

"It's all right, sweetheart," she crooned to the sobbing child. "We'll fix her."

"She's dead!" The sobs grew more uncontrollable by the minute as Carrie contemplated the destruction of the toy that had been her constant companion since she was old enough to carry a doll. Kellie couldn't count the number of times her mom had made new dresses for the worn doll and patched up holes so Sissy's stuffing wouldn't escape. But the loss of a limb had never occurred, and Carrie was not taking the injury lightly.

A pair of long, gray flannel legs walked up and paused beside them. When they squatted to bring their owner down to Carrie's level, Kellie looked over into the sympathetic brown eyes of Dan Brennan.

"Do you have an emergency, young lady?" he asked Carrie in the same soothing tones Kellie recognized from their first meeting, when she flew in with the hit-and-run victim.

Carrie's loud crying lowered by only a decibel, but she nodded at the tall, soft-spoken man with a pair of glasses pushed to the top of his head.

"Emergencies are my specialty," he assured her seriously, giving Kellie a friendly smile over the youngster's blond head. "Maybe I can help."

"I...I think she's...d-dead." Carrie hiccuped through her tears.

"Let me check." Gently Dan took the doll from Kellie and the unlucky arm from Carrie. Kellie smiled gratefully, again impressed with the compassion he seemed to have in such abundance.

Carrie's sobs subsided as Dan led her into an empty examination room followed by Kellie and Rachael. With tender care, Dan used a stethoscope to listen for signs of life in Sissy's cotton chest. Then he hunched down beside Carrie again. "I have some good news, young lady. Your friend... What's her name?"

"Sissy."

"Sissy is alive, but I'll have to perform a serious operation. Will you sit up here beside me and be very calm and quiet while I operate?"

Carrie nodded and sniffled. Dan lifted her onto the examining table, then reached for a tissue and helped her wipe away the signs of her tears. "It's important for Sissy to know you're being brave. Okay?"

"Okay."

Kellie watched, again enthralled as Dan showed such patience and understanding with a child whose world was in turmoil. She grinned as he squinted, the glasses on his head obviously forgotten, over the sturdy emergency-room sutures he used to reattach the doll's arm. All the while, he talked soothingly to a wide-eyed Carrie. By the time the surgery was over, Dan had the child smiling again as he explained that Sissy would need gentle treatment to help her recover completely.

"Who is this guy?" Rachael whispered, her voice filled with admiration.

"Don't know." Kellie shrugged, not taking her eyes off the big, brawny hands that had taken such care in sewing a doll back together. She prayed her shrewd sister wouldn't detect her reaction as Dan's soft, patient voice hummed through her. She hated to admit it, even to herself, but she was responding to much more than Dan Brennan's magic touch with youngsters. "He's new. I met him the other day."

She realized as she said it that she wanted to know more. A lot more. A thrill of panic shot through her as she acknowledged how quickly Dan was tearing down her usually steadfast defenses.

"Mommy, look!" Carrie ran toward her, holding up the rag doll for inspection. "Dr. Dan saved Sissy's life!"

"That's wonderful, sweetheart." Kellie leaned over to hug Carrie close, then looked up at Dan. Back off, she warned herself. Unavailable or undesirable, remember? But she wasn't sure how successful she was at snuffing the approving light in her eyes when she looked up at him. "Thanks, Dan. I owe you one."

A crooked grin he only half hid told her he read the interest she was trying to squelch. But before he could respond, Carrie's shrill voice broke in. "What if Sissy gets worse?"

Dan looked down and smiled at Carrie, then back at her mother. The warmth in the curve of his lips and in his eyes grew perceptibly warmer. "For you, young lady, I think I could arrange a house call."

HER SMILE was dazzling. But the hint of a blush stealing over her cheeks when he made his crack about house calls was what did him in. *Women don't blush anymore,* Dan told himself as he watched the trio head down the hall toward the exit. *Especially women who pilot helicopters,* he suspected, shaking his head over her conflicting image. How, he wondered, could she seem so guileless, so genuine, and still have the tough edge it must have taken to become a helicopter pilot? A pilot good enough to cinch the Birmingham Memorial job, at that. He'd pulled her file; she had even arranged for private, intensive training in combat and emergency conditions in order to be better qualified for the job.

And on top of that, she had the most maddeningly exotic eyes he'd ever seen.

Her eyes were like his brother's prized cat's-eye, a large marble with a surface that changed from blue to green when you turned it in your hand. All the kids had coveted the aggie, especially Dan, but no one had ever won it away from Steve.

Kellie's eyes had mesmerized Dan completely. But it was what he had seen in her eyes that fascinated him most—a look that spoke of the first stirrings of interest at the same time that it said, "Hands off."

Dan looked around absently, trying to remember where he had been heading when the tragedy of the disembodied doll waylaid him. He spied the charts on the examining table.

Admission reports. He was headed for his office with yesterday's admission reports. But as soon as he finished figuring out what additional computer equipment would be necessary to modernize the process, he vowed, he would get in touch with head pilot Kellie Adams.

As he waited for the service elevator, Dan was suddenly uncomfortably aware that getting tangled up with Kellie wouldn't make things any easier when the time came to evaluate the air-ambulance service. Granted, right now everything about her seemed to reach out and embrace the world. But it might not seem that way for long where Dan was concerned.

Nevertheless, the urge to return her illusory embrace was powerful.

"I THINK HE WAS FLIRTING with you." Rachael raised her eyebrows and dared her sister to deny it as they made their way back to the car.

"Hardly," Kellie protested, hoping her sister was wrong. She hadn't done anything to reveal any of the crazy ideas she was having, had she?

Carrie tugged on Kellie's hand. "Mommy, what's 'flirting'?"

A smug look from Rachael said she thought even her effusive sister would have trouble with that one. But Kellie always made it a point to answer her daughter's questions candidly, a practice that had resulted in a youngster who never hesitated to query anything of interest.

"Flirting is . . . trying to let someone know that you'd like to be friends without coming right out and saying it."

"Why?"

The answer to that, Kellie knew, wouldn't be as easy for an openhearted child to understand. "Sometimes grownups are afraid to be that honest with each other. Someone might not want to be friends, then the other person would feel bad."

Carrie gave the idea thoughtful consideration. "Is Dr. Dan going to be your boyfriend?"

Kellie unlocked the station wagon, and Carrie clambered into the back seat.

"No," Kellie announced firmly. "We just work together. That's all."

As she fastened her seat belt, Carrie slumped down and hugged Sissy to her chest. Her sun-browned face was dejected, and her voice was a perfect match. "Oh."

Rachael cleared her throat conspicuously in agreement with Carrie's disappointment.

Warning her sister with a glance to keep her thoughts to herself, Kellie climbed behind the wheel and turned her face to her daughter before starting the car. She had long ago given up her hopes of finding someone who was interested in making a commitment to a woman tied down with a child. Especially when she discovered that every man who stuck it out past the first date or two seemed to expect her to fall into bed with him.

But casual romance, as far as Kellie was concerned, was no romance at all. Try to explain that to a first-grader.

"Do you want me to have a boyfriend?"

Carrie picked at the frayed yarn of Sissy's hair. "Heather told Daddy you're weird. 'Cause you don't have a boyfriend." She looked up, a defiant set to the dimpled chin she inherited from her father. "So you should get one. Okay?"

Fighting to keep her expression from revealing her aggravation, Kellie wished she could simply tell her daughter that her love life was none of Heather's bloody business! But she hadn't spent years learning to be civilized to her ex-husband only to have his bride botch things up now. She wondered how long it would take Heather to learn that children Carrie's age would repeat anything said in front of them.

"There's nothing weird about not having a boyfriend, Carrie." Kellie hoped her voice was undefensive enough to fool a six-year-old. Judging from the amused grin Rachael was trying to hide, she wasn't fooling her sister at all. "When the right person comes along, I'll have a boyfriend. But I need a special boyfriend, because he'll need to love you *and* me. So he may take a little longer to find. Okay?"

Carrie smiled, clearly satisfied to learn that once this elusive boyfriend was found, she would be a part of his life, also. "Okay."

As the station wagon at last roared to life and Kellie heaved a sigh of relief that she had once again survived an exploration of the ways of the world with her inquisitive daughter, Carrie's voice piped up from the back seat.

"Dr. Dan liked me," she said, her meaning apparent.

Kellie chuckled, leaning her forehead against the steering wheel in defeat. "Tell you what, kiddo. I'll keep that in mind."

CHAPTER THREE

THE BEEPER on her belt bleated sharply.

With the sudden startling sound, Kellie's waiting came to an end. Adrenaline kicked in. She tossed her full can of diet soda into a trash can and double-timed it back to flight headquarters.

"It's at the Walker County line." Margo's clipped voice carried an undercurrent of tense anticipation as she relayed the location of the call when Kellie rushed into the office. "Good terrain for landing...."

Picking up the telephone triggered the familiar tightening in Kellie's throat and chest. She dialed the National Weather Service to check conditions: cloud cover, storm fronts in the direction they were headed, visibility, even the temperature, which affected the safe weight capacity of the chopper, so they could make last-minute adjustments in supplies if necessary.

Each time the dispatcher asked air ambulance to answer a call, the pilot made the decision whether the chopper would respond. Sometimes it felt like playing God, because the decision could mean the difference between life and death.

For that reason, Kellie made it a point not to know anything about the patient until they were in the air. It could be a sixty-five-year-old suffering a heart attack or a college student who broke his neck in a diving accident. Those facts couldn't color her judgment. She had to make the call based solely on how safely the flight could be made given the current weather and landing conditions. Now—with dusk falling quickly as their shift drew to a close—those conditions could be especially important.

While she tapped a pen impatiently on the flight log and waited for her contact at the weather service to come back on the line, she barely heard Margo's muffled question. "Are you sure you're up to this, Chip?"

Phone still at her ear, Kellie turned to catch sight of Chip shrugging off the question as he pulled his flight jacket on over his bony shoulders. "I'm fine."

Margo's dark face grew cloudy as she muttered, "How long do you think you can keep this up?"

Chip's voice was threateningly deliberate. "Back off, Margo."

Uncertain she had heard the exchange correctly, Kellie made note of the report from the weather service.

"Everything looks go," Kellie announced as she ended the call. "What's wrong here?"

"Nothing's wrong, dammit!" Chip snapped, loping off in the direction of the helipad.

Margo forced a tight smile. "If he doesn't stop sweet-talkin' me like that, he's gonna turn my head."

Before Kellie could press for an explanation, Margo followed Chip. Dismissing the exchange as another of Chip's displays of crossness, Kellie put the scene out of her mind.

Since the helicopter was always restocked for the next call as soon as one call ended, they were in the air and on their way less than five minutes after an air ambulance was summoned.

"Lift-off!" Kellie's nervous excitement spilled over in the usual way as she straddled the control stick. The steady vibration that signaled the helicopter's rise into the evening air hummed through her while the chopper climbed.

When the flight smoothed out, Kellie made contact with the hospital dispatcher to learn her specific destination and settle on an estimated time of arrival. She then gave her exact position, a step she would repeat every five minutes for the duration of the flight. Because the Birmingham airport was always so busy, she also checked in with the traffic control tower there, so they could better regulate flight patterns in the vicinity.

The ritual reminded her of their vulnerability as they floated through an overpopulated sky in her rotor-propelled bubble. If the helicopter went down, the regular location reports would help another rescue team find them quickly.

As they flew northwest of the city of a half-million plus toward rural Walker County, the galvanizing excitement Kellie always felt in the first few minutes of a flight ebbed.

"What have we got?" she called out to Margo.

"Teenager off a bridge into the Warrior River." Margo's terse message came to Kellie through her headset. "Probably drinking and hot-rodding."

Kellie pursed her lips, contemplating the potential for a wasted life. The rural counties north of Birmingham were full of hard-drinking, hell-raising teens trying to forget the coal and iron ore mines that awaited them after high school. Teen accidents were too frequent and too often tragic.

A check of the time told Kellie they would reach their destination about fifteen minutes from the time the call came in. A minimum of ten minutes on the ground and ten minutes back. That would get the patient to medical care in about thirty-five minutes—a task that would have taken at least ninety minutes on the crowded highways in and around the city.

This was the part of the flight Kellie always enjoyed—the short spurt between those active moments right after takeoff and those equally busy moments when they landed. From the first time she had swept through the air with Brian at the controls, Kellie knew she loved flying more than anything she'd ever done. Seeing the world spread out at her feet was a thrill every time she went up.

"When can I go up in your plane, Mommy?" Carrie had asked for the first time last weekend as they'd readied the boat for a sail around the lake. Always before, the prospect of going up in the air had intimidated the child. Returning to school seemed to be boosting her confidence.

Kellie had promised to take her up soon, but that hadn't been enough. "Can Daddy go, too?"

"Probably not, sweetheart." Kellie almost laughed out loud at the prospect of Brian's irritation when Carrie took her first flight with her mother.

Carrie was silent for a few minutes, then said unexpectedly, "Can Dr. Dan go?"

Her grandmother's ears had perked up at Carrie's offhand question, and Ellen Carpenter's maternal prying had turned the peaceful day of sailing into a nonstop inquisition for Kellie. Rachael had taken inordinate pleasure not only in their mom's nosiness but in Carrie's not-so-subtle matchmaking.

As the accident scene came into view, Kellie felt a familiar sinking in her stomach. Despite the encroaching darkness, her destination was easy to spot; lights from emergency vehicles flashed garishly, and hordes of thrill-seekers and rubberneckers congested the area. Even the camera crew from a local television station had pulled in close to the emergency vehicles.

"We've got an audience," Kellie shouted.

"And no place to land," Chip added. The crowd was scurrying wildly to move a rescue squad vehicle to make way for the chopper. Kellie hovered overhead, ticking off the wasted seconds until she was sure everything on the ground was well out of their way.

Darn! she fumed to herself after she'd touched down. Fifteen minutes later and this would have been the problem of the 7:00 p.m. to 7:00 a.m. crew. Instead it was cutting into her twelve-hour break between shifts. And turning into a headache, besides.

Every trained paramedic within driving distance had converged on the spot, and every passerby with a certificate in cardiopulmonary resuscitation seemed to have stopped to lend a hand and feed on the excitement of a real emergency.

That meant chaos reigned.

And that meant the crowd of gawkers and well-meaning volunteers robbed Chip and Margo of precious time in getting to the patient.

Kellie kept the engine running while Margo and Chip worked with the injured boy. She also kept her eyes peeled for curious people with more sense of adventure than common sense, so she could warn them away from the dangerous whir of the rotors.

A big, broad man in camouflage clothes, whose size reminded her of Dan Brennan, was typical of the crowd. But his similarity to Dan ended with his size. He had appointed himself master of ceremonies at this three-ring circus where everyone seemed to have forgotten the reason for the gathering. A fat plug of tobacco bulging in one cheek, he was bringing his buddies in for a closer look and generally making a nuisance of himself.

When he motioned his awestruck pals to approach the chopper, Kellie opened her door and leaned out.

"Move away from this area, please," she called out.

The big man smirked at his friends and pointed at something else along the side of the chopper, ignoring Kellie. Displeasure now turned to anger, and Kellie yelled, "Clear the area or I'll have you hauled in, bud."

He balked, a surly frown darkening his face as he debated the loss of face in front of his friends if he gave in to the threat from this bossy woman.

"Flight headquarters, this is Charlie-Able-91," Kellie said into her headphone, loudly enough for the show-off to hear. "Need to report interference at the scene. Can you report and request backup?"

Surliness turned to rage on the ruddy face of the big man. Kellie quaked as he took a step in her direction, one meaty hand clenched in a white-knuckled fist. What in the world would she do—could she do—if he yanked her out of the cockpit?

Before the man could take a second step, his friends grabbed his shoulders and held him back. For a few moments, he made a show of throwing off their restraining arms. Finally he stalked away, salvaging his reputation with a stream of venomous obscenities as he passed the cockpit.

For once, Kellie's adrenaline failed her as she slammed the door shut and settled back weakly.

GLASSES FORGOTTEN on his head, Dan squinted at the report propped against his thighs. He drained the last of the juice in one long swallow, pleased that his two-mile run had given him the extra spurt of energy he needed to finish another couple of reports.

Although, with no secretary, he wasn't sure why he was in such a lather to churn out the work. Until he interviewed and hired somebody, nothing would move very briskly, he knew.

The TV news was a comforting murmur from its niche between oversize posters, one of the Rocky Mountains and the other of the Chicago skyline. The colorful posters, burgundy miniblinds and the cream-colored leather sofa, armchair and director's chair complemented the vivid royal-blue walls.

One more report out of the way, he promised himself, massaging a stiff calf muscle under his worn gray sweatpants. Then he'd treat himself to a Scotch and soda on the balcony before he called it a night.

He was startled by the irritating chirp of the cheap phone he had picked up to replace the last cheap phone, which finally bit the dust last week. Tossing the report on the glass-topped coffee table, Dan rubbed his burning eyes as he reached for the receiver.

"Caused any trouble down there yet?" His brother's voice boomed cheerfully across a thousand miles.

"Steve!" The room suddenly seemed friendlier, warmer than it had moments before. "No more trouble than you're causing up there, I'll bet. How's it going?"

"We're great. Mom's healthy as a horse. Angie and the kids are fine."

While Steve filled him in on the latest, Dan, as always, was flooded with mixed emotions. Thinking of his nephews—a thirteen-year-old who loved horses and a ten-year-old whose greatest ambition was to amass a fortune designing the video games of the future—made him ache for a family of his own.

"So business is good?" Dan asked as Steve finished an anecdote about the day his ten-year-old tried to drop out of school to help with the family nursery and landscaping business.

"Too good. Mom's the only one who can keep up."

When their father died after his third heart attack, Steve stepped in to help their mother run the family business in Iowa. Their father's death had made them both aware of how harmful their tendency to overachieve and overwork could be. Dan had been frightened into a low-cholesterol diet and regular exercise. Steve meant well but couldn't quite give up steaks and TV for exercise and grilled fish. At least returning to the family business had been the perfect excuse to ease out of Denver's rat race.

Dan finished catching up on family news, then talked for a couple of minutes to each of his nephews. Just as he hung up and reached for the report he wanted to finish before bed, the television caught his eye.

Although the sound was too low for him to catch the report, he didn't need to hear what was being said. He watched, the tempo of the blood pounding through his veins rising, as Birmingham Memorial's unmistakable tan-and-green helicopter hovered over the scene of an accident. With the river in the background and a chaotic crowd of spectators in the foreground, the action that had been taped earlier in the evening looked more like a ghoulish carnival than anything else.

Dan moved closer to the TV, straining to identify the person hanging out of the cockpit. But the TV camera hadn't zeroed in on the chopper, and Dan could distinguish no details to help him identify the pilot. Before he could get closer to the TV to improve his view, the camera panned to a close-up of the reporter, whose serious face now hid most of the activity captured on tape.

Holding his breath, Dan saw the chopper take off, making it safely out of the sea of spectators.

He stepped into the kitchen to pour the Scotch he had promised himself, the pilot he had been unable to identify on the eighteen-inch screen now taking shape in his imagination. Could the pilot have light brown curls and a pair of eyes that held secret messages he would love to decode?

He tipped the liquor bottle for an extra splash over his ice cubes, ignoring the thought that even if Kellie hadn't been on the scene tonight, she no doubt flew into situations just as hair-raising.

The realization shouldn't have bothered him, but it did.

Tomorrow, he told himself, he would find out whether anyone at the hospital cared that they were part of the entertainment on tonight's late news.

"SEE LEN ASAP."

The to-the-point memo in Chip's big, bold script was posted on the message board when Kellie reported for work the next morning.

Taking ten minutes to catch up on the news from Andy's shift and change out of her street clothes and into her flight suit, Kellie wondered what Len Baldwin wanted. The director of nursing services, including air ambulance, rarely set foot in flight headquarters and rarely asked questions. In fact, he hadn't impressed Kellie as someone who was vitally interested in anything that went on at the hospital.

Perhaps because of that, the command performance on the executive floor caused a few jitters as she slipped into the chair across from Len's desk. If he wanted to see her, it must be a big deal.

Len, as usual, pretended to study paperwork instead of looking her straight in the eye.

"I hear things looked extremely out of control at the river last night, Kellie." Len darted a nervous glance over the top of his reading glasses. "One of the TV stations carried the report and, from the looks of things, a bystander could have been hurt."

"No one *was* hurt," she pointed out, wondering if he ever actually made eye contact with anyone. It pumped up her confidence to realize she might make him more nervous than he made her.

"But someone could have been, and we certainly don't need that kind of publicity," Len said. "Besides, I understand it appeared so chaotic that the hospital looked bad."

Kellie's jaw tightened in aggravation. He seemed more concerned with appearances than with the actual danger of the situation. In either case, she didn't see how she could keep crowds from congregating before she even arrived on the scene. And once she landed, leaving the helicopter to disperse the crowds would be futile as well as dangerous.

"Do you have any suggestions for keeping crowds away from an accident scene?" she asked coolly. "That's always a problem, whether a chopper is involved or not."

Len frowned and stared over her head. "True, but it's a more visible problem when the air ambulance is involved and we're splashed all over TV. In any case, it's been called to my attention, so I wanted to call it to yours. Maybe you should consider some kind of crowd safety recommendation...." His voice tapered off lamely.

Kellie fumed silently, picturing Len's lack of support when someone had come down on him this morning. *Nice to know the boss will back you in a pinch,* she thought dryly. "Who brought it to your attention?"

"Dan Brennan. He's—"

"Dan Brennan? What business is it of his?" Kellie was flabbergasted at the nerve of some emergency-room attendant marching into her director's office to complain.

"He's the new vice president for patient services." First Len straightened his glasses, which didn't appear crooked. Then he restacked the perfectly stacked papers on his desk. Kellie expected sweat to pop out on his forehead any moment. "He's been brought in to...look over the ways we serve patients. The admission process, billing, emergency-room procedures, the whole nine yards. Now if you'll excuse me..."

Wondering if Len had ever bothered to read the safety procedures she had worked on for months before the air ambulance's first flight, Kellie stalked out of Len's office.

So Dan Brennan was the hatchet man Margo had mentioned. Now everything fell into place: his authoritative air the day they'd brought in the hit-and-run, his probing questions about helicopter safety. Could the air ambulance be on Dan's chopping block? No wonder Len was edgy. A new VP to sweat over. A VP with a reputation, at that.

Kellie had thought all along Dan couldn't be as nice as he seemed, and it looked as if she had been right. All he wanted was to spy on her and catch her screwing up!

Feeling angry and violated, Kellie spotted the shiny new sign she had missed on her way to Len's office.

Dan Brennan. Vice President for Patient Services.

Kellie stared at the mahogany door only as long as it took to talk herself out of counting to ten.

It's bad for your blood pressure to hold it in, she told herself, grinding her teeth and giving the door a shove.

THE CRASH OF HIS OFFICE DOOR against the wall warned Dan of an intruder.

But the warning didn't prepare him for Kellie's indignant accusations as she confronted him over the systematic clutter of his desk.

"How dare you spy on me!" Kellie brought her fist down on the desktop, sending in all directions the admissions reports he had spent the past hour organizing. "And then go around behind my back like some grade-school tattletale and—"

"Hold on, Kellie." Dan stood in self-defense. But he wasn't sure his extra inches were much protection from the blazing anger of the young woman in the beguilingly snug flight suit. "Why don't you start by letting me in on what you're so hot about?"

"Don't play games with me! You know perfectly well what's wrong!"

Dan sighed. When he'd taken his complaint to Kellie's boss, he'd known his opinion probably wouldn't be welcome. And once he'd learned from Len Baldwin that Kellie had been at the controls, Dan had grown even more adamant about the apparent lack of safety measures. Besides, Len Baldwin seemed like such an unpleasant little weasel, Dan hadn't minded making him squirm.

He realized now that he should have expected the spineless administrator to take it out on Kellie. He also realized that he should have expected Kellie to have the guts to storm into his office and challenge him this way. She'd seemed plenty gutsy before—the work she did every day proved that. And the way she had upbraided him about dashing out to meet the helicopter had been another good indication that Kellie Adams wasn't afraid to wade into a fray.

He liked that. He liked it a lot. At most hospitals where he was hired to revamp services offered to patients, the people whose kingdoms he upset often fought him behind his back, using office politics to ignore or undermine his recommendations.

Dan was glad Kellie wasn't that type. It never worked, anyway. He only hoped he could make her understand the job he had to do and the fact that it was nothing personal.

At least, he didn't think it was personal. He wondered fleetingly whether his strident march into Len's office this morning had been justified. Or had his heart-in-throat concern when he'd watched the chopper hovering over the accident scene on the late news last evening been overreaction?

If it had been overreaction, what had prompted it? Apprehension over this new job? Legitimate concerns about helicopter safety? Or Kellie Adams?

His reaction to Kellie's physical presence this morning seemed even more dangerous than the chaotic scene on the riverbank. Anger brightened her exotic eyes and let slip a hint of the drawl he had missed before. His heart was suddenly pumping as furiously as it had the previous evening. Only this morning, there was no danger to explain his agitation. Was there?

"Kellie, why don't you sit down so we can talk about this?" He pointed to one of the high-backed tapestry-covered chairs facing his desk, mentally damning the job that so often brought him into conflict with people he might overwise enjoy knowing.

"If you wanted to talk about it, why didn't you come to me first?" she demanded, her anger subsiding in the face of his calm. Didn't anything fluster this man?

"Because that isn't the way they want things done around here. They want me to go through channels," Dan said quietly, sitting down and waiting patiently for her to do the same. "That might not be the way I'd prefer to do things, but I don't run the show here."

His unspoken "yet" came through loud and clear.

Kellie sat, her fury at him turning to disgust with herself for her lack of control. Why did she always let anger get the better of her? And why had Len's wishy-washy scolding riled her so this morning? She suspected it was her discovery that the conversation with Len was the result of a complaint from Dan Brennan.

Dan Brennan, whose deep voice and airy grin had been about to make her forget past experience. She could tell herself all day he was just like the rest, but something about Dan had threatened to lure her out of her self-imposed hibernation.

Now, Kellie realized as she faced him, she had really made a fool of herself, storming in here and attacking the hospital's newest honcho for doing what was apparently his job.

"How *are* things done around here?" she demanded, stubbornly refusing to back down, although she now wanted nothing more than to have this confrontation over with. "By spying?"

"Kellie, I wasn't spying."

Unlike Len, Dan at least had the nerve to look her straight in the eye. She almost wished he wouldn't. Those soft brown eyes mingled with his seductively warm voice were more potent than her flash-in-the-pan anger, which was deserting her now that it had boxed her into a corner.

She remembered now why she always regretted not curbing her temper; just like her mom, she, too, often wimped out in the heat of battle.

"What do you call it, if it wasn't spying?" She didn't intend to give Dan Brennan the satisfaction of seeing her wimp out this morning. She held on to the unfriendly edge in her voice, although her eyes were traitorously concerned with the way his pin-striped suit tapered perfectly from broad shoulders to lean waist.

Who cares about his perfect physique? she asked herself, trying to ignore the stirring inside her that had nothing to do with her now totally dissipated anger.

"I call it doing my job," Dan replied with quiet authority. "I won't make decisions about how to run an operation until I've spent time there. So I always try to get hands-on experience. I had no idea you didn't know who I was. I was wearing a name tag like everybody else. The emergency room doesn't leave much time for niceties."

Grudgingly Kellie had to admit he was right about that. People scurried around emergency all day, and she had no idea who they were or what function they served. Taking care of patients was the bottom line. Polite introductions and routine explanations took a back seat.

"I'm sorry if Len was rough on you," Dan added, the concern in his eyes genuine. "What happened last night wasn't your fault, I know. But situations like that could turn the air ambulance into a major black eye for the hospital unless we address them."

Although Kellie was dizzily aware of his physical presence, she tried to bring her thoughts back to the battleground that seemed to be spreading itself before them and away from the fire slowly kindling somewhere deep inside her.

"Then I expect we'll see a lot of you in flight headquarters," she snapped. Could he guess, she wondered, that she had turned to a warm puddle inside?

"Yes, I expect you will."

His crooked half smile softened the threat in his voice. But only a little.

FINISHING UP the previous day's flight log, Kellie twisted the tie to seal the interoffice envelope. She didn't mind the paperwork required both by the FAA and the hospital administration, but this morning her qualms over the two vexing scenes with the hospital higher-ups made it harder than usual to concentrate.

As she left her desk in the flight apartment to drop the report in the in-house mailbox downstairs, Kellie had to admit the confrontation with Len took a distant back seat to her audience with Dan when it came to nettling her. And it was more—much more—than her concern over the air-ambulance service that had her rattled.

Although she had vowed to rid herself of the mental image of Dan's melted chocolate eyes, she was having little luck. But if her job was on his target list, she had no intention of making a fool of herself by developing some kind of adolescent crush.

Chip was popping a pill onto his tongue and washing it down with a swallow of coffee when she rounded the corner.

"Anti-aging potion?" She teased as she dropped the envelope into the mailbox and reached for her own coffee cup. "Or hangover cure?"

Slipping his prescription bottle into his pocket, Chip grimaced. "Len may be on your back, babycakes, but that doesn't give you the right to abuse the hired help."

"Oops. It *is* a hangover, isn't it?" She took in his red-rimmed eyes and his grouchier-than-usual response to her amiable goading.

"Hay fever. My head's splitting."

He flopped into a chair and closed his puffy eyes, a pose she recognized instantly. When they weren't in the air, Chip spent most of his time these days slumped in his chair.

Kellie had no doubt that a bad bout with hay fever accompanied by a chronic sinus headache could account for his increasingly sharp tongue, too. Chip had never been known for his sunny disposition, but lately he had been crankier than a teething baby.

She wondered, quietly leaving Chip to his sinus headache, why someone at the hospital couldn't prescribe something that would give Chip a little more relief than he was getting from his present medication.

Checking her belt to make sure her beeper was in place, Kellie headed outside for a walk around the hospital grounds. The playground for visitors' children was usually crowded, and a grown-up to push swings or keep seesaws in motion was always welcome. And Kellie craved the mindless preoccupation. She was restless and verging on crankiness herself this morning.

But then, she might have her own chronic headache to worry about—a brown-eyed headache named Dan Brennan.

KELLIE'S FOOTSTEPS FADED down the hallway. Chip resisted the impulse to place his hand over the dull ache that was slowly subsiding in his chest. If anyone saw him looking even remotely as if his heart were bothering him, it would be all over.

As long as he could keep getting his hands on the medication he needed to calm his heart when he felt these pains, everything would be fine, he told himself. The pains were mild. He knew where the medication was kept, and he'd been around Memorial long enough to know the routine that would let him slip in and take what he needed undetected.

He had also been around Memorial long enough to know that an emergency-room nurse with a heart problem would quickly be shuffled into a boring desk job. Put out to pasture at forty-five. It wasn't a fate he was able to accept. He had watched his own father wither from the inactivity when a heart attack had forced him into early retirement. It wouldn't happen to him, he swore.

And he wouldn't put his mother through that again, either. With a weary smile he thought about the tiny woman who was no doubt bustling around his two-bedroom condo planning their dinner right now.

At seventy, Jane West was happier and more energetic than her son had ever remembered. No more exhaustion from working two jobs to keep food on the table and fuel oil in the furnace. No more anguish from watching someone she loved slowly waste away.

She had made friends in her new town. She had her youngest son to take care of her, which meant that the social security check that was her only income was plenty. And the nightmares that came from living in a house filled with death were gone now.

Chip planned to keep it that way. But history repeating itself seemed more like a very real possibility every day.

When the hospital had been staffing the air-ambulance service, Len had been concerned that a forty-five-year-old nurse wouldn't be up to the added stress of the job. Chip had convinced him otherwise.

Then the bouts of weakness started. And the pains. Just small ones. Nothing he couldn't take care of himself. If it grew any worse, he would head straight for the doctor.

But for now, he told himself, he could handle it. No one else needed to know. Especially not the people he worked with. Especially not his mother.

CHAPTER FOUR

THE BRISK TAP of Margo's heel on the linoleum signaled Kellie that her friend's patience was running out.

"Half the medical district's already there, girl," Margo prodded as Kellie smoothed her paisley skirt and stuffed her rumpled flight uniform into the tote bag she brought in every morning. "They'll drink all the beer before we even show our faces."

"You don't want me going out of here with wet hair, do you?" Kellie ran her fingers through her damp curls, wondering if she could manage to back out of this somehow.

"You're stalling. Shake a leg, lady."

Margo had convinced Kellie that she needed a night of fun, not another night at home alone. So they were heading for the Medicine Chest for a drink at the end of their Friday shift. But Margo hadn't bargained on cooling her heels while Kellie showered, then called Carrie so she could hear the youngster's voice.

The call was a mistake. Only Brian had been home. Right about now, stepmother Heather was pulling up in front of the dance studio for Carrie's first lesson.

And just before Kellie hung up, Brian took another little dig. "Heather gets along great with the kid. And she's got so much time to spend with Carrie. I can't imagine things working out any better."

Why, she wondered, did she have the feeling Brian had more on his mind than what a great little stepmother he'd found for his daughter?

As she headed out of the hospital and down the sidewalk with Margo, Kellie was provoked once more by the memory of how easily Brian had bullied her into letting him have his way about the dance lessons. But Heather had filled the child's head so full of excitement about ballet slippers and bright-colored leotards that Carrie's big, pleading eyes had been the only secret weapon Brian had needed to carry the day.

"At least we won't be tripping over Len down here," Margo commented as they grabbed the last empty table in the crowded tavern. In her street clothes—floral corduroy jeans and a hand-painted sweatshirt she'd designed herself—Margo would never have been mistaken for the imposing nurse who rarely took a wrong step. "Lordy, I've seen that man more in the past week than I've seen him in the past year."

"How can you be sure he won't follow us?" Kellie joked, not at all certain Len wouldn't turn up underfoot here, too. He had been lurking at her heels every time she turned around this week, questioning her judgment and picking her flight logs to pieces in search of a detail out of place.

"No way. I don't think his wife lets him out after dark."

Margo didn't realize that it wasn't really Len who had haunted Kellie all week. It was Dan Brennan. Although she hadn't seen him since her embarrassing explosion in his office, she was certain Len's here-there-and-everywhere presence was Dan's doing. With the new vice president breathing down his neck, Len was making a great show of his interest in the air-ambulance service.

From where Kellie stood, Brian wasn't the only man trying to run her life these days. Dan now topped the list.

Every day, she waited for him to show up in flight headquarters, almost looking forward to the chance to tangle with him again. But Kellie's desire to confront Dan was more than a need to redeem herself for letting anger get the better of her. She also wanted to prove to her errant hormones that she had misread her reaction to him in his office. He was tall, but probably not as tall as she remembered. Surely her memory had exaggerated the broad shoulders and the deep chest. And what could be so special about a pair of appealing lips half hiding under a sandy-brown mustache?

Kellie didn't have time to contemplate the question. She and Margo weren't alone for three minutes before people from Memorial started dropping by to chat on their way to the pool tables or the jukebox.

Then, in the middle of the latest news on upgrading the computerized admissions process, Margo abruptly excused herself. Kellie followed her friend's progress through the crowded bar until the nurse stopped to strike up a conversation with an imposingly good-looking man wearing a beeper and a turquoise golf shirt.

A doctor, Kellie speculated as she twirled the stem of her wineglass. An attractive, almost-forty doctor. Kellie wondered if Margo had really wanted another draft beer or if she'd had her eye on the turquoise golf shirt all along.

Margo had been right about the Medicine Chest, Kellie conceded as the admissions clerk they'd been talking to saluted with her wine cooler and returned to the group she'd come in with. It did beat going home alone with another long night stretched out in front of her. She had made great progress in stripping the woodwork. But her nails were ruined and her back was stiff and she was sick to death of being alone with only the radio for company. Before she finished the job, she'd have to con Rachael or her mom into lending a hand.

Looking toward the back of the bar to see if anyone she knew was playing pool, Kellie half listened to the snatches of conversation swirling around her.

"This guy's arteries were so bad . . ."

"Listen, I wouldn't marry a doctor if . . ."

"I'm quitting. Tomorrow. If I never see another hypodermic needle, it's too soon for me. Mother was right. Think I'll be a truck driver . . ."

"No doubt about it. The inventory's down. Somebody's raiding the pharmacy. But they're gonna crack down . . ."

That conversation, directly behind her, caught her attention.

"What kind of stuff's missing?"

"I don't know and I don't want to. The less I know, the better."

"But they figure it's somebody at Memorial?"

"That's right. Somebody with a problem, most likely."

Drug thefts at Birmingham Memorial! Kellie shifted uncomfortably. She didn't want to eavesdrop, but she couldn't quite drag herself away from the conversation.

"Somebody's either taking what they can use or taking what they can sell so they can buy what they use."

The idea of drug abuse going on somewhere in the hospital made Kellie uneasy. She read enough to know that drug abuse was rampant everywhere, but somehow she never expected to come in contact with it. Just overhearing the gossip made her feel like part of a conspiracy.

Kellie's eavesdropping was interrupted by a pudgy nurse from the nursery. Within minutes, the young woman was regaling Kellie with a series of anecdotes about the triplets born at Memorial the night before.

"You should have seen the look on the grandfather's face when he walked away from the window," she said, dimples flashing. "I thought we were going to have to call someone from coronary."

Kellie smiled, trying to listen but catching very little of the story.

Maybe, she thought, she would ask Margo about the drugs. Or Chip. If there was anything to it, they would know.

The overheard discussion nagged at her as she sipped her wine, which had long since lost its chill. No point in mentioning it to Margo or Chip, she decided. It was probably just idle gossip.

DAN ALMOST TURNED AROUND and walked out when he saw how crowded the Medicine Chest was. Friday night. He'd forgotten. Weeknights, the little bar in the heart of the medical district was cozy but not crowded. Tonight, the small, dim pub buzzed with anticipation of the weekend ahead.

Then Dan contrasted the crush of warm bodies, the sound of laughter mixed with fifties' rock and the blur of smiling faces with the deadly silence of his condo.

Even the madness of Friday's happy hour beat the sounds of a jazz album settling over the depressingly tidy furnishings. Mary Ann came on Fridays. The petite whirlwind of a housekeeper would have swept away every bread crumb under the toaster, straightened every towel and polished every ring left by an abandoned glass of juice. After Mary Ann finished working her miracles, the place might just as well be uninhabited, he thought wryly.

Thinking back to his long phone conversation with Steve and his rambunctious nephews earlier in the week, Dan doubted that even the best housekeeper could keep Steve's home looking uninhabited. He had spent two weeks with his brother's family just a month ago, before making the move to Birmingham. And right now, he missed the cheerful mayhem of family life.

He always missed it. But these first few weeks in a new town, with the liveliness at Steve's still so fresh in his mind, made him miss it even more.

At the bar, he loosened his tie and rolled up his shirt-sleeves while he waited for his Scotch and soda, then scanned the room for a familiar face. Anna Robinson had said she might drop in, but he didn't see her crisp, mannish suit or her salt-and-pepper topknot.

Birmingham Memorial's admissions director was about the only person he'd befriended. Dan had discovered, as he worked closely with the no-nonsense grandmother, that he enjoyed her company. Long hours at work had segued into more than one stop for a sandwich together on the way home. And they had cheered through a high-scoring pro football game on the Medicine Chest's wide-screen TV one Monday night, filling in the halftime with talk about family and tennis and careers.

His friendship with Anna was a welcome change from his experiences at other hospitals around the country. *If you expect to kick butt and take names,* he thought, *you can't expect to be invited to join the fraternity.*

As it had every time he saw it, Kellie Adams's face stopped his thoughts cold as his eyes swept the pub. She was sitting at a table near the wall, her almond-shaped eyes scanning the crowds near the pool tables. A soft cotton sweater was even kinder to her generous curves than her flight suit.

While his first sip of Scotch burned its way down, Dan absorbed Kellie's every move. She seemed lost in thought for a few moments as a look of puzzled concern crossed her face. Even when a plump nurse sat down and started talking to her, Dan would have sworn that Kellie's smile was forced.

After a couple of minutes, however, her infectious smile reappeared. Whatever had been on her mind, she seemed to have forgotten.

Dan wondered if Kellie was still bent out of shape over his talk with Len earlier in the week. He had purposely stayed away to give her a chance to cool off. Whatever negotiations they might have over the helicopter ambulance service would come soon enough. He already regretted that she would be going into any discussions with her mind made up that he was the enemy.

As the young nurse left the table, Kellie's eyes darted over him, then halted as abruptly as his straying gaze had halted when he'd seen her. Involuntarily her hand lifted as if to gesture in his direction. Then she dropped her hand, nodded briefly to acknowledge him and turned her gaze back toward the pool tables.

Dan felt, unexpectedly, like a failure. For the first time in longer than he cared to admit, he had run into someone who piqued his interest, someone who seemed fresh and intelligent, someone with intriguing twists and turns in her personality. And she thought he wore a black hat.

Plenty of other people had thought of him as the villain, at hospitals where overstaffed departments were reduced to lean efficiency and old ways of doing things were abandoned in favor of methods that made life easier for the patient. But thinking that Kellie Adams saw him as the cutthroat administrator made him feel like a loser.

It wasn't a feeling he relished. It wasn't a feeling he knew how to tackle . . . except head-on. Tossing back the rest of his Scotch, he looked hard at the ice cubes clinking around in the empty glass, then signaled the bartender to hit him again.

Armed with a second drink of hard liquor, which he seldom allowed himself, Dan headed for Kellie's table.

Before he could reach her, he cursed to himself as a jazzy-looking black woman walked up to Kellie, accompanied by a man in a turquoise shirt. Dan watched, still inching his way through the swarm of people, as Kellie shook her head and flashed the couple a smile. They headed away and Kellie reached for the canvas bag draped over the back of her chair.

She stood just as he reached her table.

"Don't leave." He wanted to gulp down the rest of his Scotch. *Which is why you always limit yourself to one,* he cautioned himself as he watched her study him. He saw no anger in her green eyes, only wariness.

"I really have to go." Her voice was hesitant. Her clear, precise words reminded him of the trace of a drawl that had slipped out when she was angry.

"Why?"

He watched as she opened her mouth to speak. But when nothing came out, she suddenly smiled, that radiant smile that always made him want to reach out and trace the soft line of her full lower lip.

"See. No reason at all." He pulled out her chair and waited for her to sit again. Then he sat across from her, draping his suit coat over the back of his chair. "Can I buy you a drink?"

"No, thanks."

Now what? he wondered. *Come here often? What a great line. It's bound to impress her. Should I try to clear the air about the other day or just forget it and hope she will, too?*

In his mind, he could see the knowing half-smile on his dad's craggy face when something went wrong and his younger son tried to slink away without confessing. "Just spit it out, son, and get it over with. Less painful that way."

Did father really know best? Dan decided to test the theory.

"I'm sorry things got off to a bad start this week. I'm really not the ogre people think I am."

Her eyes widened, obviously surprised that he knew the scuttlebutt making the rounds at the hospital. Then she smiled again, a smile that was almost teasing. Verging on timid flirtation. "Are you sure?"

Dan laughed, unable to respond any way but happily when she smiled. Dad always had been right. "Pretty sure. The image just seems to go with the territory."

"Sorry I came storming into your office," she reciprocated, her thumb fidgeting with the silver-and-garnet ring on her left hand. "Len managed to get my back up."

"I didn't mind." He remembered the flush of anger on her high cheekbones and the fire in her eyes. He hadn't minded at all. "Len could raise anybody's hackles."

Unless he planned to talk about the hospital, which seemed guaranteed to cause waves, that exhausted the topic. The noisy bar did nothing to ease the awkwardness that hung between them just a moment too long while he searched for another opening.

"How's the broken doll? Are her stitches holding?" Children. Children were always safe.

She didn't warm up instantly, but as he prodded her with friendly questions about Carrie, the tension of unfamiliarity started to melt. Kellie found it hard to resist anyone who would let her brag about how quickly Carrie was zipping through her schoolwork.

"You said before she's with her father. You share custody?"

"Uh-huh." Her response didn't invite more questions. Always unwilling to open up with men in settings that were prime for a pickup, Kellie wasn't completely receptive even to Dan's easy charm and seemingly sincere interest. She tried to redirect the conversation.

"Do you have children?" She already knew the answer to her question. While she'd talked about Carrie, she had seen the envy in his eyes. She had seen the same envy in too many of her friends whose busy careers had kept them from starting families. She often saw that look of longing in Rachael's face when her sister watched Carrie splash in a pool or put together a jigsaw puzzle.

"No. My ex-wife has a family now, but we never had children."

Now why the hell did I say that? he wondered, impatient with himself for even thinking of Lauren. He never thought of Lauren. It had been years since he'd even seen his ex-wife. True, he'd learned during his recent visit at Steve's that she finally had her doctor husband and the perfect little family she'd always wanted, while he was still struggling to find his. But why bring her up now? Probably because he hadn't known what else to say once he realized mentioning Kellie's ex-husband had been yet another blunder.

"You're probably lucky in a way," Kellie said, remembering Carrie's bewildered, tear-streaked face when she tried to explain that Brian would no longer live with them. The toddler's hurt and confusion, not Brian's insistence, had been the reason she'd agreed to joint custody. "Divorce is hard on kids."

The furrow in his brow deepened momentarily, shadowing his soft brown eyes and signaling thoughts that were less than happy. Kellie wondered if everyone these days had baggage from a marriage gone bad or dreams gone sour. It almost made it easy to understand why so many men—and women, too—wanted nothing more than a warm body to keep the loneliness at bay for the night.

Almost, but not quite. Kellie could imagine nothing bad enough to make her settle for less than the real thing in an intimate relationship.

Dan looked up and cleared his dark expression. "It can't be easy, managing Carrie alone."

Kellie had no intention of dragging out her memories of nursing a child through the flu alone or having no one to share her pride the first time Carrie rode a bike. Not to mention the emptiness of knowing that she had missed other big steps in her child's life during the six months when Carrie was with her father.

"This is the easy part," Kellie answered flippantly, regretting that she'd told him so much about herself. "Wait till she hits thirteen. That's what my mom tells me."

Dan sensed her withdrawal. He wasn't sure if she was leery of him personally or only of him as Memorial's new VP.

"When did you lose your drawl?"

The question startled her. She had worked hard to rid herself of her Southern accent and wondered what had tripped her up. "What makes you think I ever had one?"

"Just a hunch." He wasn't ready to tell her that her Southern roots surfaced when she was angry.

"I had to dump the drawl for my radio work." Rachael had teased her unmercifully when she'd started working on her soft, slow speech so she could go on the air. "They didn't mind if Dolly Parton sounded like she'd just stepped off the plantation when she sang. But they wanted me to sound like a network newscaster when I did traffic reports."

He was right about her. There was more to this young woman than you'd know from looking at her fetching eyes and voluptuous figure. He remembered the extra training her file reflected. When she was determined, she apparently let nothing—not a drawl, not the wrong kind of experience—get in her way. "Wasn't that tough?"

"Not really."

Her terse response told him her discussion of her radio career had ended as abruptly as the conversation about being a single mother. Again he groped for a neutral topic. What was he doing wrong, he wondered, to turn the world's biggest smile into this stony face?

"This is the best hangout I've found since I moved to town, if you overlook the fact that it's elbow to elbow with medical types." He wondered what it would take to make her let down her guard completely. He had the urge to reach across the table and still her long, graceful fingers, which hadn't stopped fidgeting with her ring. "Do any civilians come here?"

Kellie was grateful to him for letting her slip out of a personal discussion.

"Rumor has it a banker came in one time," she said, repeating the tall tale Chip had told her on her first visit to the Medicine Chest. "By the time he left, his nose had been remodeled, his heart transplanted and his appendix removed. That was five years ago, they say, and no one outside the business has darkened the door since."

He laughed, a soft, warm sound that shimmied all the way down to her toes.

"Well, I like it in spite of that. Which is high praise from a semiprofessional pub crawler. By the time I've been here a year, I'll be able to point you in the direction of all the neighborhood spots where you can get good music, reasonable prices and friendly faces.''

"So that's what you do when you aren't on duty.'' Now that her nerves were calming, Kellie found it hard to keep her eyes from devouring him. She lowered her gaze but only succeeded in catching sight of the fair hair glistening on his forearms. His skin was golden brown against the starched white sleeves he had rolled up halfway to his elbows. The only safe thing to do was leave, she thought. "You're a barfly.''

He laughed again, and once more the sound trembled through her in ways that reminded her of how it felt to be a woman. "It's a time-honored avocation among medical types.''

"Aha! And I thought you were just another bureaucrat,'' she said, beginning to realize that her heart-racing reaction to him earlier in the week had not been a fluke. What was it about a silk necktie hanging loose around an open collar that seemed so much more intimate than no tie at all? she wondered. "That's why you fooled me when I saw you in action in emergency. You didn't act like a desk jockey.''

She hit so close to home that Dan almost flinched. Yes, he could have been a doctor if he'd wanted to. At one time, he had thought that was exactly what he wanted. The knowledge that he'd walked away from it sometimes gnawed at him still.

But this chance meeting certainly wasn't the time for a detailed chronology of his divorce and his retreat from medicine. Besides, it wasn't a story he especially wanted making the rounds at the hospital.

"I planned to be a doctor once, but changed my mind.'' The sharp, clipped words didn't sound like him, and he knew it. *And you wonder why you don't get close to people,* he chided himself. *Spit it out.* He heard his father's words again and for once doubted the wisdom in them.

Dan drained the last of his watered-down Scotch, then studied the expectant face across from him. He was sunk and he knew it. If her smile didn't get him, her eyes would. Remain uninvolved? Judging from his reaction to her, that seemed pretty unlikely.

Besides, he felt instinctively that his story wouldn't make it back to the hospital grapevine. And his instincts always served him well.

"I was as close to being a doctor as you can get without actually winning your stethoscope," he said, hiding his ambivalence behind a glib line. "When I finished med school, I had my choice of some pretty good internships. Instead I walked away."

"Why?"

"I let that goal—to become a doctor—rule my life for years." Dan stared blindly into his empty glass. "I put everything else on hold. Wife, children, enjoying my life."

Dan pushed his glass around the lacquered tabletop, as if intent on spreading the ring of moisture around the table. "One day I woke up and saw that being a doctor would always be all consuming. You don't doctor eight hours a day." Dan looked up, shaking off the seriousness in favor of a smile. "I wanted more out of life than that. So I gave it up."

Kellie mulled the dozen questions that his brief explanation brought to mind. What kind of man had the courage to give up a future of prestige and good money because he wanted more out of life? How much more?

She dismissed her curiosity. Why worry about getting him to open up when she certainly had no intention of being the subject of any personal probing. "How long ago was that?"

"Seven years."

Kellie wondered if that was also when he gave up the wife he had mentioned. Something haunted him more than the spare details he was revealing, something she could see in his vulnerable eyes. She looked away, uncomfortable that his eyes were so open that his private thoughts seemed to spill out. She was sure no one had ever looked that deeply into her private thoughts. It was a lonely feeling.

"Are you glad you did it?"

Was he glad? Dan asked himself. That was the real issue, after all, and she made it sound so simple. He *was* glad. He was even glad, when it came down to it, that in walking away from medicine he'd learned the truth about his blond, elegant wife. What Lauren really wanted out of life was a doctor for a husband. Not necessarily Dr. Daniel M. Brennan. Any doctor. And not Dan Brennan without the title in front of his name.

"Yes, I am glad," he admitted, astonished at how much he'd told her. If his instincts were wrong, the entire hospital would know by next week just as surely as if he'd sent around an interoffice memo. "I like what I do—figuring out how to make a hospital visit a little less impersonal, a little less frightening. I like the feeling that I help. And I've never regretted the fact that I don't get called in the middle of the night to deliver babies."

Noticing that Kellie was avoiding looking him in the eye, Dan cursed himself for getting off on such a serious subject. *That's what two Scotches will do for you, pal. Remember that.* "Ready for more wine?"

"No. I really do have to go." She wasn't sure she wanted to look into many more of Dan's private thoughts, tonight or any night.

"Would you like to get dinner first?"

Kellie's mouth went dry. A plate of anything with those well-muscled shoulders across the table beat the heck out of a frozen pizza with a TV rerun for company.

But why, she wondered, was he being so persistent? Was he really interested in her? Or did he hope to find out more about the helicopter service by oiling the machinery with good food and drink and a hefty dose of charm?

"No. I really do have to go."

She might have a date, you dope, he told himself, again blaming the extra glass of Scotch for his lack of finesse. "At least let me walk you back to the hospital parking deck. It'll be dark by now, and this neighborhood... well, let me put it this way. I understand it's a good thing there are so many hospitals nearby."

Agreeing more because she wanted to put off her solitude than because of any fear, Kellie began to regret her decision as they threaded their way to the door. If being with Dan in a crowded bar seemed dangerous, how would it feel to be alone with him? She wasn't sure she trusted herself to find out.

Their shoulders brushed as he held the door for her, and Kellie knew she had been right. The almost nonexistent touch hit her with a powerful surge.

The busy Southside neighborhood street looked anything but dangerous—or romantic—as they walked out onto the brightly lit sidewalk. Traffic whizzed down the wide four-lane thoroughfare. Even foot traffic was brisk. People dressed in hospital whites and UAB students in miniskirts and acid-washed denim were on their way to the delis and shops squeezed between banks, hospitals and doctors' offices.

"Actually this isn't such a bad neighborhood anymore," Kellie pointed out as they strolled up the hill to the parking deck, searching for something impersonal to take the charge out of the atmosphere. Climbing the hill was not the reason she felt breathless, she knew. "Twenty-five years ago, it was pretty rough. But not now."

"What happened to change it?"

"UAB. When the University of Alabama opened its Birmingham campus, young people started moving in."

He listened while she described the once-distinguished Southside neighborhood. Her face was animated as she painted a picture of the imposing stone manors that had grown up side by side with graceful, columned homes fashioned after Southern plantations.

Then, she explained, most of the people with money moved to ritzy suburbs ringing the city. Their big old homes became boarding houses or were bulldozed to make way for high-rise student housing, parking decks or the expanding medical complex that grew up around UAB.

"But the long-haired kids enrolled at UAB in the seventies liked the old boarding houses better than the student housing," Kellie concluded.

Though they didn't touch as they turned off the busy four-lane onto the quiet side street leading to the parking deck, she could feel the warmth from his nearness. Her skin carried the too-vivid memory of the moment her shoulder had brushed his as they left the bar. The slow-burning fire it had kindled hadn't stopped, even though she tried to concentrate on her story.

"So when the hippie students grew up and became yuppie doctors and lawyers, they started bringing the neighborhood back.... History 101. Introduction to Birmingham. Chapter One.''

Rachael would say she had talked too much, Kellie thought as they rounded the corner into the parking deck. But Rachael probably wouldn't have been as terrified of being wrapped in the moonlight with a man who made her go soft inside. The chatter helped Kellie ignore her awareness of the searching glances he gave her as they walked.

''When do I get Chapter Two?''

Anytime you say was the answer on her lips as they waited for the elevator. Trouble was, she meant it. She decided to try the words as a casual retort, so they could both walk away from the moment untouched. A quick quip, after all, was supposed to be her specialty.

But when his deep, dark eyes caught hers in the halo of the overhead light, Kellie's throat tightened, trapping the unspoken words.

He wanted her.

She wanted him, too.

Neither of them moved when the elevator chimed its arrival. A gentle sway in his direction and their lips would meet.

It was too late to walk away untouched. But she had to try.

''Thanks for the escort. I'll be fine from here.''

Her words echoed like a slap in the face through the empty parking deck.

Without waiting for him, Kellie stepped into the open elevator. He watched her until the doors eased shut, not speaking, refusing to release her wary eyes from his captive stare.

Leaning weakly against the walls of the metal cubicle, Kellie knew she had just looked into the eyes of the one man who could make her forget her caution, who could make her accept a casual romance if that was all he offered.

CHAPTER FIVE

MORNINGS LIKE THIS, Kellie knew without a doubt what it meant to be thirty-one.

Forget the occasional gray hair. That was nothing compared to puffy eyes and stiff shoulders and a dissatisfied feeling that said something was missing.

The coffee scalded her tongue, and she swore crossly, oblivious to the clarity of the sun-drenched sky and the flaming leaves drifting to the ground near her back deck.

"My, my, we're a bear this morning." Rachael's voice was disgustingly chipper. So was her shining face as she sat down across the redwood picnic table where Kellie was trying to bring herself slowly to life. "Is it safe to join you?"

"Probably not," Kellie mumbled, yawning. "I'm holding a cup of hot coffee, and I'm not alert enough to be responsible for my actions."

"Hmm. Maybe I won't ask if you'd like to go bicycling later today, after all."

"Can't. Brian's bringing Carrie soon. He's got to take Heather to her grandmother's funeral in Montgomery."

Rachael didn't miss the sudden sharpness in Kellie's voice when she mentioned her ex-husband.

"Your lovely mood this morning wouldn't have anything to do with Brian, would it?"

"Ballet lessons!" Shaking her groggy head, Kellie wiggled her toes to make sure the rest of her wasn't still in bed asleep. "The ballet lessons have started. And guess who goes with her? Heather."

"That's neat! You do want Carrie to get along with her stepmother, don't you?" Rachael said rationally. "Besides, I always wanted to take ballet, too, only Mom was sold on piano."

Kellie eyed her sister suspiciously.

"'That's neat'? Did I hear you say 'that's neat'? My only child is bonding with her stepmother, and all you have to say is 'that's neat'?"

Kellie realized instantly that her sister's muffled cough was an attempt to cover up a chuckle. She wondered if Rachael would ever understand the seriousness of raising a child.

"I think it's neat," Rachael said. "What's wrong with it?"

"What's wrong with learning softball with her mother, instead?" Kellie countered.

"Kellie, don't you think you're overreacting? Would you rather she hated her stepmother? Besides, dance will be good for her. And as long as she enjoys it, I can't see the harm." The two sat in silence for a few moments. Oscar padded up from the yard and placed his head in Rachael's lap. She rubbed the dog's head for a few moments, took a deep breath and spoke.

"Don't smother her, Kellie." She raised a hand to silence the protest that rose to her sister's lips. "She shouldn't have to live up to your expectations any more than you've ever wanted to be hemmed in by anyone's expectations of you."

"That's not fair! It's not like that at all!"

"Isn't it?"

Kellie looked away from Rachael's searching gaze. Pulling her knees up to her chest, she huddled against the sudden chill in the September morning air. "I just don't want her turning out to be Brian's idea of the perfect little girl."

Rachael grunted her doubt. "She's your little girl, too, sis. I seriously doubt that she'll let anyone turn her into something she doesn't want to be."

Kellie stared across the back lawn at her neighbors' yard, where two youngsters were already busy with a game. An ache of longing pierced her—a longing for all the times she couldn't be with Carrie. The youngster had grown so fast. One day she was barely out of diapers, and now she was enrolled in a dance class. Kellie harbored the illogical fear that she would pick Carrie up from Brian's one day and find her wearing lipstick and mooning over some pimply-faced adolescent boy. Or packing for college. Overnight, it sometimes seemed, Carrie was growing up. And Kellie was missing out on half of it.

"I just feel so...left out, sometimes," she muttered, her chin resting on her knees and her eyes focused on scenes her sister couldn't see. "I don't want her to grow away from me."

Rachael searched for the right words to reassure Kellie in her uncharacteristic insecurity. "You're a great mom, sis. Carrie worships you."

Kellie sighed. "She's the only thing I've got, Rachael. But she's only half mine. The rest of the time, I feel like a helicopter with no rudder. Where am I supposed to be going? What am I supposed to be doing with my life?"

"Living it, Kellie. And not for Carrie." She leaned over to bring herself into Kellie's field of vision as she made her point. "You're more than a mother. Start acting like it."

Shaking her tawny curls, Kellie shifted uncomfortably on the bench and didn't speak.

"You can't expect to bring up a daughter to be the kind of independent person you want Carrie to be if you show her with your actions that being a mother is the be-all and end-all of life," Rachael prodded softly.

Kellie's feet shot back to the deck. She stood and grabbed her coffee mug in preparation for a retreat to the solitude of her side of the house.

"Who appointed you Dear Abby?" she grumbled, upset with herself for having no coolheaded, logical arguments with which to counter her sister's assessment of the situation. "Besides, I'm more than just a mother. I'm a pilot, too."

"But when are you going to start being a woman?"

The words hurt. Kellie's inability to argue with them hurt even more. She remembered how she had frozen the night before, as panicked as an inexperienced teen at the idea that Dan Brennan might want her. And worse, at the idea that her own traitorous body might return his longing.

"It's cold out here," she said abruptly. "I'm going in."

Rachael smiled, amazed at how much preaching her sister had let her get away with before she withdrew into her shell.

Just before she closed the kitchen door behind her, Kellie heard her sister's final words.

"Don't you hate it when I'm right?"

With a forceful shove, Kellie slammed the door shut.

DOES ANYONE SEND FLOWERS anymore? Dan wondered as he paused in front of the hospital gift shop on the way to his office. The baskets of shiny dieffenbachia and ivy weren't very romantic, but the African violets captured his eye.

A cloud of lacy pink blossoms floated over the spray of dark, fuzzy leaves. The fragile plant in its beribboned basket was every bit as luxuriant as the ones his mother specialized in back home.

Dan felt almost like a traitor at the thought, then excused himself with the fantasy of a silver-haired woman bent lovingly over a tray of the exotic plants in her Deep South hothouse, a woman who looked like his mother and smiled like his mother. A woman who, like his mother, nurtured her crop of African violets because her husband had always given them on special occasions—birthdays, anniversaries, the birth of children.

Only love could produce such lush plants, Dan decided as he peered through the gift-shop window.

The furrow in his brow deepening, Dan turned toward the elevators. Kellie Adams probably wouldn't be impressed by a basket of violets, he thought. Lauren hadn't been. He'd had to explain, after his fourth gift of violets died from neglect on the kitchen windowsill, why violets meant so much to him. His ex-wife had smiled indulgently and absently fingered the soft leaves of gift number five.

It had died, too.

It was his own fault, Dan had told himself, for giving violets to a woman whose heart was closed to sentimentality.

No, Kellie Adams wasn't the sentimental type, either, Dan decided as he unlocked his office door. Maybe she wasn't worth the bother.

But as he opened his briefcase and drew out the reports he had worked on all weekend, he couldn't stop racking his brain, as he had the past two days, for a way to break down Kellie's resistance. Violets were the last in a long string of things that didn't sound quite right.

Kellie had made it clear on Friday night that any attempts to brush her off her feet would be met with chilling, unyielding stubbornness. In fact, her vanishing act had been downright ego crushing.

Or would have been, if Dan hadn't seen the spark of undeniable interest in her eyes. Her breathlessness when he had stared deep into her eyes had been almost palpable. And Dan was determined to touch that breathless naïveté.

But how?

Romancing a pilot had to be different from romancing a mere mortal woman.... How could he convince Kellie Adams he was worth coming down to earth for?

Dan turned his attention to the reports in front of him. But throughout the morning his train of thought was interrupted by the memory of the seductive slant of a pair of bright green eyes; of the soft feathering of short, tawny curls; of a wide, full mouth that trembled between effusive happiness and timid uncertainty.

A single rap on his open door wrested Dan's attention away from his reverie.

"You planning to eat admissions reports for lunch?" Anna Robinson's arms were folded across the ample bosom of her navy suit, a stern expression on her moon-shaped face. "Or can I drag you down to the cafeteria for spaghetti?"

Pushing his glasses onto his head, Dan grimaced. "Spaghetti in the cafeteria? That's sacrilege. Marry me and I'll show you what Italian food really tastes like."

Anna laughed, a big, throaty sound that filled the room and floated down the hall. "How can I trust a man named Brennan who claims to be an expert on Italian food? Doesn't ring true."

"Okay, you don't have to marry me." He raised his hands in mock defeat and rose, grabbing his jacket from the couch, where he'd tossed it hours earlier. "But it'll cost you a tennis match one afternoon to find out how much a fourth-generation Irish-American knows about marinara sauce."

"You're on, Brennan. I've got a mean backhand, even for an old broad with a broad backside."

Anna Robinson had been one of the few people whose welcome to Dan had seemed genuine. The director of admissions, fifty-five and on the plump side, had been willing to share friendly horseplay and dead-serious insights, revealing to Dan the hospital's official structure—and its not-so-official political structure. She had also made it clear that she supported his plans to make hospital procedures more patient oriented.

"How close are we to deciding how to bring our computer out of the Dark Ages?" Anna asked, selecting the smallest slice of peach pie for her tray as they went through the cafeteria line. "Are we ready to make a report at the board meeting this afternoon?"

Dan shook his head. "Let's hold off one more week. I've given everything a thorough look. I've narrowed it down to two systems that will do what we need, but I'd like to know a little more about them before we throw it open for discussion."

"So what's next? A cost analysis?"

"Exactly. Let's put our heads together this week, and we should have that by next week's board meeting."

"Good." She followed Dan to a table for two near the door. "That'll give me time to hit you up about helping us set up an employee grievance committee."

Dan shook his head decisively as he pulled the plastic wrap from his salad. "You're wasting your breath, Robinson. I'm not biting. I'm going to have enough wars to wage for a while without volunteering for another."

"But you're a natural, Dan," she protested. "You haven't been here long enough to have any built-in biases."

"Except for Len Baldwin," he reminded her.

"That's not bias. That's just good judgment," she retorted. "Besides, if you help with this committee, it'll go a long way in helping you get to know people around here. You may not have heard this up there in your executive suite, but the word is out that you're bad news. You could use some good PR."

Dan remembered the finality with which Kellie Adams had shut him out of her evening Friday. Maybe Anna was right. Or maybe he was right and he needed the edge that being an outsider gave him, especially in these first months of reorganization. Maybe that was part of what had made him successful everywhere else.

He covered a sigh with a forkful of wilting lettuce and a frost-bitten radish. Perhaps Kellie Adams had shown better sense in shutting him out than he had shown in pursuing her.

DAN SHUFFLED THROUGH the folder of data needed for the weekly board meeting, impatient at the thought of the work piled up on his desk while he sat through hours of rhetoric. Budget amendments and building reports and grounds reports and personnel changes.

At hospital business meetings, Dan sometimes lost sight of why he worked in hospital administration. So did the others responsible for running a hospital. And that was why Dan hung in through discussions of money and new equipment and the creation of a new tier of bureaucracy. He wanted to make sure the focus continued to return to the patient. To the purpose of healing that overrode efforts to run efficiently and save money and get the paperwork done.

He had just salvaged Birmingham Memorial's chaplain services, which were in danger of being cut to save money and office space. Dan had refused to bend in his vehement argument that the emotional well-being of patients and their families played as important a role in their recovery as the number of injections they received each day. So the other administrators had given grudging approval to negotiations with the chaplains for less office space and clerical help as alternative ways to save money on the service.

Dan glanced unobtrusively at his watch, then at what remained on the agenda. The report on the hospital's efforts to recruit minority nurses was the last thing to be covered before adjournment. The meeting had run longer than expected by half an hour; already, Dan could see dusk settling over the skyline through the window. Another ten minutes at most, he estimated.

But with the recommendations on admissions that he had to draft, he would be lucky to hit the sack before midnight.

Especially if he were lucky enough to find Kellie on duty tonight. Just to say hi. He thought of how quickly she could dispel the past two hours of stuffy discussion with nothing more than a smile. Or, if he was really lucky, one of those musical laughs of hers.

Dan shifted in his chair as the report ended, anticipating a quick adjournment. But before he could coax his lazy muscles to life, hospital president Bill Walton put a halt to his thoughts of escaping the boardroom.

''I know we're all ready to get home, but something came up today that we need a quick decision on before we take off," Bill said, peering over his bifocals at the others sitting around the table. "The FAA called this morning, asking quite a few questions about our new air-ambulance service."

Dan was instantly alert. Whatever the Federal Aviation Administration's interest might have meant to him a month ago, it now also meant they were interested in Kellie.

"Len and I can't be sure what this means," Bill continued, "but they've asked for a report on our safety measures. They indicated it's a routine request—one they're making of all new start-ups in the past year. But you can't be too careful when a federal regulatory agency starts nosing around."

Dan felt his unease growing. The feds seldom gave a clear reason for wanting information. Did this mean they planned to crack down and simply wanted support data? Were they doing it for show because someone else was on their backs? And if they were cracking down, where would his allegiance fall? Would he come down on the side of getting patients to the trauma unit as quickly as possible, even if it meant a greater margin of danger? Or would he throw support to eliminating the dangers that might also afford some patients their only chance at survival?

What really made Dan uneasy, however, was a sudden realization that more was at stake than a judgment regarding patient care.

If the FAA planned to force the issue, he could find himself party to making a decision that would affect Kellie Adams. Her safety and her livelihood could be in his hands.

He didn't like the feeling.

"We have every reason to believe Len planned our service after taking a close look at every conceivable safety issue," the president went on. "But because this is such a new practice, crashes all over the country have been very visible."

"You mean the press has hopped on them like flies on honey," quipped another hospital administrator.

"Now, Dick, you know I'd be the last one to compare the media to filthy little insects." Everyone laughed, knowing Bill Walton's infamous mistrust for the news media. "Right now, my question to you is this. How should we handle this request for a report?"

Surely, Dan reassured himself, Kellie saw to it that every possible precaution was taken when she was in the air. She might have flown off the handle that day in his office, but that didn't make her irresponsible.

Did it?

Whatever the case, Dan had a sneaking suspicion that the Kellie Adams he knew wouldn't take kindly to a bunch of bureaucrats snooping around her helicopter service.

"Can't we simply ask the people who run the service to give us a report on the safety measures they established when they set up the service?" asked Dick Harper, Memorial's comptroller.

Dan was glad someone else had asked the question.

The administrator who served as the hospital's liaison with the attorney it kept on retainer answered cautiously. "Is that going to satisfy the FAA, or are they more interested in an evaluation of how effective these measures have been? And if that's the case, how objective would the people who operate the service be?"

"Can you really evaluate the effectiveness of something that's been in operation only six months?" Dan asked.

"Whether we can or not isn't the issue," Dick responded. "The issue is that the FAA's getting involved here, and they license the whole shooting match, anyway."

"Now, hold on a minute," Bill Walton protested. "Our license isn't at stake. Let's not overreact. We've been asked for a simple report, and I don't think we need to blow this thing out of proportion."

"But it could be a volatile situation, and we have to be ready to handle it," the legal liaison said calmly.

"Let's keep in mind," Bill added, "that we decided to establish this service to counteract our public image. Birmingham has a number of progressive, innovative hospitals, and Memorial hasn't been one of them.

"But is the service safe?" The silver-haired president paused for a moment to let them ponder the question. "Who knows? Were heart transplants safe? And if they weren't, was it worth taking the risk so they would be fairly routine one day?"

"How many crashes are we talking about?" Dan asked.

Bill looked around the table. "More than a dozen around the country in the past year."

The figures didn't sound too high, but Dan still felt his stomach lurch at the thought of Kellie becoming one of those statistics.

"Doesn't sound that high, I realize." Bill seemed to read his thoughts. "As I read FAA, their main concern is that we don't create a monster. If this kind of service truly is a hazard, they'd rather nip it in the bud than wait another ten years until every town in this country has some hotshot pilot playing hero in airspace that's already overcrowded."

As the hospital's governing team started to choose sides, Dan realized for the first time that the air-ambulance service probably hadn't been easy to sell to this group. And with the federal government giving them a harder look, panic could easily set in.

He wondered how committed Kellie was to the work she did and how she would react if it came under siege.

Equally important, he wondered how he would react if the facts showed that the odds were against Kellie doing her work safely.

KELLIE SEEMED anything but safe when Dan set eyes on her a few minutes later in flight headquarters. He had walked down the stairs planning to warn her what was coming. But now, seeing her up close again, Dan realized that wouldn't be smart. She was just the type to go off half-cocked and storm Len's office.

Dan knew if he was smart he would turn and run. But he could only stand in the doorway and grin as he took in her long, shapely legs, propped on the counter in the cluttered office, the firm curves of her fanny testing the limits of her tan jumpsuit. Tugging fiercely on a golden brown curl at her temple, Kellie was absorbed in the paperback novel in her lap, her expression changing slightly every second or so as she responded to the story.

"You'll need a two-by-four to get her attention." Chip startled Dan out of his reverie. "When she gets started on one of those silly love stories, it takes an earthquake to move her."

He seemed to be right. Kellie showed no sign of having heard anything Chip said. Dan smiled, somehow pleased that this self-sufficient woman who had etched out an unconventional life for herself could still lose all sense of the world around her by reading a simple love story.

Maybe this was what he had missed in all the other capable, intelligent career women he had met in the six years since Lauren walked out of his life.

"I'm not much for swinging two-by-fours," he told the tall, thin nurse, who was sitting in a chair near Kellie. "Think I should leave her alone?"

Leaving her alone wasn't a bad idea, he thought, especially in light of his recent vote with the rest of the administrators to ask Len to work with Kellie to prepare a report on the air-service's safety measures and their reasons for choosing those measures. But he couldn't stop drinking her in. He hadn't noticed before what a cute dip her slender nose took right at the end. Vastly superior to all those turned-up noses out there, he decided.

"Let me handle this." Chip leaned forward and gave Kellie's feet a shove, sending them and her book toppling to the floor.

"Hey, what's the bright idea? He was just about to ravish her senseless!" Kellie grabbed the book and thumbed through it to find her place.

"I couldn't see the TV through your big feet, baby-cakes," Chip said. "Besides, you have a visitor. I told him you weren't worth the trouble, but he thought otherwise."

At last, Kellie looked in the direction of the door and almost dropped the book again when she saw Dan's burly form draped casually against the door frame. Her face lit up with a smile she was powerless to squelch.

"Hello!" She stood, self-consciously smoothing her jumpsuit. The excitement of the frenzied kisses in the now-forgotten book mingled with her own nervous excitement over the presence of the sandy-haired man before her. She realized for the first time that the lusty pirate in the book had materialized in her imagination as a broad-shouldered blonde with a crooked smile, despite the author's descriptions to the contrary.

"How about a soft drink?"

Kellie felt like a kid with a crush. And even with her back to Chip, she knew he was soaking up every inch of her flustered agitation.

She nodded, but as soon as they were out of range of Chip's big ears, she grabbed Dan's arm to stop him. "Do you really want a drink? Or would you settle for a walk around the grounds, instead?"

A walk around the grounds had much to recommend it over a watery soft drink in a brightly lit snack bar. They were already out the door and turning the corner toward the playground before Kellie remembered it was past sundown.

She recalled her panicked reaction to her last solitary walk with Dan Brennan. *There's nothing to panic over,* she warned herself. *You're overreacting. He's not a swashbuckling hero out to sweep you off your feet. That's pure fantasy. You just work together.*

Rachael's dig echoed in her mind. *When are you going to start being a woman?*

Nonsense, Kellie thought. *It isn't like that at all.*

"Fresh air. I get so tired of being cooped up," she said, unconsciously lowering her voice to suit the velvet night that had fallen around them. She forced herself to ignore the sliver of a moon that lit the sky, concentrating instead on the outdoor lights that served the purpose of safety well.

"I forget there's an outdoors after nine or ten hours locked in boardrooms," Dan agreed.

His deep, low voice shivered up her spine. The quivery softness that had frightened her so the last time they'd walked under the evening sky was definitely less intimidating now. She was on duty. Her tan-and-green flight uniform was her armor against his seductive magnetism. The beeper on her hip was her shield.

They walked in companionable quiet for a few moments, until they came to the playground gate. Kellie looked up, a playful look in her eyes. "Do you like to swing?"

"Can't say that I've done it for a while. My backside's probably outgrown the seats."

She walked toward the swings, laughing. "Don't be silly. I don't think swings can be outgrown." She sat down in one to prove her point. "Come on. It feels like flying."

As soon as he sat down on the narrow plank, hemmed in by the familiar iron chains, Dan realized his legs were too long and that unwedging himself from the low, snug swing would be an awkward endeavor.

But Kellie didn't let her long legs get in her way. Giving herself a few good pushes with her feet, she was soon flying high into the night air, legs stretched out in front of her to avoid dragging the ground. Dan watched, fascinated, as she sailed by, the wind sweeping her short hair away from her heart-shaped face. She forced herself higher and higher, until Dan grew worried that she would sail right off the swing.

His moment of anxiety reminded him of his earlier fears, and he stood abruptly, backing away from the swing and trying to bring back his vicarious pleasure in watching her. He again felt an urge to tell her about the FAA report; it would be the friendly thing to do. *Friendly isn't your job,* he warned himself. *Even if you'd like for it to be.*

When at last she stopped and walked back toward him, he saw the reflection of the moon's silver sliver in her eyes.

"Maybe it seems silly," she said breathlessly, "but I rediscovered swinging after I became a mother, and now I'm hooked. I love it."

He pushed away his thoughts of the FAA and helicopter safety. It wasn't his place to discuss the report with her, anyway. That was Len's job. He tried instead to concentrate on the little-girl wonder of the woman standing in front of him. How could the woman who had withdrawn from any hint of emotion last Friday have become the same woman who could now turn something as simple as a child's swing into a vehicle for reaching the sky?

"Do you love swinging for the same reasons you love to fly?"

Kellie impulsively took his hand and maneuvered him to a small merry-go-round. She pulled him down with her and started the wooden ride in a slow, lazy circle.

"Most people think I fly because of some romantic notion like feeling as free as a bird, or because it's adventurous." She stared at the ground, her voice thoughtful. "I started flying in college. I had wanted to for years, ever since my brother flew helicopters in Vietnam. I worshiped Sam. He was six years older than me, and I thought the sun rose and set on him. I was twelve when he went into the army."

She smiled fleetingly, remembering how handsome Sam had been in his uniform and how romantic it had seemed that he was going off to war. The memories dissolved into a lump in her throat.

"Hard to believe that was almost twenty years ago."

Dan heard the catch in her voice and knew intuitively what was coming.

"Anyway, Sam never came home. But when I was in college, years later, an old army buddy of his looked me up. I told him I used to daydream that Sam would teach me to fly, so he ended up teaching me, instead.''

Kellie tilted her head toward the sky, looking absently at the moon as they spun slowly around. Her face was serene.

''Flying made me feel close to Sam again, and getting to know his friend finally helped me accept Sam's death.'' She met Dan's understanding gaze and paused to enjoy the shadowy light flickering over his well-chiseled face. ''I found out Sam worshiped me about as much as I worshiped him. That helped.''

Dan reached out to brush a hand against the smoothness of her cheek. ''I'm sorry. That wasn't easy for a kid to deal with.''

Kellie closed her eyes and leaned into the gentle touch of his hand for a moment. ''I read somewhere that death is easier to handle if you had a good relationship. I guess it's true.''

''So flying helps you feel closer to your brother?'' Dan kept his voice low, hoping she would tell him more. He had already learned how little about herself Kellie was willing to give out.

''That's how it started, anyway.'' Her familiar smile was beginning to surface. ''For a while, I stuck with it because I liked being different. I never wanted to be ordinary. I liked stopping conversation at parties. I liked having something that set me apart.''

He felt the evening brighten with the return of her wide grin.

''But when Sam's friend decided he didn't want me to keep it up, I was stubborn enough to do it just for spite.''

Dan wondered uneasily if Sam's friend was still around. ''Why didn't he want you to fly? Still hung up about Vietnam?''

"Maybe." She shrugged, then her face brightened in a devilish smile. "No. Not really. He just didn't want to lose control. By then he was my husband, and he wanted me doing more . . . conventional . . . things. Wifely things."

Dan grinned in response to her light tone. He could imagine how easily her brother's friend had been captivated by a youthfully exuberant Kellie. And how he had tried to mold her to his own expectations once he had her within the safe confines of marriage.

He already knew how unsuccessful that had been. And he could read in Kellie's eyes her warning that she had learned more than flying from her first husband. Men expected her to fit into a conventional niche. And she had no intention of cooperating.

He wondered how much his own failed marriage colored his reactions to women. More than he would admit, he suspected.

"Could I interest you in a little unconventional activity right now?" he asked, the mesmerizing effect of her eyes glittering in the moonlight suddenly more than he could resist.

"Such as?"

But she knew. She could see it in the darkness of his eyes as they roamed her face. She could feel it in the poised tension of his body as he leaned toward her on the merry-go-round. Her heart was thumping as thunderously as it had in the parking deck a few nights earlier. But not, this time, from fear.

He knew she had seen the answer he didn't need to voice. Responding to the languor in her eyes, he reached out once again to feel the heat of her cheek against his fingers. He lowered his lips to hers, one slow inch at a time, aching for the sweetness at the same time that he wanted to prolong the magic of anticipation.

When at last his lips touched hers, it was lightly, teasingly, permitting only hints of soft fullness, only fleeting tastes of moist sweetness. It was not a first kiss of uncertainty, of safe exploration, but a kiss designed to leave behind the promise of passion.

CHAPTER SIX

KELLIE FELT guilty.

She knew she should feel nervous. Or at least properly obsequious. But facing a man in a three-piece suit across a polished oak desk—even when that man held the key to her paycheck each week—seemed like a piece of cake after some of the things Kellie had been through. Natural childbirth. A three-year-old with a stomach virus and a soaring temperature. A private plane that had dropped unexpectedly out of a bank of clouds directly in front of her chopper.

Those were things to be nervous about.

But a summons from Len Baldwin was just another minor irritation in a day that had started out badly. A day that had started with a bad case of the guilts.

After a fitful night, Kellie woke with the guilty memory of letting Dan Brennan kiss her. And the guilt had followed her into work, in fact right up here into Len's office, resisting her efforts to concentrate on anything but the gentle pressure of Dan's lips against hers. The brush of his soft mustache. The violent storm of response his tender touch had stirred in her.

She could barely keep her thoughts on Len, the memory was so vivid. The steady hum through her body hadn't stopped all night, Kellie was certain. Thankfully Margo was here with her. If heads were going to roll—although why, she couldn't imagine—at least Margo would be able to fill her in later, when her power to think clearly wouldn't be clouded by the ghost of Dan's kiss.

"I'll keep this brief." Len tapped a pencil methodically on the desktop, obviously uneasy over the task at hand. "The FAA has requested a report on the safety measures for the helicopter service. The board discussed it last night and agreed that you would be the best ones to make the report."

The quivery warmth flowing through Kellie quick-froze into ice. She swapped glances with Margo, then turned back to Len. On the surface, the request didn't seem particularly serious. But Kellie knew better than to take anything that came from the FAA too lightly. And the stocky, balding director seemed less than thrilled with the news, too.

While she pondered how extreme Len's discomfort seemed, Kellie was suddenly struck with the realization that Dan must have known this when she saw him last night. When he kissed her. When he looked down at her in the moonlight....

She now understood the chain-of-command protocol that didn't let him confide in her. But uneasy flutters warned her against sharing something as intimate as a kiss with a man who couldn't tell her all he knew.

The hospital grapevine called him a hatchet man. Why should she feel so confident she was right and everyone else was wrong about Dan Brennan?

"I've prepared an outline of the points the board feels should be addressed," Len continued, passing each of them a computer printout. "Doesn't have to be lengthy, but it should be as comprehensive as you can make it. If my secretary can help you run down any statistics or other documentation, just give her a call. No big rush. Is a month reasonable?"

Margo looked questioningly at Kellie, who gave an almost imperceptible nod as she studied the printout.

"We should be able to do that, Len," Margo said. "Is there any special reason the FAA wants this report now?"

The tapping of his pencil stopped, but Len didn't raise his eyes. "None that we know of. Just the usual, routine concerns about whether we're doing enough to assure safety."

"But we've only been in the air six months," Kellie pointed out, her irritation over FAA scrutiny obscuring for the moment her thoughts of Dan. "We filed a report on all of this when we first went after our license. Why so soon?"

Len looked up and tried to muster an unconcerned expression. His eyes drifted to the left of her face. "I honestly believe it's just a little bit of governmental chain yanking. You know, remind the new kids on the block that this is serious business by making them do everything in triplicate. If I thought it was more serious than that, you'd be the first to know."

Kellie hoped her skepticism didn't show. These days, it seemed she was the last to know about everything. "Should we look for any information that would compare air-ambulance safety to the safety of standard vehicles?"

"No," he answered hastily. "I don't think we ought to go on the defensive at all. Let's just give them what they asked for and be done with it."

A few minutes later, Kellie learned that Margo was as skeptical as she.

"Do you think they'd take our license away?" Margo asked as they stepped off the elevator.

"Only if we screw up," Kellie responded, pulling the rolled-up printout from her pocket.

"Your reassurance is comforting."

"You know, I don't care what Len says. I think I'll work on a few more safety recommendations while I'm at it. Find out if the other hospitals are doing anything we aren't."

"Why bother if he doesn't want it?"

Kellie wasn't ready to share her suspicions that the hospital's new vice president might have a bias against the use of helicopters. If she could anticipate his objections—his reaction to the chaos at the river was a good example—it might save headaches in the long run. But she didn't want Margo or the others with the flight service to worry that they were on the new hatchet man's hit list.

"I just like to be prepared," she responded.

Margo ran a hand through her tight curls. "Seriously, the FAA can't take away our license before we're up for renewal, can they?"

Kellie raised her eyebrows. "Uncle Sam can do anything he darn well pleases. Haven't you noticed how much of your paycheck he helps himself to each week? Would you trust anyone who would do that to us poor working stiffs?"

Margo grunted her agreement.

"What's Len's complaint this time?" Chip asked as they walked back into flight headquarters.

The two women explained the outcome of their meeting. Chip, if anything, seemed even more upset than Kellie at the idea of the FAA wanting to know more about the air operation.

"Great!" he fumed, slamming his coffee cup onto the counter. "Just what we need! A bunch of bureaucrats poking around where they aren't needed."

Margo gave him a sharp look. "Don't get in a tizzy, old man. Nobody's gonna be poking around. We've just got to write a report, that's all. And even if they did decide to come down here and give us a look, there's nothing to worry about. Right?"

Kellie had started writing a memo explaining the report to the nurses and pilots who staffed the other shifts, and didn't notice the long silence that preceded Chip's reluctant reply.

"Right. It's just the idea of it. We have enough to sweat over without having the FAA on our backs. That's all."

THE COLD SWEAT was an icicle down his back. He prayed his voice would sound normal as he reached over the half door leading to the hospital pharmacy to let himself in.

"Terry, I'm coming through," he called out to the young pharmacy technologist who manned the room during the lunch hour. To Chip's ears, his own voice sounded strained, ready to crack. "Gonna pick up this medication for Dr. Holton in emergency."

"Right, man," came the response. "It's in the ER bin."

Chip quickly found the medication he had volunteered to come for, then listened for the sound of Terry's crepe-soled step. Chip slipped between two shelves of prescription drugs. Searching for the now-familiar vials, he paused to look and listen as a final precaution before palming the drugs.

"See you later, Terry," Chip said as casually as he could, then left. He tried to walk slowly, unhurried. But by the time he reached the corner, he was almost jogging, one hand shoved deep in his pocket, wrapped in a sweaty clench around the medicine.

Panic electrified his nerves when Chip almost ran into a doctor wheeling around the corner. The doctor couldn't possibly know what he'd done. His sweaty palm tightened around the drug vial. No reason for him to suspect anything, Chip reasoned with himself as he forced a friendly grin. No more reason than the FAA or Margo or Kellie had to be suspicious.

But by the time Chip slipped into the men's room, he was on the verge of nervous tears. Locking himself in a stall, he slumped against the door.

There has to be a better way, he told himself once again.

His father's gray, listless face filled his head. His mother's weary, shuffling step as she returned from her second job late every night echoed in his memory.

Chip wished desperately for someone to confide in. He felt sometimes as if he locked himself deeper and deeper into solitary confinement with each petrifying visit to the hospital pharmacy. Maybe someone else—Margo or Kellie—could help him think of another way to handle this.

Then he envisioned the dread in his mother's face. He felt the emptiness of being forced into a deadly desk job or asked to retire early.

There was another way. But not a better one.

DETERMINED TO PUT the upsetting news about the FAA out of her mind, Kellie wedged her way into a break in the lunch-hour foot traffic streaming up and down the sidewalk in front of Birmingham Memorial. She snuggled into her leather flight jacket and zipped it against the autumn wind as she headed for the bookstore in the next block.

Now that Carrie was in the first grade and was learning to read in earnest, her ability had far outstripped the simple books that lined the built-in shelf above her bed. Kellie wanted to restock the shelf with more challenging books, since Carrie now insisted on reading the bedtime stories aloud herself.

Absorbed in her mental debate over whether to look for simple versions of the classics that would be appropriate for Carrie's reading level or to buy books that might better depict today's world, Kellie didn't hear the voice calling her name from half a block away.

Dan was at her elbow before his deep, mellow voice sounded in her ear. "Do you always walk like the finish line has just come into view?"

The tingling rush of his kiss. The not-quite-justified sense of betrayal. The fear of her own powerful emotions. All these tugged at Kellie's senses as he moved up beside her on the sidewalk. His arm was too close. His lips too far away. His eyes saw too much. And said far too little for Kellie to be sure how she should react.

Her insecurities took charge. "Only when I'm being followed."

His half smile told her the waspish retort didn't put him off. She turned to stare straight ahead. The red-and-white striped awning of her destination was only four storefronts away now. But even with her eyes rigidly focused on the store, she could hear the light teasing in his voice.

"So I was right. You *were* trying to lose me in the crowd. I've watched enough old detective flicks to recognize evasive action when I see it."

Not even pausing as she pushed open the door under the candy-striped awning, Kellie kept her voice even and cold. "Then consider yourself lost. If you have business to discuss, leave a message on the board in the flight office."

The jangle of the bell above the door quieted for a moment before Dan's entrance set it off again, which told Kellie she had stunned him at least temporarily. She wandered, aimlessly fingering the books on display at a sale table, her mission forgotten as she pondered her reactions. The complication of the FAA report faded as Dan's magnetic presence moved into the foreground again. He was behind her now. Without even looking, she could feel him studying her. She could remember the power of his kiss, whispering over her lips like early-morning fog on the lake. Her body shivered to awareness under the businesslike cotton of her flight suit.

Kellie faked an avid interest in a coffee-table book on the French Impressionists.

"You've talked to Len, haven't you?" The teasing tone was gone.

Calmly closing the book, Kellie braced herself to meet his soft brown eyes. She turned, determined to be firm. "It's a good thing, isn't it? I wouldn't know a thing about you if it weren't for Len filling me in, would I?"

The furrow in his forehead deepened, shadowing his troubled eyes.

"Len has nothing to do with us." His tone was even and measured, each word carefully chosen. "The hospital has nothing to do with us. The work we do back there has nothing to do with us. I want to keep it that way. Don't you?"

Frustrated with his calm logic, Kellie turned away briskly and scanned the store for the children's section. "I don't know what you're talking about. But I'm busy right now."

Before she could move away, Dan's hand encircled her wrist. A current shot through her, a sizzling jolt of electricity that robbed her of her awareness of anything except the man who had captured her arm so tenderly. So inescapably.

"Quit playing games, Kellie." She heard the determined edge of someone accustomed to giving orders. But his hand on her arm, his hand sparking shooting stars through her body, made it impossible for her to rebel at the authoritative tone. "I'd like to get to know you. And

I think you'd like to get to know me. But we're both professional enough to know that we have to leave the hospital behind if we're going to..."

Kellie jumped at the opportunity his hesitation created. Snatching her arm from his hand, she backed away from him. "Why do you want to get to know me? So you can keep an eye on me for the FAA?"

The working of his jaw made Kellie wonder just how far Dan's patience could be stretched.

"No. I just want to make sure you have plenty to keep you angry and on the defensive." He shoved his hands into the pockets of his pleated dress pants. "I think I'm doing a damned fine job. What do you think?"

Kellie wondered if Dan's irritation mirrored her own and had a pretty good hunch that it did. An image of Carrie, pouting angrily at such imagined injustices, sprang to mind, and it was all she could do to corral her threatening smile.

"Listen, I'm sorry. Maybe I overreacted." She shrugged. "It wouldn't be the first time. I'm famous for it."

His dark eyes warmed again, and the tension ebbed from his jawline. "Good. I like a volatile woman."

Her leather jacket was too hot for the small store, Kellie realized. She unzipped it, but that didn't seem to help. She had felt safer when Dan was on the verge of anger and she had a wall of righteous indignation to hide behind. She smiled nervously, her mouth dry, her heart a furiously ticking time bomb.

Pointing toward the aisle of children's books, Kellie started to make her excuses and her escape.

Dan shook his head. "Not until you promise."

"Promise what?"

"Promise to help me use these tickets." From the breast pocket of his suit, he pulled two tickets and waved them in the air.

"What kind of tickets?"

"Football. Saturday. Alabama versus somebody." He stopped long enough to look at the tickets. "Georgia Tech. Big game. When these two teams get together, you can throw past records out the window."

She chuckled at the football cliché and thought greedily of the thrill of a Saturday afternoon at Legion Field. The stands were a sea of red as the college team ran for touchdowns and tried to trample the opposition. Tickets to Crimson Tide football games were difficult to come by. She wanted to go. Most of all, she wanted to go with Dan Brennan.

But single mothers have to learn to let opportunity pass them by.

"I can't, Dan. I have Carrie this weekend." She couldn't help but feel a little guilty at how much she regretted missing the game. Missing an afternoon with Dan. *You'll be with Carrie, for goodness' sake,* she reminded herself.

"Great! Does she like football? Bring her, too."

"But—"

"She doesn't like football? What kind of daughter are you raising?" His eyebrows shot up, teasing her with pretend horror. "I thought this was Alabama, where football reigns and basketball is just a pastime until it's time to toss the old pigskin around again."

"Of course she likes football. But two tickets won't get all three of us in. Besides—"

"Leave the ticket problem to me. What time should I pick you up? Kickoff is at two."

"But—"

"I hear the traffic is awful. Is noon early enough?"

"Dan, I don't think—"

"Great. It's settled. Noon." He took her arm and laced it through his. "Now what book are you looking for? Maybe I can help."

It wasn't until later in the day that Kellie realized how easily Dan had bullied her into accepting his invitation. But as Saturday drew near, she simply couldn't work up any real aggravation over the fact.

GIVING THE STITCHES that had saved Sissy's life a thorough examination, Dan turned to Carrie's upturned face. He almost smiled at her motherly concern for the doll, then remembered his own role as the kindly but serious doctor.

"You've been taking good care of Sissy, just the way I told you, haven't you?" he asked, placing the doll gently in Carrie's arms.

"Yessir," she said solemnly. "No more swinging her by the arm. Not even her good arm."

"Good. She seems to be one hundred percent healed now, so I must say you've done a commendable job." He patted Carrie on the hand, unable to resist smiling as her wide little-girl grin reminded him of her mother.

"'Commendable'?" Carrie repeated the word, excited to encounter another long word to add to her list. "What's that?"

"It means you should get a pat on the back for doing such a good job."

"Oh. Okay." She waited expectantly. "Well, aren't you gonna pat me on the back?"

Dan laughed and did just that, thinking he would gladly give her a hug to go along with it if he knew her a little better. *Someday,* he promised himself as Kellie appeared from upstairs. *Someday I'll know them both a lot better.*

Since she had answered the door and disappeared upstairs, Kellie had capped her light brown curls with a rakishly tied lavender silk scarf that matched the stripes in the slacks she filled out so fetchingly. Dan admired her effortless stylishness, which he also saw reflected in her living room.

The room, he had decided, was just like Kellie—a little unexpected, a little too flashy to be ordinary. A brightly colored Mexican piñata hung in one corner over a wicker papasan chair with a circular cushion that cried out for someone to curl up with a book or in front of the TV. Oriental rice paper curtains were a shade of pale orchid that was repeated in splashes of silk flowers and hand-thrown pottery and a stuffed fabric fish mounted tongue in cheek over the fireplace. A few antiques—the old trunk doing duty as a coffee table, an art deco lamp with fringed shade and a stiff-backed corner chair that served as home for a solemn-eyed marionette—looked as if they'd been salvaged from someone's rummage sale.

Dan had smiled as the warmth of the room surrounded him with its message that life was too much fun to be taken too seriously.

"Have you given Sissy her clean bill of health?" Kellie's eyes were bright as she greeted him again.

"She's just like new," Dan proclaimed, hoping Kellie couldn't see the hunger in his look. That first kiss—their only kiss—had kept him on edge for days. He had felt the leashed yearning in the tentative touch of her lips and longed to push her past whatever reservations held her back.

But today would not likely be the day for that, he reminded himself as Carrie's impish voice interrupted his thoughts.

"Why can't Rachael go with us, Mommy?" Carrie asked as she shrugged into her pint-size denim jacket.

"Because she has other plans today." Kellie's hands fumbled awkwardly with the metal buttons on Carrie's jacket as she suddenly realized how grateful she was to have her six-year-old as a buffer. She wasn't sure she was ready to handle Dan Brennan alone.

"With Elliott?" Carrie asked, excitement lacing her voice.

"With Elliott," Kellie affirmed, watching nervously from the corner of her eye as Dan studied the collection of books hemmed in by the brass bookends. Would he, like Brian, think that her selection of favorite novels was shallow?

To heck with him if he does, she thought, almost missing Carrie's next question. "Are they going to get married?"

Kellie couldn't stop a chuckle. Her daughter had been preoccupied with the idea of marriage ever since Brian had announced his impending wedding. Carrie was no doubt anxiously awaiting another opportunity to wear an overpriced dress and sprinkle rose petals in the church aisle, while imagining herself to be the center of attention.

"Just because they are dating does not mean they will get married." Kellie repeated the phrase like a robot and rolled her eyes for Dan's benefit, hoping he wouldn't think Carrie had picked up such an idea from her.

"TAKE A LOOK at the replay, ref!" Kellie's voice, ringing out from their forty-yard-line seats, was almost lost in the roar of the crowd. "That's no fumble!"

Discovering that Kellie and her daughter were big sports fans had been like discovering a bud about to open on one of the lush plants lining his folks' greenhouse—it made something already special seem even more so. And now that they were part of the crush of people packed in Legion Field, wolfing down nachos and soaking up the sunshine that tempered the September chill, he was equally delighted to discover that Kellie was not a ladylike spectator.

"I might have known," he said when they settled back onto the bench after cheering in the first touchdown of the game.

"Known what?" Kellie asked, warming to the sight of Carrie perched on his knee, intent on shaking the red-and-white pompon Dan had brought back with their first round of soft drinks and hot dogs.

"That you'd be a rude and raucous fan. I like that in a woman."

"Don't get carried away admiring me," she teased in return. "I have my bad points, too, you know."

"Such as?"

Their conversation was put on hold for a moment while Kellie joined the crowd in a roar of approval as the kickoff landed deep in Alabama territory, leaving the Georgia Tech Yellow Jackets with more than ninety yards to go for a touchdown.

"You were about to fill me in on your bad points," Dan prompted Kellie when she finished her cheer.

"I was?"

"Umm-hmm. It's called truth in advertising."

"Do I get another hot dog first?"

"After."

Kellie puckered her brow in a poor imitation of giving the matter thoughtful consideration. "Bad points, huh? Well, I get crazy in rush-hour traffic."

Carrie registered the conversation and turned to face them. "That means she yells at other drivers. And runs yellow lights."

Dan nodded gravely and brushed back a strand of hair that had escaped Carrie's braid.

"I'll tell this, sport. You just watch the ball game." Kellie tweaked her daughter's nose. "And I'm always hungry because I'm always on a diet. That's about it."

Dan nodded deliberately. "At least you've been completely honest with me." He studied her face carefully, wondering at the propriety of stealing a kiss from a woman while her daughter wiggled on his knee. "You're sure I won't find any darker secrets later?"

"Absolutely not," she assured him. "Except for those things, I'm a saint."

"If that turns out to be true, I'm going to be an extremely disappointed man."

Kellie's impish grin faded and her pulse quickened at the clear message in the honey-brown eyes sweeping over her face. If she didn't turn her attention elsewhere in a hurry, she was likely to create a scandal right here in front of seventy-five thousand people, one of whom was her six-year-old child. *Single mothers can't afford to feel this way,* she chided herself.

"And I'm going to be extremely disappointed if we have to punt the ball here," she said, straining to sound normal as she directed their attention back to the game.

By halftime, Kellie was more than ready for a chance to move her fidgety limbs. She was also ready to stand up and distance herself from the steady pressure of Dan's brawny shoulder against her arm. Every time Carrie moved—which was even more often than the ball was snapped on the playing field—the jostling and shifting brought Kellie into physical contact with Dan. Sitting shoulder to shoulder with him for the past ninety minutes had been a bigger strain on her self-control than she would have imagined.

When Kellie unfolded her long legs and Carrie climbed onto the bleacher to tug on her mother's arm, Dan didn't budge.

"Maybe you're new at this, Dan, but milling around at halftime is an important football ritual." She gave Carrie a hug but resisted lifting the fifty pounder into her arms. "Otherwise, you might end up seeing part of the halftime show. And that could turn you off football forever."

"Yeah, come on, Dan." Carrie reached for his hand, trying to coax him out of his seat. "I need ice cream."

Dan faked a protesting groan and allowed Carrie to pull him up from the bleacher. "And the wooden planks were just beginning to get comfortable."

"Is that one of yours?" Kellie asked as they eased their way through the crowd.

"One of my what?" He smiled, watching the fluid rhythm of her hips as she climbed the steps leading to the concession area.

"One of your bad points?" she said, harking back to the conversation two touchdowns and a field goal earlier. "That you're too lazy to get up during halftime?"

His nod conceded the point. "No point in trying to hide it now."

"What else?"

"Did you notice, during the second quarter, how quick 'Bama's quarterback is?"

''You're avoiding the issue,'' she protested, noting the twitch of his lips under his dark blond mustache as he threatened to smile. ''You were about to tell me your bad points.''

''I was? I find that hard to believe.'' He leaned over to capture Carrie's attention now that they were out of the flow of traffic. ''Which direction to the ice cream, short stuff?''

Carrie pointed and took him by the hand again.

''You're not going to distract me,'' Kellie warned as she caught up with them.

''But can I bribe you?''

Kellie's eyes brightened. ''Ice cream for me, too? In one of those plastic football helmets?''

''Whatever you want.''

What Kellie wanted, at that moment and for the rest of the afternoon, was Dan. She ate ice cream, but she tasted his lips. Her eyes dutifully followed the players up and down the field, but she didn't miss a single one of Dan's moves, either, as he put his crooked grin to work charming both her and her daughter.

By the time the game was over and they had finished dinner at a burger joint, Carrie was worn out. But Kellie was even more keyed up than she had been when the day started.

As she tucked Carrie into bed, Kellie resisted the urge to shake the sleeping youngster's shoulder. A few good nudges and an exhausted Carrie could be counted on to cause enough sleepy-eyed ruckus to scare off even the most ardent of dates.

Dan sat downstairs. Waiting. Waiting for her to finish being ''Mommy'' for the day. Waiting for her to come back downstairs and engage in a little contact sport of their own.

She had seen the waiting in his eyes all afternoon. Every look they had exchanged had simmered with promise.

How dare Carrie desert her now, when she needed her most!

Drawing a deep breath, Kellie pressed the back of her hand to her cheek. Hot. No doubt visibly hot. She felt the same way all over.

Carrie sighed and shifted on her narrow bed but merely snuggled closer to her rag doll. Admitting she had stalled as long as politeness would allow, Kellie left the room and started slowly down the stairs. Dread put lead in her feet.

What she dreaded most, she knew, was putting her own willpower to the test. Drawing an evening to a graceful close hadn't been hard when her dates hadn't inspired much response. But sending Dan home would be another matter.

The dread mixed with restless longing when she saw Dan, his broad frame sprawled on the couch. The gray, camelback couch looked, suddenly and unaccountably, too small for both of them. Fleetingly she thought of sinking into the round papasan chair. But that wouldn't be, she knew, proper date etiquette.

An insistent throb, telling her he was near but not near enough, intensified the moment she sat beside him on the couch. She had felt it off and on all afternoon, all evening. When she fed him a spoonful of her butter pecan. When he laughed and wiped the dot of ice cream from her chin. When she wondered how his well-defined arms, then wrapped protectively around her daughter, would feel wrapped tightly around her.

Kellie sat facing him, curling her feet beneath her. Her knees brushed a solid thigh, and the shock waves traveled to the roots of her hair.

When Dan reached out to trace her jaw with the lightest touch of a finger, the reverberations quaked her. The almost indiscernible rise and fall of his chest inspired her with an aching need to seek out the thundering heartbeat that must surely match her own.

"I've wanted to kiss you all day." His voice shuddered through her, a pledge of tenderness. "I watched your lips while you reviled the Georgia Tech coach and held myself back with the utmost restraint while you licked the ice cream from the corners of your mouth. All in the name of waiting patiently."

Kellie waited breathlessly for him to continue. She could almost feel the touch of his lips and knew it would be the first sip of wine to one who couldn't stop until the bottle was empty.

"And now I have the feeling you want to keep me at arm's length."

Disappointment tainted her appreciation of his ability to read the subtle shadings of her behavior. He was right and he was oh, so wrong. She wanted him to leave before the embers smoldering in her burst into white-hot flame. And at the same time, she wanted him to ravish her until she forgot the rigid code she had imposed on herself as a single mother. She wanted him. Period.

"Am I right?"

Kellie saw in his eyes the faint hope that she would deny his words, a hope that dimmed with her silence. She wanted him to understand but couldn't face airing all her feelings of uncertainty and insecurity.

"Dan, I . . ." How could she tell him that she wanted him and she didn't? It sounded crazy and he would probably march out of her house never to darken her door again. It didn't happen that way in those love stories she lost herself in. But this was reality, where people really screwed up and never had a chance to get things right again. She grabbed the first cowardly excuse that came to mind. "It's Carrie. She wakes up easily and I'd be afraid that if we...that she might..."

What the heck, she told herself weakly, he'd never know that Carrie, just like her mom, wouldn't wake up if a bulldozer was bringing the house down around her.

Dan's attempt to hide his disappointment was commendable. *But he'll never make it to stage or screen,* Kellie told herself. *Maybe I blew it, after all.*

For a fleeting moment, Kellie toyed with the idea of backtracking and telling him the truth. That she was just plain afraid of her emotions because she had stayed away from men for so long. That she sometimes felt guilty even thinking about giving a man the same amount of love and attention she gave her daughter. But she held back. *Maybe it'll be easier later,* she convinced herself, *when I know him better.*

If there is a later.

"Maybe I'd better go now."

He didn't sound angry, but Kellie reminded herself that Dan could be the silent, seething type instead of the hurl-angry-expletives type.

She followed him to the door, trying to sort out a way to salvage the situation without making it worse, instead. But her brain was a muddle of conflicting emotions. Should she give him time to get over being upset? Or would that just give him time to stew about the way she sent him packing tonight?

Oh, goodness, I've really done it now!

Kellie felt light-headed when he turned at the door and placed his hands gently on her shoulders. "Do you think one kiss before I go would be safe?"

He was teasing her. She could see the wicked gleam in his eyes and the cockeyed grin that said he didn't buy her excuse for a minute.

"Barely safe," she admitted, melting into him as he pulled her into his arms.

Dan eased his hands over her back in lazy circles as he covered her lips with his. His touch wandered from the soft curls at her nape down to the flare of her hips, lingering there tantalizingly but stopping just short of caressing the womanly fullness not disguised by her pants.

Straining to concentrate on the delicious teasing of his lips, Kellie was distracted by the press of his broad, firm body. She wanted to snuggle into the firm bend of his arm and lean against him the rest of the night. But the slim, hard waist against her hand and the length of muscular thigh against hers lulled her into a state of mind that asked for more than friendly comfort. As she had known it would.

Too soon, Dan returned his hands to her shoulders and ended the kiss that had echoed through her.

"Good night, Kellie." He matched his whisper with the fluttering brush of his fingertips along her jaw. Kellie ached with longing for him to stay.

What made him different? she asked herself minutes later as she watched from an upstairs window while his sports car pulled away from the curb. What made him impossible to resist when others had been so easy to tell no?

And why now, of all times, when she had finally met a man who seemed so much more real than most of the single men she had met since her divorce, was she trying so darned hard to shut him out of her life?

Grabbing the flannel gown that hung like a disapproving accusation from the hook inside her closet door, Kellie got ready for another night of snuggling up alone in the middle of her queen-size bed. Tonight, her body wanted fluid silk, and here she was bedding down with the same old faded flannel. Giving her pillow a resentful punch, Kellie closed her eyes to the darkness.

Before, knowing that Carrie slept peacefully in the next room had made up for the loneliness of knowing she would fall asleep alone and wake up alone. Tonight, it didn't help.

Tonight, Kellie wondered if the comfort she took from Carrie would survive the invasion of a new stepmother. With that threat, the last thing she needed was a man in her life to steal her attention from Carrie. It would take all her energy and determination to keep their relationship strong.

But right now it was taking all her energy and determination to still the waves of response that swept through her every time she remembered Dan's kiss.

CHAPTER SEVEN

FEAR SKITTERED AROUND the edges of her consciousness.

The chopper moved through an endless sea of white. Nothing ahead of her, nothing to the side of her, nothing above or below but clouds. It might have been beautiful, were it not so treacherous.

The voices on the other end of the radio were Kellie's only reality. The calm male voices crackling in and out. Every time one of the voices disappeared for a split second, the victim of a patch of turbulence or a competing broadcast, the fear fluttered a hairbreadth closer to the surface.

If the voices helping her interpret the readings on the instrument panel in front of her disappeared for good, she and Chip and Margo would be doomed, as would the farmer who had collapsed with massive heart failure just minutes earlier.

They had been on the ground longer than usual, trying to stabilize the forty-six-year-old man before heading back to Birmingham with him. And the cloud cover had rolled in faster than anyone had predicted.

So Kellie had no choice but to fly by following the instructions of the popping, fading voices from the control tower and hospital dispatch. She had no choice but to trust the truth of the instruments on her flight panel when they assured her she was flying straight ahead instead of toward the ground. She had to believe someone in a control tower miles away when he told her she was headed into empty airspace and not crashing into another aircraft also feeling its way through the clouds.

The fear escalated into a prickle of panic as the voice of the air-traffic controller backfired into silence once again and was gone too long for comfort.

Kellie flew by instrument as well as anyone, but she was always aware how vulnerable she and her passengers were when she depended on air-traffic controllers to guide her safely to her destination. Normally she would bring the chopper down below cloud cover or set down and wait for an ambulance to come after the patient rather than take the risk. But Birmingham's skyline was too close right now to let them lower their altitude without risking a crash with the side of a skyscraper. And they were almost as close to the hospital as they were to the nearest landing site. So Kellie had made the reluctant decision to spend the extra three minutes in the air and take it on home.

It was the right decision, she reassured herself as she kept an edgy eye on the instruments that measured her altitude and her speed and pinpointed her exact location. *I'm a skilled pilot with ten years of experience. It's not like I'm a rookie.*

But plenty of skilled pilots lose it flying instrument, another inner voice admonished. Every pilot could tell stories of colleagues who'd lost their equilibrium, whose instincts had told them they were flying straight ahead when their instruments and the people in the towers told them they were headed for the ground. It happened.

Kellie tried to calm the involuntary racing of her heart. She concentrated on the instruments and pushed the scare stories out of her mind. She shivered. Even under her flight jacket, she could feel the gooseflesh.

"Location?" The voice of the hospital dispatcher crackled over the radio. Kellie gave him her altimeter reading, her shiver now verging on a constant tremble.

Get a grip on yourself, she commanded as she registered the instructions from the tower to move twenty degrees to her right. Was it another aircraft breathing down her neck? she wondered. A building? How close? And what if she actually needed twenty-two degrees? They could be wrong.

A film of perspiration broke out on Kellie's upper lip. The hand gripping the control stick that turned the main rotor was damp, too, so she switched hands long enough to wipe the dampness on the leg of her flight suit. Then she gripped the stick with both fists. Almost instantly, they were damp again.

Even Chip and Margo were deathly quiet in the cloud-enshrouded chopper. Only a faint whisper passed between them from time to time. Did they feel her uncertainty? she wondered. Did they know panic was ready to rise in an uncontrollable giggle from the lungs she could scarcely fill with air?

I'm going to kick your behind when we get this crate on the ground, she reproached herself. *You're a pro. Act like it.*

Grappling for a way to calm herself, Kellie fixed her sights on the billowing clouds that obstructed her view of anything identifiable. *You're close to the hospital now,* she told herself. *Just below you is the side of Red Mountain.* She strained to envision the slashes of rusty-colored iron ore rising in a sheer, magnificent cliff on either side of the four-lane highway that had been carved into the heart of the mountain. *Any other day,* she told herself, *I could glance straight down from here and see cars creeping across the mountain. Just like a thousand times when I did traffic reports.*

She was able to draw a long breath without shuddering. *Now I'm in sight of Vulcan,* she continued her pep talk, calling to mind the sixty-ton iron statue of the Roman god that had been built for the 1904 World's Fair, then brought back to straddle the crest of a hill in this city known for its iron industry. She could see his fist now, wrapped around the beacon pointing skyward.

Next was the glistening side of a glass-fronted office complex, her signal that they were in the home stretch.

Her heart slowed its frantic pace. Her imaginary tour was doing the trick. Blotting her upper lip with the sleeve of her jumpsuit, Kellie willed herself to focus on her returning calm.

Her radio snapped with the message from the control tower that it was time to start the descent that meant she would soon be in sight of the helipad at Birmingham Memorial.

As she lowered the craft toward the pad and the world came into view through the Plexiglas bubble, Kellie breathed a silent prayer of thanks and steeled her hands to stop the hint of trembling that remained.

THOSE MOMENTS of terrifying disorientation wouldn't leave Kellie alone.

When she stumbled out of the chopper, knees wobbly, throat dry, she didn't expect the welcoming party that waited at the door leading to flight headquarters.

The bearded, heavyset dispatcher who had helped lead her through the clouds had taken a break to give her a thumbs-up salute.

"Great job, Kellie!" His woolly face broke out in a friendly grin. "I've never had to listen in on anything like that before. And I don't mind sayin', this old country boy was scared spitless.''

Kellie forced a tight grin. "Thanks, Ted."

"Was it really dangerous?" A passing nurse who heard Ted's praise stopped.

"Hell, yeah! Why, you've gotta have nerves like steel to..."

Ted's effusive, if exaggerated, assessment of the situation followed Kellie up the stairs to the flight apartment. Her lungs still felt deprived of oxygen. The crazy part was, Ted was way off base. Though flying by instrument wasn't easy or desirable, it was an everyday occurrence. But once in a blue moon, a pilot panicked.

Today had been Kellie's turn.

No one had guessed at her terror, and Kellie could think of no graceful way to tell them their pilot had been so cowardly she was ready to sail them into oblivion at any moment. Filling them in on the episode in the clouds would be a dirty trick to play on people who depended on her skill as a pilot.

The apartment cot offered no escape. Ever her own bed and the comforting darkness of her familiar bedroom were no consolation the next few nights. Every time Kellie dozed off, she could see once again the unyielding bank of clouds that had threatened to rob her of good sense. And she could find no way to excuse herself for the way she had reacted.

Carrie offered no distraction. In fact, when Kellie picked up her daughter for a rare weeknight dinner following the episode, it took every bit of strength she possessed not to cry as she wrapped her arms around the six-year-old.

"Gee, Mommy, don't squeeze so tight," Carrie complained, trying to wiggle out of Kellie's panicky grip.

Fighting back the tears, Kellie remembered every recrimination Brian had ever thrown her way about the dangers of flying. The thought of leaving her irrepressible Carrie motherless was more terrifying, even, than her panic during the flight had been.

But she wouldn't be motherless, a heartless inner voice jibed as Kellie finally released her hold on the slender child and steered her toward the station wagon. *She has a stepmother just waiting to take your place.*

Kellie almost pulled out into the path of a bakery delivery truck when the thought struck her that Brian would love to know about her lapse. His hints that her job left too little time for mothering were making Kellie nervous that her ex-husband had more than needling her on his mind. Like a scene from a bad daytime soap opera, she could see slender, red-haired Heather dragging a wailing Carrie out of a courtroom, never to see her mother again.

By the end of the week, Dan's invitation to spend some time together seemed like another possible distraction. Especially with Carrie back at her dad's, Kellie knew she would need to fill the long Saturday. She vetoed his invitation to dinner, hoping to avoid candlelight and wine and a repeat of the explosive feelings they had shared after the football game. Her counterproposal of attending a Saturday afternoon folk-music festival at a farm outside of town seemed like the perfect way to keep things light.

Dan showed up right on time, taking her breath away when she opened the front door. The cable-knit sweater in smoky gray accentuated the leanness of his hips in his neat but faded Levi's. Forcing herself not to let her gaze linger over his body, Kellie looked up into a pair of brown eyes that told her instantly that Dan was not in his usual easygoing mood. As close to the surface as his warmth and openness always were, she now discovered that his displeasure was equally easy to spot.

She tried to coax him out of his mood, but found that her smile did not work its magic.

"Banjo music!" Kellie snapped her fingers. "Banjo music is just what you need to cure the blahs left over from a bad week. We'll head out to Horse Pens and—"

"I didn't have a bad week." Although his forehead was creased in a ferocious frown, his voice held no anger. "I had a bad night."

She wished she knew the secret of his calming touch, so she could use it herself and brush away whatever was brewing in him. "I'm sorry. Today will be—"

"Can we sit down for a minute?"

Kellie's spirits sank to the orange-tipped toes hidden inside her ankle-high, lace-up boots. What had happened to the promise of toe-tapping music, a picnic under the trees of Horse Pens 40 folk farm, maybe even the thrill of an occasional kiss only slightly restrained by the nearness of other people? Why couldn't he shrug off whatever was bothering him?

While Dan perched, stiff backed, on the couch, Kellie burrowed down in the wicker papasan chair to face him. Even his moodiness, she noted, couldn't spoil his good looks and their effect on her.

"I heard about your flight the other day."

Kellie frowned, her fingers automatically starting to twist the garnet ring on her left hand. She didn't even have to ask which flight. Ted's tale grew with each telling, and emergency-room personnel had talked about it all week. The other pilots, especially Frank, had teased her about her notoriety. And one of the younger nurses, who'd heard the tale in its final, most embellished version, had threatened to quit if ever forced to fly with a pilot who couldn't see six inches in front of his face.

Do we have to go into that again? she thought. *That's what Saturdays are for—forgetting work. Besides, if he thinks I'll enjoy a little more praise, he's dead wrong.* "Oh, that. Wasn't a big deal."

She moved as if to dismiss the rest of his comments, but his somber voice arrested her.

"That's not the talk in emergency. Everybody says it was pretty dangerous. Was it?"

The question wasn't idle, Kellie's instincts told her. But she wasn't quite sure why he was asking. Was he proud of her? Or was it more than that?

"It's nobody's favorite way to fly," she said defensively. "But pilots do it every day."

Dan wasn't satisfied. "But was it dangerous?"

Kellie squirmed at his persistence. If an admission that she had faced a little more danger than usual would get her out of this conversation, she was all for it. Then maybe they could get on with the fun they had planned.

"It's never as safe to depend on someone in a control tower to talk you through the air as it is to be able to see what you're flying into," she admitted brusquely.

"Then why didn't you land? Let someone bring the patient in by ambulance?"

The probing questions raised Kellie's suspicions and sparked more than a hint of anger. Who was he to question her judgment? she fumed. And what business was it of his how she did her job?

Unless he was looking for information to take back to the hospital board....

The idea startled her. Why shouldn't his interest be more than personal? she wondered. After all, he was part of the executive board that requested the report for FAA.

"Why don't we let this drop for now?" Kellie folded her arms stubbornly across her chest, determined to clam up if his intention was to use their relationship to get information for his stupid board.

Dan was stunned by her reaction. Maybe he was right, after all. Maybe she had used poor judgment and wasn't willing to admit it. When the dispatcher in emergency had told him about the hair-raising flight, Dan had felt sheer panic, although the danger had long since passed at that point. But the fear had been as real as if Kellie were still suspended in the clouds, just waiting to collide with an aircraft she couldn't see.

Instead of bottling that fear inside himself, Dan knew he had to get it out on the table. Kellie knew her job and he didn't, and stewing over things he didn't understand wasn't his way. A few minutes with Kellie, he had told himself, and this thing would be cleared up.

But Kellie's response was no consolation at all. He had half expected her to laugh it off and explain that it was all part of a day's work. So why was she acting so defensive, unless there was something she didn't want to admit?

Dan was quietly insistent. "I don't want to let it drop. I want to know why you decided not to land and let someone else finish the call."

Cardiac arrest, for starters, Kellie wanted to blurt out, but she stubbornly bit back the words. If the hospital administration wanted to know that the patient in the chopper that day had experienced cardiac arrest twice on the way in and that his blood pressure had dropped to a life-threatening level, they could get the information somewhere else. Likewise the information that her choices had been a five-minute flight to an emergency landing site versus an eight-minute flight to the hospital, which made the choice almost moot.

But if Dan Brennan thought he could become the pipeline from the air-ambulance service to the hospital's executive offices, he could think again.

"I made the best professional judgment I could," Kellie said heatedly, determined to march upstairs and lock her bedroom door behind her if he didn't drop it. "And if the hospital doesn't agree with my decision, I'll discuss it on their time and not in my living room on a Saturday afternoon."

Dan's bewilderment at her reaction started to clear up. He should have realized that Kellie would feel he was questioning her professional judgment. He winced. Maybe that was what it boiled down to, come to think of it. But what he really wanted was for her to ease his apprehension.

"I'm sorry, Kellie. I don't think I've handled this very well." Dan took a deep breath and wondered how to salvage the conversation. "I was just worried about you, up there risking your neck to save somebody else's life. It scared the devil out of me. I . . . I guess I just wanted you to tell me you knew what you were doing and help me understand a little better, so I wouldn't be so worried next time."

His words helped some but brought in another set of concerns that were just as disconcerting. Was Dan going to become as overprotective and as inhibiting as Brian had been? She wasn't ready for that, no matter how goose bumpy he made her feel when they kissed.

Besides, she still didn't feel like talking about the flight. What if she managed to communicate her momentary phobia to him? If her flying scared the devil out of him now, what would it do if she told him she had been so panicked she was almost ready to disregard everything the tower was telling her? Ready to disregard their instructions and the logical information she could read on her instrument panel and fly straight into the side of Red Mountain simply out of uncontrollable fear?

Kellie hadn't noticed him stand up and walk over to stoop in front of her chair. But his hands on her knees brought her instantly alert and aware of a much more immediate danger than a flight gone awry. The heated power of his hands through the soft flannel of her skirt was as real a threat to her sanity as flying through the clouds had been.

Every inch of her resistance—to both his worried concern and his gentle touch—melted away like heated wax dripping its lazy way down the side of a candle.

"You do take care of yourself up there, don't you?" He pleaded softly for reassurance.

A tentative smile pushed aside the last of the indignant anger on her face. "Of course I do. I've got better ways to spend my time than filling out accident reports."

Her lighthearted retort didn't completely rid him of the dread he felt when he contemplated that Kellie wouldn't be the one filing the report if her chopper went down. But he knew it was all the relief he was going to get right now. He made up his mind to follow her lead toward a less serious twist to the conversation.

"Can I get your solemn oath on that?" A half smile replaced the furrowed brow he had worn into the house.

"Solemn oath." She traced an X over her heart, regretting it instantly when his hungry eyes followed the movement of her finger.

"I was looking for a more—" he hesitated pointedly, deepening the crooked grin under his sandy mustache "—a more adult way to seal the bargain."

He leaned closer, sliding his hands up from her knees so that his powerful arms framed her thighs. She was agonizingly aware of the slight movement of his fingers on her hips.

"Any way you want to seal it," she answered breathlessly, ready to lean into his kiss until his raised eyebrows alerted her to the full import of her last statement. She chuckled, a husky, throaty sound. "Well, almost any way."

His mouth hovered over hers, tempting her to a kiss. His mustache was a tickle of softness against her lips, his breath sweetly warming her. But no matter how openly she welcomed his kiss, he held back.

With a satisfied sigh, Kellie leaned forward until their lips touched, surrendering to his insistence that she make the final move to turn his invitation into a kiss. The velvet caress of his lips on hers was an instant blaze, leaping to life in secret places. Slipping the tip of his tongue tentatively between her lips, Dan began a gradual seduction. He forayed and withdrew, then forayed again as she used the tip of her own tongue to tempt him back.

The swell of her breasts and her taut nipples strained for his touch, but his hands were preoccupied with the gentle massage of her hips. Liquid response poured through her in waves, giving life to the sensuous undulations she tried to hold back.

Dan deepened the kiss, drawing her tongue into seductive, lazy play with his. She leaned toward him in the chair, unmindful of her skirt hiking higher and higher until his fingers grazed her thighs. With a muffled gasp, Kellie shivered against his touch, which grew bolder as she showed no resistance. His fingers traced the triangle of silk. She arched to meet the gentle exploration that took him past the silken barrier to the moist warmth of her passion.

Their kiss dissolved into her tiny whimpers, and he buried his face in the yellow cotton covering her inflamed breasts. Barely aware of his moans against her, Kellie was lost in the heat he brought to her with his ever more insistent caress.

"There's no one who'll wake up now," he whispered hoarsely.

The words broke through the turmoil of her emotions only slowly. He wanted to make love, just as she did. But Kellie knew that she didn't fully trust herself to let go with him. Even if he didn't plan to use his power at work to control her, using his personal power to control her would be even more insidious.

Besides, making love was something for which she wasn't prepared—in more ways than one.

Drawing a shuddering breath, Kellie straightened in the chair, reluctantly feeling his retreat. She struggled to find her voice. "I know. But I don't ... It's not ... safe."

Dan smiled a weak, wry smile. He was glad to hear she wasn't constantly prepared for lovemaking. There was comfort in that these days. But he also wondered if there was more to her unwillingness than being unprotected. She had used her daughter as a shield before. And now this. Kellie didn't open up easily, he suspected, and drawing back from making love could be one more way to avoid letting him see behind her facade of cheerful frivolity.

He dropped a tiny kiss on her thigh and felt her quiver in response. "Then we won't run any risks," he promised, looking up into the passion-softened timidity in her eyes. "But that doesn't mean we can't make love."

He watched the uncertainty in her face disappear as he hooked his fingers through her panties and slowly rolled them away from her. Her cheeks darkened, the barest of pink heating her face.

"But . . ."

There was no protest in her hoarse whisper as his hands crept back up her legs. When she closed her eyes and dropped her head back on the chair, he lowered his lips once again to the firm softness of her thigh. Trailing damp, wet kisses along her flesh, he breathed in her fragrance. Intoxicating. Maddening. His kisses moved toward her heat.

Wanting to fight her loss of control, Kellie was powerless to act. His lips robbed her of all reason. Only her senses remained. She writhed to his touch, to the feel of his lips caressing her flesh, his teeth nipping gently higher and higher along her inner thigh. She was his, with no reservations, as his powerful hands slid beneath her hips and raised her to him.

With a soft moan, she opened herself to his intimate kiss. His lips were soft against the folds of her womanhood. His tongue alternately seeking deep inside her and swirling against the tiny bud of flesh that tightened at his caress. He was slick and soft and hot. She heard him sigh against her, felt the intensity in his lips, in his tongue, in the hands that tightened on her full, round flesh.

A convulsive, surging warmth rose along her thighs, tingled along her breasts and grasped at her loins. All feeling converged. All warmth met. And held her in its grasp for long, shivering moments. His lips and tongue pulsed against her, meeting the fury that welled within her.

Then slowed, as her gasping sighs slowed.

When her movement stopped, when her cries of pleasure died, he rested his cheek against her belly, wondering if he could ever explain that his fulfillment went as deep as if he had spent himself inside her.

THE ROLLING HILLS of north Alabama were still green, with the oranges and yellows of fall barely singeing the edges of the lush foliage. Once they left the freeway for the winding country highways leading to Horse Pens 40, Dan was struck by the differences between the southern countryside and the more prosperous midwestern farmland he was accustomed to.

Small farms dotted the hills or crouched next to the highway, some comfortably cared for but others unpainted, their vistas spoiled with rusted cars and ramshackle barns. Ribbons of clotheslines strung with overalls and flannel shirts decorated side yards. Chickens pecked at the rusty red earth, oblivious to traffic whizzing past. People waved from front porches as the snazzy sports car sped by.

"I thought all the ghettos were in the cities," Dan commented as they turned into the long driveway leading to the forty-acre farm devoted to preserving Southern folk art.

Kellie glanced at him, still feeling a little shy about the complete abandon with which she had reveled in his touch less than an hour earlier. Her body was seized with a wave of knee-weakening emotions when she let herself remember the adoring look in his eyes as he reluctantly helped her straighten her clothes.

"My grandparents were subsistence farmers," Kellie commented as they paid their admission and wound up the dirt road to the field used for parking. The clean simplicity of string-band music teased their ears once Dan killed the car's engine. They followed the lilting mountain tune, holding hands as they walked. "Born, lived and died within a ten-mile radius. My grandfather was peddling eggs the day he died. Grandmother hoed the garden from a cane-bottomed chair once she got too old to do it standing up."

She pointed to an ample woman in a homespun housedress and a wide-brimmed straw hat near a quilting frame ringed by nimble-fingered women hard at work. "That's what she looked like. Except that her face was as brown as old shoe leather, in spite of the hat."

"Look over there." Placing his arm lightly around her shoulders, he pointed toward a bonneted woman toiling over a bubbling caldron. "What's that smell?"

Kellie took a deep breath of the aroma coming from across the meadow. As sweet as it was, it was only half as sweet as the weight of his arm on her shoulders. She stifled the thrill that shot through her but not the smile that came with it. "Apple butter."

"Want to go sample some? Or shall we listen to the music first?"

"I'm not hungry yet. Let's listen."

They spread out the floral tablecloth Kellie reserved for picnics near a towering rock formation, then settled down to watch and listen to the musicians. The thin, high voices of the folk musicians punctuated some of the simple tunes; for others, the only addition to the music was the steady thump of clapping hands or an occasional rebel yell of appreciation.

Children roamed the hills, chasing recklessly through the checkerboard of blankets marking picnic space. Kellie and Dan had chosen a spot farthest from the stream of sightseers.

"There's not much of the country girl left in you," Dan commented, leaning back to prop on an elbow and look in her direction.

"I know. Canning vegetables and piecing quilts have never been in my repertoire." She tried to ignore the dusting of pale curls along the back of his hand, glistening now in the autumn sun.

Never one to be still for long, Kellie was satisfied with sitting and listening to the music for only a short time. Soon, they left their tablecloth spread out to mark their spot and started roaming the farm. They listened to a mountain storyteller, a rotund woman whose dark, rich voice was resonant with feeling. They watched a woman spinning yarn on an old wooden wheel, yarn that was then transferred to a nearby loom and transformed into woolen fabric. Baskets were woven and chairs caned before their eyes. And the apple butter bubbled in its caldron, filling the fresh mountain air with the fragrance of fruit and spices.

"That...smells...like...heaven." Each word was punctuated with a pause as Kellie sniffed in the aroma of the thick, sweet spread.

"How about a jar to take home?" Dan pointed to the plank bench lined with the jars, each tied around the lid with a calico ribbon.

Kellie shook her head in spite of the mouth-watering aroma. "No, thanks. I don't need the calories. And if it isn't grape and swirled together with peanut butter, Carrie won't touch it."

"Oh, go ahead," he urged, picking up one of the jars. "A little apple butter on your toast won't hurt a couple of times a week."

Entertaining visions of herself standing on the bathroom scales while she wolfed down a hot buttered biscuit topped with a generous dollop of creamy calories, Kellie shook her head even more emphatically. "No. I'm serious. I don't need it."

"We don't *need* plenty of things. But that doesn't mean we don't *want* them." As if that answered all her arguments, Dan dug into his pocket for his money clip and passed on a bill to a young woman in an appliquéd apron.

Kellie stared at the jar he placed in her hands, mildly irritated that he would ignore her wishes and at the same time pleased with a gift she knew would remind her of what had already become a very special day. Shrugging off the aggravation, she thanked him and placed the jar carefully in her oversize shoulder bag.

"I'll bet people don't live much like this where you're from," Kellie said as they continued their ramble. His arm was around her shoulders again, but she couldn't quite work up the courage to hook her arm around his waist. In spite of the jittery emotions Dan's touch inspired, Kellie couldn't think when she had last had more fun. Unless it had been at last week's football game.

But today was even more special, she told herself with a guilty thrill. Today, they were lovers. At least, sort of lovers. She went soft and warm again at the thought. And without Carrie, Kellie hated to admit it, she felt more free to be herself, more open to walking arm in arm with him, accepting an anything-but-casual kiss on the cheek.

"Sometimes I think I was the only kid in the world who really grew up in a *Father Knows Best* kind of family," Dan admitted. "We were always close, always able to talk."

Dan's voice took on a satisfied, almost dreamy quality as he talked about his parents and their nursery in a small town in the Midwest. She could almost see his crusty, broad-shouldered father and the gentle woman who was his mother. Kellie sensed, as he talked about the summers and weekends he worked in the family business, that Dan had inherited his father's looks and his mother's nature. She warmed to his tales of letting his older brother lead him into the harmless predicaments most teens get into, realizing how much like Rachael and herself the two Brennan brothers must have been. She felt as if she knew the dog who had been part of the family for years and the high-school sweetheart who had become his sister-in-law.

Dan didn't talk about his own marriage. But that, Kellie decided as they roamed the sunny hillsides, would come another time. On a day that wasn't bright with sunshine and energized with the snappy coolness of autumn.

"Oh, look, a pony!" she exclaimed as they neared the corral and barn.

"And an overprotective mother." Dan pointed across the field to a mare whose ears had pricked up at their approach. As Kellie leaned over the fence to dangle her hand toward the spindly legged colt, the mare snorted uninvitingly. "I don't think she appreciates your admiration for her little one."

Kellie ignored his warning as the colt moved forward cautiously to nuzzle her hand. "Feel his nose, Dan. It's so soft!"

She reached for his hand to guide it toward the colt's velvet nose. Instead he pulled her back just as the powerfully built mare galloped up. Startled by the sudden movement, the pony bolted away from the fence. The mare ambled after him.

"You scared him away!" Kellie exclaimed.

"Better that than have his momma eat you for lunch."

"She wouldn't have hurt me," Kellie protested, peeved that Dan again seemed determined to make her decisions for her.

"Maybe not." He shrugged, his half smile showing his amusement at her disappointment. "I admit I'm better

with plants than I am with animals. But I couldn't see
giving her a chance to toss you into the next county.''

"She's a horse, not a bull.'' Kellie frowned and walked
away. There he went again, trying to tell her what to do.
The most irritating part was that he was probably right
this time. But being right, Kellie told herself stubbornly,
didn't give him license to go trying to take care of her.

By the time she had rounded the dilapidated barn and
spotted the haystack, Kellie's pique had dissipated once
again. A haystack. Just like the ones in books, in movies,
in idealized paintings of American country life. Kellie
couldn't resist. With a whooping holler, she headed full
speed for the pile of straw and dived into the top of it.

Giggling and wiping the prickly hay out of her face and
hair, she came up for air to find Dan standing by with
hands on hips.

"What if—?"

"I know. What if there had been a pitchfork in here?''
Kellie refused to listen to his admonition. "My dad tried
those same lines on me for twenty years. In fact, he's still
trying and they still don't work. Give it up, Dan.''

"Maybe you need somebody to—''

She reached for his hand and with a quick yank pulled
him into the haystack with her. "No, I don't need somebody to take care of me.'' Still feeling slightly giddy from
her running jump into the hay, Kellie allowed herself the
boldness of pressing herself more tightly against the body
lying next to hers. Granted, the straw was pricking her in
the most inappropriate places, but she wasn't about to let
this romantic cliché go unexplored. "That isn't what I
need at all.''

His arms tightened around her as she entwined her long
legs with his. "What do you need, then?''

Raising her face only a fraction, she could feel his mustache brushing against her upper lip.

Reluctantly pulling her lips away from his, Kellie placed her hand on his chest and closed her eyes. "This may be what I want," she said, breathlessly paraphrasing his earlier argument, "but it isn't what I need."

"Now who's sounding like somebody's parent?" His finger traced along her ear, then trailed down to the hollow at the base of her neck.

"I *am* somebody's parent."

"That," he said, his fingers still lingering at the collar of her blouse, "is totally irrelevant in the present situation."

She tried to collect her thoughts as he toyed with her top button, a finger grazing her flesh as he did so. She had to put a stop to this, she told herself.

"Maybe we should finish our walk," she said weakly, forcing herself to shift away from his touch. "I'll bet our blanket is gone by now."

Sighing and leaning back, Dan gave her a resigned smile. Then, after a brief pause, he said, "Maybe you're right."

As they walked through the grassy meadow overlooking hillsides covered with verdant trees, they held hands. Kellie felt shy. She also felt warm and liquid and agitated.

"Thank you for understanding."

"I do."

She really felt he did. It was a new experience for her.

But as they topped a steep hillock, the protective hand at her elbow guiding her along the uneven path wasn't a new experience. In fact, it felt irritatingly familiar. In spite of having such a wonderful time with Dan, she wouldn't have bet a nickel that he wouldn't always feel obliged to try to take care of her.

And all the beautiful lovemaking in the world wouldn't be worth putting up with another man who wanted to baby her.

CHAPTER EIGHT

NOTHIN' SERIOUS, lady. Cable just snapped, that's all.

The baby-faced mechanic had probably been right, but the minor malfunction shook Kellie up anyway. Going over the scene at the airport again, she was barely conscious of the paint sticking to her hands as she and Margo capped the cans of leftover paint in the hospital basement.

The routine refueling after a morning flight had been disrupted when Kellie realized the altimeter wasn't working on her instrument panel. It wasn't a big deal—a snapped cable, not the kind of thing that can be anticipated.

But as she'd dropped onto the helipad at the hospital, with Margo behind chattering away about her daughter's college entrance exam scores, Kellie could only think of the day she had been forced to rely on her instrument panel to get her through the fog. If the altimeter cable had picked that day to snap, she would have been helpless.

Now she was having trouble keeping her mind on the paint cleanup. A group of third-shift workers, including pilot Andy Payton, had stayed through the morning to finish painting the scenery for Birmingham Memorial's fund-raising carnival, which was now just weeks away. She and Margo had offered to spend their lunch break cleaning brushes and putting away the cans of paint and generally straightening up so the next stage could begin—hanging the fairyland scenes their more artistic co-workers had created on canvas.

"Where's your head?" Margo brought over a large plastic garbage bag and held it open for Kellie. "You haven't heard a word I'm saying."

"Sorry. I'm a little preoccupied." Too absorbed in her thoughts to care, Kellie shrugged and started filling the bag with throwaway foam brushes and plastic sheeting daubed with spills and splashes of vivid pink and vile green. She was making too much of the altimeter cable, she knew. But she couldn't help thinking how Dan Brennan would react if he heard about it and put it together with her hair-raising experience in the fog the week before. Just another example of her not being able to take care of herself, she thought, bristling once again at how he had mother-henned her at the folk festival on the weekend.

It had been too much like a rerun of the same old hassles she'd had with Brian for so many years. By the time the day was over, she had half convinced herself she shouldn't see Dan again.

She had tossed the jar of apple butter in the trash before turning in for the night.

But by 2:00 a.m., when she gave up trying to sleep and sat up to read, instead, her conviction had weakened that Dan wasn't for her. And when the torrid love scenes in her novel paled in comparison to Dan's lovemaking, Kellie wondered if she would ever again sleep undisturbed by thoughts of him.

When she woke the next morning, she retrieved the apple butter.

"I was asking how you thought the report was coming along," Margo repeated, spinning the bag closed.

"Fine. We'll have it ready in plenty of time." Kellie fastened a twist tie around the bag while Margo held it aloft, forcing into oblivion the thoughts that had shimmered through her consciousness and prickled her aching body at the most inopportune times the past few days. "I was thinking, though.... Maybe I shouldn't file a report on the altimeter cable."

Margo raised a thin, dark eyebrow. "Oh, yeah? If they found out, it'd be your funeral, girl."

Kellie sighed. "You're right. I just couldn't help but think that our new vice president might latch on to that little fact and blow it out of proportion."

"You're awfully preoccupied with our new vice president. Is he giving you some kind of grief I don't know about?"

Kellie's brief chuckle was humorless. "You could say that."

"Tell me more."

"Some other time. Let's grab a quick sandwich." Kellie could think of no easy way to explain that Dan turned her into one of the hot-blooded women in the romance novels she loved to read, but that she wasn't sure she was ready to grant any man that much power over her. She hadn't even been able to talk to Rachael about it. "I just think he's too eager to criticize air ambulance. And I don't want to do anything to foul us up."

Absently picking up her flight jacket, Margo stared intently at the gaudily painted canvas spread across the basement floor to dry. "I don't think a minor equipment failure is what's going to foul us up."

Her partner's voice told Kellie the comment wasn't an idle one. "What is, then?"

Margo scrutinized Kellie's face for a long time before she spoke, staring deeply into the eyes of her co-worker and friend. "I'm worried about Chip."

Kellie's heart sank. She had been worried about Chip, too, but her own personal problems had overshadowed that concern in the past weeks. His abrasive moodiness had disintegrated into sullen silence. But more worrisome than his mood was the way he looked—drawn and pallid. Already thin, he seemed to be losing weight, too.

"I've noticed, too. What do you think's wrong with him?" It bothered Kellie to learn that Margo was as concerned as she; with Margo's training, she would spot a medical problem in a heartbeat.

"Could be a lot of things." Margo's noncommittal answer didn't fool Kellie. The veteran nurse had some notions; she was sure of that. "I thought at first maybe it was just this place, the flights, making him nervous. But when he was over helping Carol study for her exams a few weeks ago, he was just as shaky."

The nurse shook her head and again stared at the canvas on the floor. "I think we ought to keep an eye on him. That's all."

The burdens that weighed Kellie down suddenly grew heavier. *Isn't it enough,* she asked herself, *that I have to worry about losing Carrie to a new stepmother? About losing my job to a bullying bureaucrat? And my self-respect to a man who turns me into jelly every time he comes near my airspace?*

"Will you let me know if...if you see anything that I ought to know about? Anything I ought to act on?"

Margo nodded, pursing her lips and keeping her eyes downcast.

Kellie felt like a traitor.

Brian was probably right. The job wasn't worth it.

ONCE AGAIN, Dan's racket fanned the air, the fuzzy ball just out of reach. *You're not hitting on all cylinders today, old man,* he told himself as he moved into position for another of Anna Robinson's mean serves. For an overweight grandmother, she was like a gymnast on her feet. And right now, she was killing him.

Although his co-worker's ability had much to do with that, his own inability to concentrate on the game was a more significant factor, Dan knew. Everywhere he turned was Kellie. It had been like that since Saturday and the folk festival, when everything he did seemed to rub her the wrong way.

Well, almost everything.

Another ball whizzed by. At this rate, Anna was going to sweep the set.

Even in his own home, Kellie's image refused to release him. The fireplace he never used mocked him with the thought of how wonderful it would be to stretch out with her in front of a fire on one of the chilly winter nights that were just around the corner. And the balcony would be the perfect place on a balmy spring night, starting with a glass of wine, a kiss, then more wine and another kiss. And from there—

Damn! Dan's thought broke off in frustration as he stumbled and missed another shot.

It was more than just desire, Dan had decided the evening before as he repotted a newly purchased African violet. He grew more dissatisfied with his home, with his solitary existence, every day. Even the delicate violet, smiling at him from its ceramic pot on the kitchen window ledge, hadn't been able to take the edge off his restless dissatisfaction. He kept seeing the cozy spaciousness of Kellie's house and longed to take part in the renovation, longed to be a part of the summer cookouts and the lazy Saturday mornings when Carrie woke up first, bright eyed and ready for TV cartoons. He was even envious of having gutters to clean and grass to mow and weeds to trim back from the sidewalk.

He was ready for the settling down he had known would be important even seven years ago, when he gave up medicine so he would have time for the kind of family life he craved. But Kellie seemed content to strive for new highs with her career. Personally, her daughter seemed to be all she needed.

"Man, you must be a million miles away," Anna chided him as she rounded the net after another win. "What's your problem? If you ran a hospital as badly as you played tennis this morning, we'd have to close the doors and send the patients home."

"Sorry, Anna." He pulled a sweatshirt on over his damp T-shirt and wiped his brow with the towel waiting at courtside with his gear. "I probably should have suggested forty-seven shots of whiskey instead of tennis this afternoon. I thought the action would clear my head, but it didn't seem to work."

"Hmm. Must be a woman." Anna fixed him with a knowing smile as they headed for the clubhouse. "See my social secretary. She'll set you up with the earliest possible appointment for forty-seven shots of whiskey. You buy. I listen."

He laughed. "How about if I just buy you one now? It'll ease my remorse at being such a lousy opponent today."

"Deal."

When the club bartender sat Dan's beer and Anna's whiskey sour in front of them on the varnished parquet bar, Dan took a long drink of the ice-cold liquid. "Better,'' he pronounced. ''Acts in seconds to cure the agony of defeat.''

''But it's not much good for heart trouble,'' Anna prodded. ''Give a reformed gossip a fix, Brennan. Are you breaking hearts already?''

What the hell, he thought. *She's the best friend I've got in town. Maybe the only friend.*

''I've seen this woman a couple of times. She acts interested, then seems to push me away,'' he admitted.

Anna eyed him speculatively. ''Does that mean you're put out because she won't sleep with you?''

''No.'' Dan frowned, trying to pinpoint the problem for Anna. ''Hell, I don't know. Maybe I'm just overeager. Afraid of getting to middle age all by myself.''

''Umm-hmm. So you're pushy and she's gun-shy.''

''Gun-shy?''

''Sure. How long's she been divorced?''

Dan raised his eyebrows. ''What makes you think she's divorced?''

Anna grinned slyly. ''Well? How long?''

''I don't know. Two or three years, maybe.''

''Let's see. Doesn't go out much. Right?'' Anna waited for affirmation and, when Dan nodded, started ticking off her guesses on the fingers of her left hand. ''Got kids? Wrapped herself up in raising her young'uns? Only outside interest is her job?''

Anna popped the cherry from her drink into her mouth and turned both hands palm up as if to say, ''See how simple?''

''How'd you know all that?''

''It's an old story.'' She sipped thoughtfully on her drink. ''She's gun-shy and here you are giving her the big rush. Give her some space, but don't give up on her. Just keep giving her one more little nudge at a time.''

"Maybe you're right."

"'Course I'm right. I'm a grandmother. All us old women know everything there is to know about how men and women carry on before they get down to business. It's called wisdom. Don't you know anything?"

"You're not old enough to be wise yet, Anna. If you were that old, you couldn't possibly have beaten me that easily this morning."

"My youngest grandbaby could've beaten you this morning, Brennan." She set her empty glass decisively on the table and leveled a no-nonsense finger at him. "If this woman's got you going that bad, you better do something about it."

"COME HERE, you big oaf!" Kellie made her voice as commanding as possible and pointed at the open back door. *Bossing Oscar around would be much easier if he didn't outweigh me,* she decided as the tail-wagging dog ignored her from the living room. But he had to go outside, or she and her mother would never make any progress in stripping the living room woodwork.

"And that's my charming, soft-spoken sister."

Kellie started at Rachael's voice on the back deck. When she turned toward the sound, she spotted the stocky young man at Rachael's side and wondered if her sister had forgotten her promise to help with the project for the evening.

"The joys of pet ownership." Kellie shrugged and ushered the couple into the house. Her sister's boyfriend had the thick neck and well-developed thighs that said he lifted weights. "A close third only to the joys of motherhood and home ownership. Which reminds me, aren't you supposed to be wielding a paint stripper this evening? Mom and I are ready to roll."

"Don't worry. Elliott just stopped by on his way home. I thought you and Mom might want to meet him."

They moved toward the living room, where Rachael introduced Elliott to Ellen Carpenter, whose silver-streaked curls were tinted dark auburn this week. As they chatted, Kellie was tempted to ask if Elliott was going to be her new brother-in-law. After all, that would have been Carrie's tactic. But Rachael would probably move out of her apartment owing a month's rent if she did that.

Besides, no one who was undergoing Ellen Carpenter's third degree also deserved a sound teasing. She half listened, taking the time to shoo Oscar into the kitchen so she could cover the furniture with plastic, while her mother found out where Elliott grew up, what he did for a living, how many siblings he had and where he graduated from college.

Kellie could have written his résumé by the time Elliott was ready to leave a few minutes later.

"Here, why don't I take him outside when I go," Elliott offered, hooking a finger through Oscar's collar as he headed toward the back door.

Ellen Carpenter's broad smile softened as she watched Rachael see him to the door, and Kellie could easily predict what was coming.

Ellen pulled her sweatshirt—one of Margo's creations, gaudily decorated with sequins and peacock feathers—over her head and folded it carefully. She smoothed the worn Mickey Mouse T-shirt she wore under the sweatshirt back into place over her full figure.

"What a nice young man. It's so nice to see Rachael dating someone regularly, isn't it?"

Kellie passed one corner of the plastic sheeting to her mother and maneuvered it over the camelback couch. "Yes, Mom. And isn't it a shame I'm not?"

Ellen blushed at her daughter's teasing remark. "Now, Kellie, I didn't say a word."

"You didn't have to. I'm pretty good at reading your mind after all these years."

"Isn't he a doll?" Rachael came back into the room. "And he is so sweet."

"Are those wedding bells I hear?" Kellie passed her sister a can of stripper and a brush for applying it to the deep oak molding along the base of the floor and around the doors and windows.

"You're as bad as Mother."

"Nobody is as bad as Mom."

Ellen tossed one of the clean rags at her older daughter. "I'll leave right now if this is the way I'm going to be treated tonight. I'm just interested in your welfare, that's all."

"Can we discuss something besides my welfare?" Kellie asked as they settled onto the floor in different areas of the room and started their chore.

"Why certainly, dear. How's Carrie?"

"Good. She's doing great in school. Reads better than I did at eight." She paused to remove an electrical outlet cover. "She asked me to show her how to write her name in cursive a few weeks ago and copied it perfectly."

"How are her dance classes going? Will she have a recital soon?"

"Don't ask," Rachael warned. "Kellie turns into a bear when she thinks about Carrie taking dance."

"For goodness' sake, why? I think it's delightful!"

Kellie grunted and concentrated on thoroughly covering the rounded molding with the thick goop that would help them restore the wood to its natural finish.

"She's just mad at Brian because he won the battle," Rachael continued.

Ellen clucked sympathetically. "Are you having more problems with Brian, dear. You know, I think—"

"I am *not* having problems with Brian, Mom. Can we drop this?"

"I just think you'd be so much better off if Brian knew you had settled down again, too," Ellen continued, undaunted by Kellie's growing irritation. "He wouldn't be so ready to push you around if he knew you had a man to rely on and back you up."

Kellie heard Rachael strangle a laugh. Taking a deep breath, she wondered what had ever made her think she was getting free labor tonight. If listening to her mother's advice all evening was the price she would have to pay, this wasn't even cheap labor. "I think I'll put on an album. Jazz or classical?"

"Now, Kellie, there's nothing wrong in thinking about looking for a man to round out your life. Look how much happier Rachael is these days. Aren't you, sweetheart?"

"Oh, yes. I'm much happier." The strain of fighting back her laughter was apparent in Rachael's voice.

"See? Besides, Carrie would be much better off if—"

"If you don't have a preference, I'll just throw on that new jazz album I got last week." Kellie ignored her mother's unceasing tirade, wondering if it really was Elliott's appearance that had wound her up on this subject. Or had Rachael been filling her head with ideas about how miserable her sister had been recently? "So choose now or—"

The ring of the telephone interrupted her. Kellie ran for the kitchen phone as if it were her only sanctuary.

"How about tomorrow night?"

He wasted no time priming her with small talk. His first words were soft and coaxing and instantly undid all the pep talks she had given herself about what a bad idea it would be to get more deeply involved with Dan Brennan.

"Dinner by candlelight with the view off the balcony. A little music. I'm the best bachelor chef you've ever met."

Kellie resisted the urge to glance into the living room to see if they were paying attention to her conversation. The last thing she needed was to add fuel to her mother's big push to handcuff her to another man. How could she convince her mother she was talking to a magazine salesperson without scaring Dan off forever? she wondered.

And why was that such a bad idea? countered the part of her that had been arguing for dismissing him from her life for days.

Right now, all she wanted to do was get him off the phone before her mother's antennae went up. Mother could smell an interested man halfway across town. Kellie chose her words carefully and kept her tone impersonal. "No, that won't be possible."

Dan sounded undaunted and amiable. "Sorry, Kellie. It's not going to be that easy. I'm not hanging up until you agree."

Kellie gritted her teeth. *God spare me,* she thought, *from men who can't resist trying to run my life.* "I'm in the middle of something now, so—"

"If you hang up, I'll be over there in ten minutes. Now which would you rather have? Me tomorrow night, with a bottle of wine and some homemade lasagna? Or me right now, still sweaty from tennis, barging into whatever you're in the middle of? You don't have a man there, do you?"

His teasing tone, which told her he didn't really expect an answer, made it impossible for Kellie to work up the fury she wanted to summon. She could just picture Dan

Brennan, tall and charming with those melt-you-down-to-your-socks eyes, wading into the middle of the living room right now. Her mother would have his family history and his marriage eligibility requirements locked into her memory in less than five minutes. She would be planning what kind of flowers would be best for a double wedding in June before the night was over.

Think fast, sport. This is important. "We're putting together scenery for the fund-raising carnival tomorrow night, starting right after work. The painting's all done, and we could use some extra hands with the hammer."

"I warn you, I'm not as good with a hammer as I am with a garlic press. But I'll be there. On one condition. Drinks at my place after."

"Fine." Kellie was willing to agree to anything at this point. The continuing silence in the living room warned Kellie that her mother had activated her radar. She could take care of Dan tomorrow night. "And thanks for volunteering. I'll see you then."

Wishing she had learned the tricks of social lying a little better years ago, Kellie took a few minutes to collect herself before she went back into the living room. "Coke, anybody?" she asked as she hid her face in the refrigerator.

Bringing three diet soft drinks into the living room with her, Kellie passed them around and put on her best non-committal smile. She knew that her mother didn't buy into the polite theory of keeping her nose out of her daughter's business, so she offered her a slightly doctored explanation for the call before Ellen Carpenter could ask.

"Someone from the hospital, wondering what else needed doing for the carnival. We're through with the painting now, and we'll be hanging scenery and building sets for the fairyland tomorrow night.''

"That's nice, dear.'' Ellen sipped her soft drink and looked up, shrewd speculation in her eyes. "I'll bet plenty of nice young men at the hospital will be there to help.''

Kellie rolled her eyes and ignored the statement. Were all mothers such a pain? she wondered. And were all men such bulldozers? Or had she simply been lucky enough to find the two who were?

CHAPTER NINE

DAN BALLED UP the front page of the afternoon paper and stuffed it into the trash can under his desk. But the words continued to swim before him.

Another helicopter ambulance down, this one in Tennessee. Four dead, including the nine-year-old patient.

Dan swore at the jangle of his phone. He was in no mood to talk to anyone.

He was in no mood for the lighthearted camaraderie he was certain would reign at the carnival work group, either. Nevertheless, that's where Kellie would be tonight, and he intended to see her, was determined to see her, especially now.

Glaring at the ringing phone, he felt for his reading glasses under the pile of reports he hadn't been able to concentrate on all afternoon. He'd never see Kellie if these interruptions didn't stop, he told himself impatiently as he retrieved the pencil from behind his ear and grabbed the phone in midring.

Memorial president Bill Walton's voice was brisk in his ear. "Did you hear?"

The pencil cracked in Dan's fist. His jaw tightened as he sent it after the newspaper into the trash. "I heard."

"The FAA isn't going to ignore this. It's the thirteenth crash so far this year."

The numbers were all too fresh in Dan's mind. The radio report he'd heard at lunch had churned through him for the past six hours, gnawing at his stomach and turning his vegetarian hoagie into a colossal case of heartburn. He'd bought an afternoon paper as soon as they hit the stands. He had read the story at least six times, word for word. But the story never changed. Four dead.

His first impulse had been to rush right down to flight headquarters. He ached to see Kellie. Some irrational nervousness drove him to seek reassurance that she was safe and sound, walking around three floors below him in one piece. If he admitted the truth, what he really wanted was to hold her in his arms, to take comfort from feeling her next to him, warm and breathing, her heart beating against his chest. That would calm him. That would ease his sickening fear.

But he had promised himself not to bring their personal relationship into the hospital. He'd agonized alone for six hours. And now that he was ready to calmly go to Kellie for the words of solace he needed so badly, the hospital president had him trapped on the phone.

What the hell did Bill want from him?

"You think it'll have some effect on K...on our report?"

"It had better have some effect on our report," Bill barked emphatically. "It had better make it more effective. At this stage, anything we send the FAA had better ring true, and it had better look good. I need somebody to make sure Len doesn't screw this thing up."

Dan suppressed a groan. Now he got it. Bill wanted somebody to keep an eye on Len Baldwin, to make sure the ineffectual little weasel did his job right for a change.

"Keep this under your hat, Dan. But I want you breathing down Len's neck. I'm not sure I trust him, and I want you to make sure he's not running a loose ship. And if he is, I don't want it showing up in that report."

Len reported to Dan, so it made sense for Dan to keep an eye on the director of nursing services. But Bill was making it clear he was holding Dan responsible for any of Len's snafus. He wanted Dan to put the screws to Len.

In other words, Dan was being held responsible for the report while keeping his hands officially off the whole business. Damn, he hated office politics.

"Am I making myself clear, Brennan?"

Dan opened his mouth to protest but was distracted by a shadow at his office door. Anna Robinson stopped to wave, then raised her brows quizzically at the belea-guered expression on his face. Waving weakly at Anna, Dan could think of no suitable response. Finally, he said, "Clear. I'll take care of it."

Like hell he would. How the hell was he supposed to keep Len in line if he had to pussyfoot around about it? Dan groaned as he hung up. It was easy to see how Bill had made it to the presidency of the hospital. He could steamroll his way through anything.

Dan gave his tie a fierce yank to loosen it.

"Easy, Brennan," Anna warned. "Our public rela-tions folks would hate to have to explain away a hospital exec asphyxiated by his own hand in the executive suites."

Dan felt like a growling bear. He hated himself when he let his frustration turn into foul temper. He tried to sum-mon his typical good humor but discovered he was no better than usual at hiding what was eating at him. Sometimes he envied men who could shove their feelings behind some macho facade and get on with fooling the world.

He headed around his desk and grabbed his coat and briefcase, then paused long enough to retrieve the news-paper from his trash can and stuff it into his briefcase.

"I'm running half an hour late, and Bill catches me on the way out to drop a bomb on me," Dan said, rushing out the door at Anna's side. It would take him at least thirty minutes to dash home and change into jeans, then another fifteen to get back to the hospital... and Kellie. "Wish I had somebody to do my dirty work for me."

"Bite the bullet, Brennan. That's what you're here for, right?"

"That's me, all right. Dan Brennan, Bureaucratic Hit Man." The words left a sour taste that burned clear down to his gut.

KELLIE STEPPED BACK from the canvas screen to survey the bold sweeps of green paint that were the forest where Hansel and Gretel would drop their bread crumbs.

"Looks great, doesn't it?" she asked Jack, the off-duty pilot who had tacked the canvas in place while she and a nurse held it. "Can I bring anybody a drink before we move on to Snow White?"

She headed for the cooler filled with soft drinks, knowing the movement was just another way to use her nervous energy. She could barely keep her attention on the work at hand. She'd arrived late and had already completed three fairyland scenes and still no Dan.

But it wasn't worry that had Kellie's green eyes straying toward the door every few minutes. Pleasurable anticipation was more like it. In spite of her determination to put Dan out of her thoughts, she hadn't been able to fight the building excitement as the workday drew to a close.

Kellie hadn't seen Dan since the weekend, and with the giddiness of a schoolgirl, she couldn't wait to see him walk through the door. She was excited at the prospect of feeling his nearness as he tapped a canvas into place. Their hands might brush as she held the two-by-fours in place for him to build another framework for hanging another scene. She looked forward to letting her eyes travel the length of his body and revel in the memory of his strong arms around her and his broad chest crushed to hers.

She shivered in expectation that his honey-brown eyes would engage in the same not-so-discreet seduction....

As she walked back to the work area sipping a diet drink, Dan's tall, broad form stepped off the elevator. He had traded his suit and tie for a sweatshirt and a pair of faded jeans. The well-worn clothes were perfect for painting but even better for admiring glances, Kellie told herself as he came toward her. The gray cotton sweatshirt molded itself to his well-muscled chest and outlined brawny biceps for her admiring gaze. And the jeans, soft from many washings and much hard wearing, were snug over his powerfully built thighs.

But the look in his honey-brown eyes as he came closer was not the look she had expected.

"Hi!" She greeted him brightly, wondering if her brusqueness on the phone the night before had teed him off, after all. He wasn't even smiling, for goodness' sake! "Grab a hammer and a handful of nails over there. I've been saving Snow White for us."

"Have you seen this?" He thrust a crumpled newspaper in her direction.

Anxiety took over the spot vacated by Kellie's happy anticipation. The seriousness in his voice wiped the wide grin from her face. Kellie took the paper from him but didn't spot the headline right away.

"Chopper Ambulance Crashes, Four Die."

Kellie sighed, then released a muttered "Damn." As she read the brief account of the Memphis crash, Kellie knew that she would feel the repercussions right here in Birmingham. It explained the telephone message from her mother that she hadn't had time to return—she would want to be first with the news and an admonition to go into a safer line of work. It explained Dan's worried expression, especially so soon after her own risky flight last week. And there would be more to come, she knew, from Brian and from the others in flight headquarters.

But the one thing she refused to do, couldn't do if she wanted to stay sane in this business, was dwell on the implications for her own vulnerability. She couldn't let those four people become real for her, couldn't let herself mourn them, couldn't let visions of their violent death interfere with her efforts to do her job.

"No, I missed it." Her throat dry, she folded the paper in dismissal. "That's rough."

Dan stared in stunned silence as she turned toward the activity behind her. "'That's rough.' That's all you've got to say? 'That's rough.'"

Kellie closed her eyes in momentary frustration. She did not want a scene. Not here. Not at all. She wanted to get on about her business and put it behind her. She knew that reluctance to deal head-on with life's unpleasantness was one of her shortcomings. But in this case, she felt it was justified. More than that, it was necessary.

"What else am I supposed to say? Come on, let's get to work."

Dan reached for her arm, exercising great control to ensure that his rising tension didn't translate into a bruising grip. "That's not good enough, Kellie. You may be able to dismiss those people and the fact that they died doing something you do damn near every day. But I can't be that casual about it."

Kellie looked up, her heart torn by the genuine confusion in his eyes. "I don't feel casual about it, either, Dan.

But I can't do anything about it. And I'd rather not discuss it here and now. We do have an audience, you know.''

Dan glanced at the half-dozen people who were beginning to turn their attention toward the little drama. Kellie was right, but he wasn't sure he could quiet the grinding nervousness in his gut long enough to create a fairy-tale world with hammer and nails. He needed to deal with reality, and he needed Kellie to help him deal with it. He looked away from the blatantly questioning looks of the other volunteers.

"Okay," he conceded reluctantly. "Later."

Dan's halfhearted response to Kellie's playfulness for the next two hours was ample clue that he was more than a little distressed. He barely smiled when she goosed him in the side and seemed unmoved when she brushed against him as she stretched to hold the top of the canvas in place for him.

By the time the canvases of gingerbread houses and castles and ballrooms and houses of straw were in place on the lightweight frames, Kellie sensed that Dan had loosened up some since he'd arrived. But not much.

"I think you need cheering up." Kellie smiled when the work was complete and they were washing up before leaving. "How about beer and pizza with the rest of the gang?"

Dan felt his heartburn flare at the mention of pizza. "I've got fresh pita bread and smoked turkey at home. Besides, you promised a drink at my place in return for my labor."

While part of her wanted to be alone with him, Kellie knew that tonight she wanted the safety a group had to offer. But the look in his eyes told her it was pointless to argue. "Sure. I'll follow in my car."

THE CONDO WASN'T what Kellie expected. Well furnished and comfortable, it didn't have any of the warmth and hominess she thought she would find in Dan's home. The leather sofa didn't invite flopping down for a Saturday afternoon read. No plants added life to the brass and glass coolness, except for a single small violet blooming in the kitchen window. No books lined the tidy shelves built into the wall on both sides of the fireplace, only a few glass and brass knickknacks that looked as if they were gifts from people who didn't quite know Dan Brennan.

Only a wall in the dining room, covered with dozens of matted and framed family pictures, told her anything about the man whose actions had been so revealing until now. A round-faced, smiling woman, standing between Dan, minus his mustache, and another man who was a carbon copy of Dan. His mother and brother, Kellie speculated. Another, larger portrait of the round-faced woman, years before her face had filled out, with a handsome man who could only have been father to the two young men in the other picture. Family portraits that traced the young family's life until Dan reached junior-high age, all in matching wooden frames and tan mats, filled out the collection. And another family portrait, of the brother, a cheerfully pretty young woman and two grinning youngsters, brought the collection up to the present.

"I like this," Kellie said. "I feel like I know them already, after all the stories you told me Saturday. It's nice to see their faces."

The words didn't seem to please him, and Kellie sensed a disquietude in him that would soon surface if she couldn't keep him distracted.

"Do your folks still run the nursery? Or have they retired?"

"Steve helps Mom run it now. Dad died a few years back." Dan longed to tell her how hard his dad's death had been to accept, how much it had shaken him to realize that death could snatch away the future of someone so content with the world and his place in it, someone who should have had many years in which to grow old gracefully, peacefully. Seeing that future end so unexpectedly, so irrevocably, had helped Dan decide to end his frantic search for success and prestige and begin the more important search for a more meaningful kind of life.

Sometimes it was a bitter pill to swallow that the meaningful life he sought still eluded him, and he wanted to share those feelings with Kellie.

But not right now. Right now, he needed her arms around him. He needed the comfort of her touch. He needed reassuring words. Tonight, they had other things to deal with.

"I'm sorry about your dad," Kellie looked again at the smiling faces of Dan, his brother and mother. "Why did you leave Iowa? You look like such a close family."

"Kellie." He put his hand on her shoulder and waited for her to turn, perplexed, back in his direction. "Kellie, come here. I just want to hold you."

He saw the surprise in her eyes before he pulled her into his arms. With her cheek resting against his neck, Dan tried to absorb her warmth, to dispel the chill that had engulfed him since he'd first heard the news of the crash earlier in the day. She was soft and round against him, as beautiful as anything he had ever touched. But, for the moment, at least, all he needed was the emotional reassurance of her nearness.

Fanning his palms to take in every soft inch that he could cover, Dan felt the tension leave him. She was here. In his arms. Safe. And his. His to hold. He brushed his lips softly over her forehead, then the lids of her closed eyes. He heard her soft, contented sigh, and his heart constricted with sweet passion.

He loved her, he realized at that moment, inhaling the quiet fragrance of her hair. And someday she would love him back.

She tilted her face to his. He released his desperate hold on her long enough to reach one hand up to caress the fullness of her lips. She captured the tip of one finger in the barest of kisses, igniting a fire that swept swiftly through him. He trailed the finger down her neck and lower still, until he captured the swell of her breast. She responded with an almost inaudible gasp, which ended in a moan. Even through her sweater, he felt the bud tauten.

Charged with desire, Dan lowered his mouth to hers, giving her only moments to accept his caress before he parted her lips and deepened the kiss. His tongue matched the growing boldness of his hand at her breast. When her timid hand slipped beneath his sweatshirt to mold itself to the ridge of muscles along his spine, the surge within him intensified.

"Kellie," he breathed her name against her lips, wanting to tell her in every way possible how deep his need for her went. "Kellie, I want to hold you close. Keep you safe. Kellie, you're so beautiful."

Dan wasn't instantly aware of the effect his words had on the woman in his arms. But soon he noticed the uneasy stirring, the subtle withdrawal that signaled he had struck a chord better left untapped.

"What's wrong?" he whispered against her cheek, hoping to recapture the moment but knowing it was unlikely. Perhaps, in fact, it was just as well. Making love might provide a temporary distraction, but it didn't solve the deeper problem.

"Is that what this is all about?" Kellie took a step backward, hoping her clothes weren't rumpled, hoping she didn't look as muddled and distracted as she felt. "My safety? Taking me in your big, strong arms and keeping me safe from the big, bad world?"

Dan's heart sank. He should have followed his better judgment instead of his instincts and presented his feelings to her logically and cautiously. Now he was off on the wrong foot before the discussion even started.

"Not exactly. Can we sit down?" He resisted the urge to pull her close to him so his arms around her could convey the message that they were on the same side even though his words brought up unpleasant topics. Instead he led a reluctant Kellie to the couch and sat down an arm's length away. "I have to talk about this crash today."

The words dredged up Kellie's unwilling apprehension, and she did her best to beat it back. Finding she couldn't easily face him with the memory of his lips still burning hers, she turned to face the fireplace.

"Dan, there's nothing to talk about. I have a job to do and I do it. It's that simple." Desire still raged within her, leaving her too weak to argue with him, too weak to resist his insistence.

"It's not that simple." Dan stared at her stony profile. "I care about you and that makes me worry about you. I need—"

The last thing Kellie wanted to hear was that someone else was worried about her. She had a life to live, and anyone who couldn't accept that could just be damned. Turning toward him, Kellie's eyes glinted fire. But her voice was in rigid control. "I'm a grown woman and I don't need a mother hen. If you want someone to protect and fuss over, you'll have to find someone else.''

Anger doubled the anxiety already knotting Dan's insides. Why was he bothering with a woman so bullheaded she wouldn't even listen to what he needed to say? ''I'm not trying to fuss over you. If you'll listen for half a minute, all I want to do is . . . is . . .''

Dan struggled for words. Maybe she was right. Maybe he had no right to question what she did with her life simply because it worried him. But dammit, he cared, and all he wanted was to talk to her about his fears, to listen to her talk about her work. Getting things out in the open would help. It always did.

''All I want to do is talk about it,'' he finished, his eyes pleading with her to understand.

''Well, I don't want to talk about it.'' Kellie folded her arms stubbornly across her chest. ''And if that's how you propose to spend the rest of the evening, I'll leave now.''

''You mean you'll just walk out?'' Dan couldn't believe his ears. What had he done to make her so damned bullheaded and dead set against talking to him?

''That's right.''

''I can't sit here and make casual conversation the rest of the night without getting some of this out in the open,'' he protested.

''Then we won't.'' Kellie clamped her jaw shut, snatched her purse off the back of the couch and was out the door before he could take in the fact that she actually preferred to leave than to talk with him.

KELLIE NURSED HER HEADACHE, ignoring Oscar's romping, tail-wagging pleas for attention. She closed her eyes, lowered the back of the webbed lounge chair a notch and willed the three aspirin to take effect before Brian showed up with Carrie. An overgrown Lab was much easier to disregard than an energetic six-year-old.

Mother would get a kick out of seeing me trying to keep up with Carrie today, she decided, wishing she hadn't tried to drown her memories of Dan's caresses in three glasses of wine the evening before. Her temple throbbed at the reminder of her mother and the telephone conversation they'd had when Ellen finally caught up with her.

Her mother's frenzied insistence that her older daughter find another way to support herself had not been the only fallout from the Tennessee crash. Margo and Chip had taken the bad news solemnly, refusing to join her in putting the incident behind her. During yesterday's shift, Kellie had faced more questions and consolation and curious stares than she had since her first family reunion after her divorce.

"You can't hide your reaction to this kind of thing forever," Chip had said at last, stationing himself at the kitchen bar next to the apartment cot, where Kellie was trying to lose herself in a paperback novel.

"I'm not hiding anything," Kellie had said casually, keeping her eyes on the page of meaningless words.

"If you don't deal with your emotions, they'll either eat you up or you'll find that the only way you can handle any emotion is to suppress it." Chip rapped his fist on the countertop to capture Kellie's attention. "Listen to me, Kellie. I know what I'm talking about. Sometimes we all need to talk to someone."

Kellie didn't notice the desperate plea in Chip's voice—or the bleak resignation.

"I promise, Chip, I won't become a crazed introvert driven by my unresolved emotions." Kellie kept her tone light and smiled, hoping to convince Chip she was fine.

"But I may commit mayhem if you don't let me finish this love scene."

Chip snorted in good-natured disgust. "Living out your love life vicariously, too. That figures."

Kellie took aim with the paperback and would have landed a blow if Chip's reflexes had been slower. "See? Your hostility's surfacing already."

Chip didn't know it, but Kellie's reaction to the latest chopper crash wasn't her only cowardice in the past couple of days. She had congratulated herself on how slickly she had avoided the calls of a TV reporter looking for her response. And when Dan had called her at the hospital yesterday, she was unrelenting in her refusal to talk to him.

"Kellie, I need to see you tonight. Can I stop by after work to talk?"

"There's nothing to talk about," she'd announced, staunchly guarding against the fluttering of her pulse at the sound of his voice. "Maybe we shouldn't see each other anymore if you can't manage to accept what I do for a living."

"I *do* accept what you do for a living," he insisted. "But you have to accept my need to talk about it with you."

"I don't want to talk about it, and I don't have to."

Her words defied him to say otherwise. Nevertheless, she was stunned when he issued a curt, "Fine. Have it your way," and hung up.

The day had seemed endless. And when she'd come home to an empty house, a glass of wine and a late-night horror movie had seemed like the perfect answer to her troubles. Instead the TV screen had yielded a grim-faced

Dan Brennan talking to the reporter she had felt so clever to have avoided.

"Certainly such an incident strikes home with us," he said, his clouded eyes firm and self-assured. "We don't hear about something like this without questioning the validity of our own operation."

Furious, Kellie switched to another channel, where Frankenstein's monster looked suspiciously familiar for the next ninety minutes. One glass of wine turned to two, two turned to three and the third glass had turned into this morning's headache.

"And that," she muttered into the barely warm sunshine on her face, "is why two is my limit."

"So?" Rachael's voice startled her. "A little too much fruit of the vine? I didn't know you had a date last night."

Ignoring Rachael's probing final sentence, Kellie opened one eye to watch her sister pull up a lawn chair. "What are you doing here? You're supposed to be at work."

"It's Saturday, sister. A break at the end of a workweek for us poor working stiffs who hold down regular eight-to-five jobs."

"Saturday. That's right. Then go take a break and leave me to my hangover," Kellie grumbled. She was in no mood to hear Rachael's opinion of her job.

"I can't leave you to suffer through this alone. I decided that while I stood at the kitchen window, eating a grapefruit and watching you stagger out to your chair and collapse."

Kellie chuckled, pleased to note that the movement and the noise didn't pound behind her closed eyes. Maybe the aspirin was beginning to work. "Come on, now. I'm not that bad."

"So what's on the agenda for today, assuming you become mobile before the day's over?"

"I'd better get mobile." She raised the lounge chair a notch, moving slowly so she wouldn't nudge her headache out of hiding. "Carrie will be here any minute. Actually they were supposed to be here forty-five minutes ago. Where the heck are they?"

"Don't panic. It's only the Kellie Factor."

Kellie's eyes snapped in Rachael's direction. "What do you mean by that?"

Guilty amusement surfaced in Rachael's smile. "Everybody knows by now that you're never on time. So we...fudge a little when we give you times. If the play starts at eight, we tell you seven-thirty. If dinner is at eight-thirty, we tell you eight-fifteen. The Kellie Factor."

"Vipers! I'm surrounded by vipers who don't even trust me to be on time."

"'Vipers'? You should be grateful for such patient, understanding loved ones," Rachael teased. "What are you guys doing tonight? Want to go with Elliott and me for dinner?"

"Why so hot for Carrie to meet Elliott?"

Rachael smiled slyly. "It's about time to find out how much he really likes kids, that's all."

"That serious, huh?"

"It might be. But not if he starts asking if it's her bedtime as soon as dinner is over."

They laughed, remembering the last boyfriend Rachael had tested for his Carrie quotient. She had decided before the evening ended that he was a child hater who would work late every night until the last bedtime story had been told. She had deep-sixed him swiftly and painlessly.

"Ask Dan to come along, if you like," Rachael said, standing to head back to her side of the house.

"No, thanks. Carrie and I will also pass on dinner."

The careful disinterest in Kellie's voice raised Rachael's curiosity instantly. "Problems?"

"No." The ache started again, but Kellie was disconcerted to note it had moved from her head to other, less easily remedied regions. His touch had left its brand, deep and poignant and not to be ignored. Was she being rash to cast him out of her life so swiftly? "We just won't be seeing each other again."

"Why not? And don't pull your silent treatment on me, big sister."

Why can't I just put things out of my mind? Kellie fumed. *Why do people always want to drag out my problems and moan over them?*

"We . . . I lost interest. That's all. You know how it is."

"Baloney!" Rachael said gruffly. "You can peddle that somewhere else. I want the—"

"Mommy!" Carrie bounded into the backyard with her father trailing behind, and threw herself into the lounge chair before Kellie could prepare herself for the onslaught. "Can we buy a dress today, Mommy?"

"A dress? What for?" Carrie had two dresses for dressing up, but getting her out of jeans and T-shirts and into one of them took an act of Congress.

"For the school program. Can we?"

"Of course we can, sweetheart." Kellie wondered if Carrie would be as enthusiastic once she set eyes on the lace and crinoline numbers filling the racks of little girls' dresses. "Why don't you give Aunt Rachael a hug before she leaves?"

"And then run your bag into the house so your mom and I can talk for a minute," Brian said.

"I want to stay here and play with Oscar," Carrie said after planting a big kiss on Rachael's cheek.

"Later, kidlet." Kellie sat up in the lounge chair, swinging her legs to the ground. If Brian wanted to talk, she probably didn't want to take it lying down. "First, do what your dad says."

Brian filled the lawn chair Rachael had vacated before she'd said her quick hellos and goodbyes, and they watched Carrie lug her backpack through the back door.

"How's it going?" His question was uncomfortably polite, a nicety designed to delay and soften whatever he planned to bring up.

"Fine."

His hesitation was a distinct contrast to Dan, Kellie thought, grudgingly admiring Dan's brand of openness, even if she didn't always want to reciprocate.

"I've been wondering if you've given any thought at all to Carrie lately, and how she might react when she hears about people dying in helicopters," Brian blurted out at last. "Has that occurred to you at all?"

The slow, methodical pounding started in her forehead again. "Has she said anything?"

"No," he admitted. "Do we have to wait for her to get hysterical before you do something about it?"

Kellie's temper started a slow steam. Dan wouldn't resort to hyperbole, either, she thought testily. And he wouldn't blame somebody else's reaction for his own concerns. Brian, however, had never been above using any tactics whatsoever to win his way.

"It really isn't your problem, Brian. And if you can avoid communicating your own biases to her, I seriously doubt that Carrie will get hysterical over the fact her mother flies a helicopter for a living.''

Brian's eyes narrowed in anger. ''That's a pretty cavalier attitude for a mother to take.''

''I have a lot more confidence in our daughter than you do, that's all.'' Kellie knew instantly that kind of statement was on her list of don'ts for working out child-raising problems with her ex-husband. But her slow steam was becoming a steady burn. ''And I don't plan to feed her fears. I expect to help her learn to cope with them.''

Brian stood up stiffly, apparently convinced that Kellie had grown no more pliant in the past four years. ''There's no reason for her to even have any fears, if you weren't so damned irresponsible. Maybe all this would be easier on her if she lived with Heather and me full-time.''

Fear paralyzed Kellie momentarily. The sharp reply she had poised and waiting died. Instead she waved an imaginary white flag, hoping to avert any discussion of a custody battle. If they could just avoid discussing it, she reasoned, maybe it would never become a reality. ''Listen, how about a truce? Fighting each other won't help.''

Brian struggled to bring his anger under control and finally nodded. ''Maybe you're right.''

''I'll talk to her this weekend, if you think I should.''

He hesitated. ''I don't know. I don't think she's heard anything on the news. Maybe I'm overreacting.''

You and everybody else, Kellie wanted to bark back, wondering if Brian would ever stop trying to run her life for her. He had tried it for years when they were married, and he was still trying to use Carrie as leverage to dictate to her.

But I didn't give in to him, and I'm not giving in to Dan Brennan, either, she declared to herself as Brian walked back to his car. *Even if I do melt into little puddles every time I see him.*

CHAPTER TEN

KELLIE'S BIG SMILE was as fake as the poison apple she had devoured in her role of Snow White an hour earlier.

The carnival that she had been helping plan for months was in full swing, complete with rides, games and side-show acts donated by a traveling fair. The live fairy tales had been a big hit. But somehow, the day was missing some of the magic Kellie always felt when she stepped back into the world of children.

"Isn't this wonderful?" The tiny white-haired woman who was tossing her quarters recklessly and ineffectually toward the plates sounded as childishly pleased as Kellie longed to feel this crisp autumn morning.

"Wonderful," Kellie responded as she passed another fistful of quarters to her equally reckless daughter. When she and Carrie had stopped to meet Chip and his mother, Jane West, the six-year-old had determined that she wouldn't budge until she won a tiny stuffed bear for landing a quarter in one of the plates.

It looked suspiciously as if Carrie and Jane West would single-handedly finance the new equipment for the children's rehab center.

"Mother, this may not be your game," Chip teased, rolling his eyes in Kellie's direction. She was pleased to note that his face, when he looked at his mother and the two nieces who were with them, lacked the apathy that had become his most common expression lately.

The frail-looking woman rapped him affectionately on the arm, a gesture Kellie had seen Chip mimic many times. "Don't be a fussbudget. You worry too much." Fishing another bill out of her handbag, Jane West turned to Kellie. "Just because I let him support me these days, he thinks he has the weight of the world on his shoulders. If he's not careful, I'll get me a job slinging burgers again."

"Mother—"

"See what I mean?" Jane West laughed. "Takes everything too seriously."

As the two continued their good-natured bickering, Kellie turned her attention back to Carrie, hoping to convince the girl to give up her quest for a teddy bear. Kellie's feet hurt. She was hungry. But most of all, she was weary of faking enthusiasm. And the sooner Carrie saw all the sights, the sooner they could leave.

Then she spotted Dan.

Kellie felt like the heroine in one of the novels she was addicted to. Standing in the middle of the hospital's temporary midway, with the sound of a calliope and a ring-toss barker swirling together with the smell of popcorn and cotton candy and Shetland ponies, she looked up and he was there.

She melted. Everything inside her slithered right down from her hot-pink sweatshirt to her acid-washed jeans, then all the way down to her lace-up boots.

She had managed to lie to herself about the reason for her boredom with the carnival until she saw Dan leaning against a ticket booth, waiting for her to notice him. Now she knew—the emptiness within her had been there since the night she'd walked out on Dan, more than two weeks ago. And even the magic of a kiddie carnival couldn't make up for the loss.

His soft, striped flannel shirt was indecently alluring, stretched across his broad, powerfully built chest. The pleats in his khaki jeans drew her eyes to his flat stomach and slim hips. But it was the look in his eyes that finished the job of turning her to melted butter. His half smile was apologetic without begging forgiveness. And his eyes said he wanted her too much for his pride to keep him away any longer.

Kellie was just about to turn and run from her own weakening defenses when Carrie spotted Dan.

"Dr. Dan!" The child ran across the midway and took him by the hand. "I need help. My quarters won't stay on the plate. Can you help me win a teddy bear? That one right there?"

It took Dan less than a dollar to win the pink teddy bear for Carrie and a yellow striped kitten for Jane West.

"Now can we ride the ponies, Mommy?" Holding Dan possessively by the hand, the bear snuggled under her other arm, Carrie was immediately ready to conquer new worlds.

And suddenly, Kellie's feet didn't hurt anymore. The calliope sounded lyrical and the cotton candy smelled like heaven and she was as giddy as a child.

Dan grimaced, giving in to Carrie's insistence that he have another bite of her hot dog.

"It's good for you." The little girl echoed the phrase her mother used to coax her into eating undesirables like green beans and corn. "Like health food."

"There goes my cholesterol allowance for the week," Dan replied, swallowing a bite of the barely warm hot dog that Carrie had smothered in catsup.

Hands aching to touch him, Kellie watched as her daughter pulled every trick she had learned in her short life for making herself adorable to grown-ups. As they had made the rounds of carnival activities, Carrie had smiled at him with shameless little-girl charm, had insisted on holding his hand instead of her mother's hand, had flattered him outrageously when he won her another stuffed toy with his target shooting. And now, after feeding his ego, she was feeding his stomach.

Where, Kellie wondered ironically, did she learn to be a femme fatale before she even finished the first grade? And why was it that her mother never learned it?

Nevertheless, she was glad for Carrie's presence, which had served as a buffer, enabling them to enjoy the past hour together without rehashing their last meeting. Kellie suspected the reprieve was only temporary.

"What's cles-ta-role?" Carrie asked, stuffing her cheeks with the last bite of hot dog.

Dan opened his mouth to explain but stopped to look at Kellie quizzically, obviously unsure how much explanation Carrie needed and could understand.

"It's something grown-ups can eat too much of, and it makes them not as healthy," Kellie said, speculating that it would take a heap more than one hot dog to make the near-perfect body across from her unhealthy.

Carrie shrugged her disinterest and attacked the rest of her soggy French fries. "I'm in a school program next week." She looked up at Dan, her eyes suddenly bright. "You can come, too. Okay?"

Kellie's startled look in his direction revealed that Dan was well versed in the etiquette of dealing with invitations from youngsters. With a jealous stab, she wondered how many other women's children had opened their hearts to him since his divorce.

That's off-limits, she chastised herself. *Just as off-limits for you to worry about as it is for him to worry about your*

*past. Which is fine for him, since you don't have any juicy
stories to tell.*

"I'd love to, Carrie, but I may have to work then." He
wiped a streak of catsup off her chin with a napkin,
winking at Kellie over the youngster's head. "Why don't
I check my calendar and I'll let your mom know."

"You could tell them about the program and you
wouldn't have to work that day," Carrie explained, lick-
ing more catsup off the side of a finger. "That's what
Mommy did."

"Who's ready for the haunted house?" Jack and his
family stopped by the picnic table.

"Me! Me!" Carrie bounced up and down on the bench.
"Will you go with me, Dan? Pu-lease?"

"Tell you what, sport." He picked her up and sat her
on his knee. "Your mom and I need to have a little talk by
ourselves. Why don't you go with these folks, and we'll be
there by the time you finish."

Carrie accepted the deal, grabbed her new stuffed toys
and bounded away in the direction of the haunted house.
Kellie wasn't sure whether to be happy her daughter responded so well to Dan or sorry Carrie had been so willing to leave them alone.

Their eyes locked and Kellie once again felt the urge to
reach across the wooden table and take his face in her
hands.

"I'm sorry," he said, raising a hand to stop the words
he could see on her lips. "Me first. Then you. I'm sorry
if I sounded overbearing and overprotective. Maybe I am.
I don't want to run your life, but I do want to be a part of
it. I like you. Quite a lot. And maybe I took it for granted
that you liked me quite a lot, too."

Kellie started to protest, but he shook his head to stop
her. "Not yet. You'll get your turn. I'm thirty-four and all

I've wanted for years is to have a family like the one I grew up in. That's why I quit medicine, because somewhere along the line I realized that, for a doctor, everything but his practice comes in a distant second. I didn't want that.''

Dan's eyes didn't stray from hers, even when they hardened with a hurt only slightly dulled by the years.

''But the joke was on me,'' he continued, his mustache twitching in a wry smile. ''After I quit medicine, I found out that my wife didn't want me anymore. Lauren wasn't looking for a family man, she was looking for a doctor, and all the prestige that goes with the position. When she found out that wasn't going to be me anymore, she couldn't show me the door fast enough.

''So there's the irony. I gave up a career for a family life and haven't been able to find that family life yet.'' His expression suddenly softened, the hint of an apology returning. ''And now that I've found the person who might make it possible, I'm self-destructing. I'm trying too hard. I admit it. And I'm sorry.''

Dan's openness touched Kellie. Although their stories were different, Kellie was moved when she learned how similar the results of following their hearts had been. Brian had wanted a traditional wife and mother; when she couldn't do that with her life, their marriage had ended. Lauren wanted the glamour of being a doctor's wife; when Dan couldn't do that with his life, their marriage had ended.

''Anyway, I respect what you do and I respect your professionalism,'' Dan concluded. ''But sometimes I'll need your reassurance, or I'll simply need you to listen and help me work through my worries. But I won't be able to handle it if you shut me out the way you did that night.''

Kellie bit her lip, ashamed of the instinctive barrier she put up simply because it was easier for her that way. What about him? What about all the others who cared about her?

"Now you can tell me to go to hell or you can throw your arms around my neck and tell me how desperately you missed me. Or anything in between," he said with a crooked grin. "But I warn you, when you finish, I'll likely do the latter."

Laughing softly, Kellie reached across the table for his hand, unable to bear not touching him any longer. His grip was solid and strong, giving her the courage to tackle the problem she had wanted to push aside before.

"I'm sorry, too," she started softly. "I did think you just wanted to tell me how to live my life. I've been through that before and I refuse to go through it again. I suspect . . . I'm pretty sure I was wrong about that."

Drawing a deep breath for courage, Kellie plunged ahead. "I also overreacted because I was feeling pretty shaky about the Tennessee crash myself. Sometimes it's easier for me if I put things out of my head instead of confronting them. I was scared, too, so it was easier to think about other things. Maybe even safer. I can't afford to be worried and afraid when I go up."

The revealing speech wasn't as hard as Kellie had anticipated when she started trying to find the right words. In fact, once she began, she thought of a million things to say to Dan to explain how she felt and why she reacted the way she did. His understanding nod and the reassuring pressure of his hand told her worlds about his ability to empathize and forgive. And because of that, she knew the millions of words waiting to spill out could wait a bit longer.

What couldn't wait was her need to hold him close, to feel his arms around her in solid reassurance that she hadn't driven him away with her stubborn refusal to open up.

Fingers loosely linked, eyes tightly locked, they stood and met at the edge of the table. In one swift motion, Dan pulled her close to him and brought her lips to his in a slow, gentle kiss of welcome. All the need she had suppressed during the past days bubbled to the surface as she clung to his broad shoulders and molded her hips to his.

Before she could lose herself completely in his arms, he pulled away and cradled her head against his shoulder. "God, you feel good. But if we don't go after Carrie now, I'll be tempted to drag you away from here and leave this hospital at her mercy for the rest of the afternoon."

Kellie laughed lightheartedly for the first time in weeks.

KELLIE COULDN'T DRAG her thoughts away from the weekend with Dan as she drove across town Monday to meet her husband's new wife for lunch. The unexpected and unexplained invitation had done nothing to redirect Kellie's one-track mind.

Easing her way through the heavy midday traffic, she replayed the weekend.

Their pizza had grown cold while Carrie taught Dan the newest video game after the carnival, but Kellie's blood had grown warm as her thigh brushed against Dan's. And his glances convinced her that his incompetence at the video game had at least as much to do with her nearness as it did with his inexperience.

The weekend hadn't ended with his heart-stopping kiss at the door Saturday night, either. He had picked them up Sunday afternoon, delighting Carrie again by squeezing her into the space behind the front seat of his compact car and Kellie by touching the back of her hand with his every time he changed gears. With the top down and the sun shining, all three of them had enjoyed the drive almost as much as the picnic they'd had later at the lake.

Kellie had been smiling all morning. Even Heather Adams, she thought, couldn't wipe the smile off her face today.

She was wrong.

Across the tiny table for two, Heather's thin face, almost overwhelmed by the cloud of fiery red curls, was troubled. She pushed pieces of her spinach salad around on the crystal plate, and Kellie discovered she was having as much trouble as her daughter's new stepmother in working up an interest in eating.

"Brian plans to see an attorney about getting custody of Carrie."

The words robbed Kellie of her smile and her appetite. She didn't even care, after hearing the chilling news, why the fact seemed to bother Heather, too.

Nothing had ever frightened Kellie as much as the prospect of losing her daughter. She would fight, she vowed. She would get a job as a secretary if she had to. She would marry the first man her mother could round up, she promised herself irrationally, if that's what it took to keep Carrie for the precious six months a year that were hers and hers alone.

Brian Adams would not rob her of her child. And neither would this model-thin redhead who had floated in on a cloud of expensive perfume.

But she was at a loss what to say next without antagonizing this woman who was part of the plot to steal her daughter. So she waited, with uncharacteristic patience. A mother's instinct to protect her young, Kellie decided, ran deeper even than the impulse to lash out in anger.

"I knew you wouldn't be happy about that," Heather said quietly, still not daring to look her lunch partner in the eye. "And I wanted you to know that I'll help you any way I can."

That was when Kellie dropped her fork. Heather was full of surprises. The invitation to lunch, too intriguing to turn down, had been surprising enough. Then Heather's bombshell that Brian might actually make good on his constant threats to seek full-time custody. And now this. Kellie didn't know what to make of it.

Is this some kind of setup? she wondered.

"What do you mean?" Kellie studied the troubled face in front of her.

Heather placed a hand over her eyes, took a deep breath and looked up. "Don't get me wrong. I think Carrie's a real sweet girl. But... well, I'm just having a hard time adjusting to being a full-time mother. I don't know if I understand kids that well. I'm almost thirty and I've never been around kids before." Three chunky rings captured the light as she waved a long, thin hand in the air. "I never seem to know the right things to say to her. And she's always talking about how you do things and what you've told her and how much she misses you. I just feel so... inadequate."

The insecurity in the voice of the woman she had considered her rival for Carrie's love stunned Kellie.

"Besides, I can tell by the way she talks about you what a mistake it would be to try to force Carrie to live with us all the time." Running a nervous hand through her untamed curls, Heather reached for her glass of zinfandel and brought it unsteadily to her lips. "She shouldn't be put through that. And I can't be part of doing it to her. But I don't know how to take a stand without... you know, without causing a ruckus with Brian."

Kellie slumped back in her chair, the wind completely knocked out of her by Heather's straightforward admissions. So this magazine-perfect woman felt inadequate! She fretted over Carrie's affection for her real mother as much as Kellie fretted over her daughter's newfound infatuation with her stepmother.

But the bottom line was this: neither woman wanted to see Carrie dragged through a custody fight.

Pushing her untouched plate of pasta away from her, Kellie suddenly wished she had shown Heather's foresight in ordering wine with her meal. *Should be an unwritten rule somewhere,* she thought. *When dining with your ex-husband's wife, order wine. You'll need it.*

"Heather, I... I don't know what to say. Except that I appreciate your telling me all this." She took a deep swallow of her iced tea. On second thought, it was just as well she didn't have a glass of wine in front of her. "Most of all, I appreciate that you're more concerned with how all this would affect Carrie than anything else. I'm just a little blindsided. How far has Brian taken this?"

"I'm not sure. But he talks about it all the time. And he's been asking around about attorneys, trying to find out who's got a reputation for custody cases." Heather bit her bright fuchsia lower lip, which was a perfect match for the silk scarf draped casually over one narrow shoulder. "Kellie, I don't know what to do. We've already had one fight over this."

Kellie sympathized with Heather, knowing how easily Brian would be able to cower this none-too-aggressive woman.

"Don't worry," she said, surprising herself by reaching out to pat Heather's trembling, ice-cold hand. "We'll take it one step at a time. Keep me posted and we'll figure out a way to make sure Brian remembers that Carrie is the important one in this whole mess.''

But she didn't feel half as confident as she sounded.

KELLIE FROWNED, tossing the rough draft of their report into the basket. After her lunch with Heather, she couldn't concentrate on the facts she was preparing for the FAA.

"I'm going to be ready for them," she declared to Chip and Margo, a stubborn set to her chin. *Brian. The FAA. I'll take 'em all on,* she thought vehemently. "I've put in calls to helicopter services all over the country that provide ambulances for hospitals. I know how many pilots they have and what kind of shifts they work and what kind of safety records they have. We stack up as well as any of them."

Chip finished restocking the vinyl bag of drugs they carried in the chopper. "So did Memphis, until a couple of weeks ago."

Kellie made a face at him, reaching for a handful of pencils to sharpen. "Terrific. A cynic is just what we need."

"Then you're in luck," he retorted. "We've got plenty of them. I talked to some of the number three crew when I came on this morning, and they're convinced it's only a matter of time before one of us goes down."

"Maybe Kellie's not worried," Margo interjected. "Maybe she's working on an inside track to the top."

"What's that supposed to mean?" Chip asked the question Kellie hadn't wanted to voice. She had a hunch what Margo was driving at and didn't want to discuss it.

"I hear Kellie was gettin' pretty cozy with the new VP at the carnival Saturday."

Knowing Margo's distrust for management, Kellie listened for a clue that her friend was irritated by the news.

But at that moment, the hot line from dispatch rang, freezing conversation as the trio realized they would likely be in the air within five minutes.

"Maybe this is our lucky number right now," Chip said sarcastically as Kellie jotted down the destination and prepared to check flight conditions.

"Can it, Chip!" Margo said sharply.

Kellie held her breath while she took the report from the weather service. As low as their spirits were, she almost prayed for some excuse to turn thumbs-down on the flight. This kind of mood could so easily spell disaster. A successful flight depended on razor-sharp teamwork.

She hung up with a tight smile. "Clear sailing, boys and girls."

As they headed down the short corridor toward the helipad, Chip glanced at the chalkboard where flights were tallied. "Cheer up, babycakes. This will be number thirteen for the month. What could possibly go wrong?"

KELLIE TRIED to block out the jarring thump of the patient jerking violently on the stretcher just inches from her elbow. She concentrated instead on the static jibberish coming through her headset from the airport control tower and the hospital dispatch office.

Behind her was a teenager, young and slim and probably cute, although there had been no way to judge that when Chip and Margo loaded her onto the stretcher. The passengers and drivers in the other four vehicles in the five-vehicle collision had not been hurt as badly. But the fifth vehicle—the one on which the girl was a passenger—was a motorcycle. The driver of the cycle would make a leisurely trip to the hospital as a D.O.A.—dead on arrival. And it was beginning to look as if the young girl's massive head and chest injuries might place her in the same category, in spite of the speedy flight back to Memorial's trauma center.

Kellie recognized all the warning signals that indicated when a patient's heart had stopped, and she knew they were now pumping electricity into the young girl's chest in hopes her heart would kick in. Once. Twice. Three times.

It was hard to give up on one so young.

It was hard not to fly faster than was safe in hopes that something could be done once they were on the ground.

It was even harder to sit in somber silence the last five minutes of the flight, knowing that Chip and Margo were keeping watch over a body that would respond no more to medical treatment, no matter how fast she could set the chopper down.

"Damn it all." Chip's voice came through the headset, flat with despair and wasted energy.

Kellie sensed Chip and Margo ceasing the life-saving activities, a step that was contrary to everything they were conditioned to do. It battled every instinct.

"Kellie, let dispatch know we're bringing in a D.O.A." Margo's dispassionate words didn't hide the emotional upheaval and frustration Kellie knew the nurse would feel for the next few minutes, until they were on the ground and could begin to distance themselves from this teenager whose injuries had defied all medical help.

Once they had landed and waited out the two-minute cool-down period, Kellie lagged behind while Chip and Margo wheeled the young girl's body toward the entrance. She took her time checking the oil levels and securing the rotor, wanting to do anything but go back inside to stare at the walls and occupy herself with paperwork and listen to Chip rehash the flight.

Darn Chip and his pessimism! This kind of work was hard enough without someone on your team who was so eager to look on the bleak side. Risk was a constant companion in flying. Death was a constant companion at a hospital. The tension from that combination never let up. Add to that a bunch of bureaucrats breathing down their necks, and they were all dangerously on edge.

What rankled more than anything was her knowledge that Dan—as a member of the hospital's executive board—would be one of the people set up as judge and jury for the safety report on the helicopter service. Dan, whose kisses left her mindlessly inebriated, might be one of the first to point an accusing finger if anything went wrong. She remembered his pointed questions about whether she had made the right decisions during that instrument flight. Was it safe? he'd wanted to know.

Why was he so concerned? she wanted to know.

Kellie left the chopper and entered the building, stopping at the chalkboard, where the number of yesterday's flight mocked her. With a quick swipe of the eraser, she removed the number twelve and defiantly logged in the number of the flight just completed.

Thirteen. *Chip's got a big mouth,* she thought. *And if I go up to that apartment and lie down on that lumpy cot and look at the ceiling, I'll be ready for a straitjacket.*

She wandered toward the emergency waiting room, looking around restlessly for something to occupy her mind. A feverish-looking old man waited, unseeing and unresponsive, while a student nurse checked his blood pressure. The tight, black ringlets on a toddler's head bobbed as she adamantly refused to open her mouth for a thermometer. Another child wailed from behind a closed door. A pregnant woman grasped her white-faced young husband's hand for security while a volunteer pushed her down the corridor in a wheelchair.

Emergency was peopled with a thousand faces, each face another story. Kellie often calmed her itchy nerves by trying to read the lives of the people in their faces, picturing the happy endings that would be the outcome of these unexpected hospital visits. But today, she was interested in only one face, a face she didn't realize she was searching for until she spotted him, helping a feeble old woman with her admissions papers.

Kellie stood by, drinking in a scene that should have been old hat by now. Never satisfied with what he could learn from official reports and hospital statisticians, Dan continued to put on a white coat and work in every area of the hospital. This week, he was back in the emergency room.

Dan squatted beside the old woman, whose stooped shoulders brought her leathery face close to the clipboard in her lap. His thighs were as alluringly powerful as ever. His broad back tempted and the sweep of sandy hair over his forehead brought an ache to her fingers. But as much as his physical presence stirred her, it was watching him at times like these that moved Kellie most.

How could she not react to the tenderness in his voice when he asked the frightened woman about her insurance coverage? How could she remain untouched when he patted the old woman's withered hand with a powerful, broad palm? How could she fail to smile herself when Dan coaxed a weak smile from a wrinkled face that had been shrouded in worry just moments before?

He works miracles with people, Kellie thought, an unexplainable pride welling up to mix with a wistful wish that he could do the same for her.

And when he tries, you cut him off short, Kellie reminded herself, catching his eye as he helped the woman into a wheelchair. She pantomimed drinking from a cup and he nodded, holding up five fingers to indicate how long he would be.

She listened as he walked past, leaning low over the snowy white head stooped forward in the wheelchair. "We're going right down the hall to a quiet room, Mrs. Whitesell, where you'll be away from all this noise. And a woman from the admissions office will be there to finish these papers in a few minutes. Pardon? No, I won't leave you alone if you don't want me to. I can wait there with you until someone else comes, if you like."

Kellie watched as he walked away, talking softly to the elderly woman the whole time. She felt better just watching him, just hearing his voice. He seemed able to do that with everyone, almost as if his voice and his touch carried the power to heal the spirit.

My spirit certainly needs healing, Kellie mused dryly as she waited for him in the snack bar. The five minutes became ten, and she could picture him sitting patiently with the old woman, keeping her company with talk about her children and grandchildren and what she remembered from the old days, while they waited for an admissions clerk.

She could also picture him last weekend, sorely tempting her to lose herself in a ravishing kiss right in front of Carrie and all the others who were gathered in the parking deck after the carnival, waving goodbye at the end of the afternoon. If only they could have slipped away long enough for her to revel in the feel of his arms wrapped strongly and protectively around her, his thigh pressed hard and insistent against hers, his lips soft and moist and seeking....

The fantasy was completely out of control by the time Dan joined her in the snack bar.

"What's behind that wicked grin?" He slipped into the chair beside her, his knee dangerously and intentionally warm against hers.

The grin deepened as the pace of her heartbeat quickened. Her daydream left her as deliciously sensitive to his nearness, to the whisper of his touch, as if it had just come to life.

"I was just remembering our ride through the tunnel of love Saturday," she said, lowering her voice so only he could hear.

"We didn't ride through a tunnel of love on Saturday." He frowned in confusion.

"We didn't?" Kellie chuckled coyly. "Then we should have."

The corner of his mustache turned up in a grin as Dan caught her implication. "I see. I think the fairground has a tunnel of love. When should we go?"

"How about tonight, after work?"

"I thought you were working an extra shift tonight?" He leaned closer, his own voice a whisper, his lips close to her ear.

"That's right." Her full lips settled into a seductive pout. "We'd be all by ourselves."

Dan groaned and backed away slightly, his soft brown eyes pleading mercy. "I can't take any more of this. I've still got work to do tonight."

Kellie's sultry looks dissolved into a weary frown. "Don't remind me."

"Bad day?"

She sighed heavily. "The pits. The Tennessee crash has pretty thoroughly fouled up everybody's mood. Chip's done nothing but harp on it. Margo said the other crews are even worse." Kellie couldn't believe she was telling him so much or how good it felt just to get his understanding nod in response. "I'll probably have to talk to them before it's over. A little rah-rah business to keep the crowd from turning ugly. And right now I'm as discouraged as anybody. How the heck am I supposed to be a cheerleader?"

"Why so down?"

Kellie pushed aside her momentary twinge of reticence. "Besides the mood in flight headquarters, Brian seems convinced I'm guilty of unmotherly conduct. And my mother says I'm breaking her heart. In both cases because of my work." She still couldn't bring herself to tell him that her fears that he might become an adversary added to her unhappiness. "I'm taking all this guff because I want to help save lives, and some days I can't even do that."

Dan's eyebrows shot up. "What happened?"

Kellie shook her head, seeing once again the battered body Margo and Chip had hauled into the helicopter. "We had a D.O.A. a while ago. Motorcycle smash-up. Just a kid. The guy with her didn't make it, either."

Dan wrapped her smaller hand in his for a moment. "Nobody, nothing, can save all of them, Kellie. But you can't forget the chance you give so many who wouldn't have a chance without you."

She felt his strength and heard the convincing urgency in his voice, chipping away at her despair. "But it's so hard to fight everybody and then have to lose the patients, too."

"What about the ones you don't lose?"

She shrugged as if to dismiss the results of the other twelve flights so far this month. And the twenty-seven last month and the twenty-four the month before. "Oh, I know, but—"

"But nothing. Come on." Tugging on the hand he held, Dan pulled her up and proceeded to lead her out of the snack bar. "I've got something to show you."

"What?"

"Never mind. Just follow me."

In less than five minutes, they were on the seventh floor, peering at a youngster whose face was as pale as her platinum blond hair but whose smile was brighter than the sunshine splashing across the hospital bed from the window.

"Dan!" The child's voice was weak but enthusiastic. "I got to go in the swimming pool today. For therapy. They said if I try hard, I'll move my legs all by myself soon."

"That's wonderful, Amy!"

Amy. This was the fragile hit-and-run victim they'd brought in the first night she met Dan. He had said it would be an uphill battle for the little girl, but here she was, looking as pleased as punch with herself and the baby steps of progress she was making. Kellie felt a catch in her throat.

"Amy, I want you to meet somebody. This is Kellie Adams. She was the pilot of the helicopter that brought you to the hospital."

Amy looked up, hero worship in her big blue eyes. "You're a lady," she breathed in wonder. "Wow! Can ladies fly helicopters?"

"Sure." Kellie found it hard to smile through the dampness welling in her eyes. This little girl would have had no prayer for survival without the air ambulance.

"That's what I want to do when I grow up," Amy declared, resting her blond head on her pillow, her voice tiring from the excitement of her swim and the visit. "Then I can save people, too."

"I think that's a super idea, Amy." Dan patted her cheek. "You're pretty tired right now, young lady, so we're going to let you get some rest. I just wanted Kellie to meet you."

"Come back soon?"

"You betcha."

Kellie fought back the tears that had filled her eyes as they walked toward the elevator. True to her resolve, she had never visited one of her patients before, had never let one of them become real flesh and blood. She realized now that translating those names and numbers on her reports into smiles and blue eyes and voices she would hear for days to come, could become the most rewarding part of her job.

And it could also, she realized, become the most devastating, on days like today, when one of them didn't make it.

"Convinced?"

"Of what? That I'm turning into an old softy?" She sniffled, grabbing a tissue from the nurses' station as they passed.

He stopped and turned her toward him, his hands strong and warm on her arms. "That what you're doing is worthwhile, even if some bureaucrats and whiners like Chip are going to make it tough on you for a while?"

She smiled shyly, a little embarrassed that he had seen her so emotional. "Okay. I'm convinced."

"Good. Now do you want to go with me to see if Mrs. Whitesell is in her room yet, or do you have to get back to work?"

Kellie wasn't sure she was up to another encounter with a patient. How did he do it without breaking his heart?

"I'd better get back. I've got to refuel."

"Can I call you tomorrow?"

She nodded and reached out to give his hand a squeeze before he headed down the hall and left her alone.

But his departure didn't leave a void as she punched the elevator button for the ground floor. He was still with her, filling her with reassurance and understanding that would help her make it through the rest of her shift.

But it went deeper than that, she knew. What he was bringing to her life was more than simply a temporary balm to her spirits. What he offered was a new door that opened onto parts of her soul no one—not even herself— had explored before. What he offered was a flight of fancy come down to earth. What he offered was love.

And Kellie realized with a start that she was ready to book that flight, no matter what the destination.

CHAPTER ELEVEN

ALTHOUGH SHE AND DAN had settled into an easy pattern of yearning phone calls and lingering glances during moments stolen from the busy days that followed, life in flight headquarters grew no more pleasant.

In fact, right now, Kellie could hear angry words, muffled but clearly heated, coming from the air-ambulance office while she was still halfway down the hall. But when she walked into the room, the argument skidded to a halt.

Averting his face, Chip turned abruptly and faked an avid interest in making a new pot of coffee. Snatching the lid off the pot, he angrily tossed the filter full of old grounds into the trash can.

Steam rose almost visibly off Margo, whose face was set in a stubborn scowl.

"What's going on here?" Half the time these days, Kellie felt like an outsider. Although Margo and Chip sniped at each other constantly, most of it was done outside her earshot. Kellie felt they were shutting her out of some significant twist in their relationship that was slowly but surely poisoning the strong bond that had made them such an effective team.

"Nothing." Chip bit off the word sharply without turning around, spilling coffee on the counter as he mutinously measured it into a fresh filter.

Margo merely grunted, then looked at Kellie and shrugged as if to say, "I can't do a thing with him."

The other three shifts were having morale problems, Kellie knew. But she had hoped for more from her trio. If she couldn't even keep peace in her own group, how could she expect to influence morale in the other shifts? Yet she had to do something. The mood in flight headquarters had gone from bad to worse in the past week. Things were so bad, in fact, that she had scheduled a meeting of the three other pilots after her shift ended that very day.

Looked as if it was her day for dealing with recalcitrant co-workers.

"Don't give me that. I want to know what's bugging you two." She waited, hands on hips, for one of them to speak up. They exchanged a wary glance, but neither spoke. "I mean it. I want to know. You two can't say three words anymore without turning it into a cat fight. And I'm tired of being in the middle of it."

Margo shifted from one foot to the other and didn't look Kellie squarely in the eye when she spoke. "I'm just uptight. That's all. Tryin' to get my girl into college and all. She's been accepted at Emory, and now I'm wondering where the money's gonna come from. I've been taking it out on Chip."

Thinking back to their discussion the day she and Margo had cleaned up after a painting session in the basement, Kellie didn't buy it. But she didn't know what to do about it short of bringing up that discussion now, in front of Chip. She made a mental note to take Margo aside soon and talk about it more. If the tension between the two nurses was solely because of Margo's concern for Chip, perhaps it could be resolved. But if Margo had learned anything that aggravated her concerns, Kellie needed to know that, too.

"Chip—" Kellie turned to him, hoping Margo's words would elicit a similar concession from the sour-faced nurse. But before she could finish her question, he had whirled around and marched past her with the coffeepot.

"I'm going to get water," he snapped. "See if you can get her off my back while I'm gone."

Stunned by his brusqueness, Kellie turned to Margo, thinking now would be the perfect time to follow up on their earlier conversation. But Margo had already grabbed her flight jacket off the coatrack and was also headed for the door.

"I'm supposed to be somewhere. Beep if you need me."

Kellie opened her mouth to speak, but before she could get a word out, she was alone. The empty room still crackled with tension.

"HOW CAN WE BE SURE we'll even have jobs once this report is made?" Jack Lambert tossed out the challenging question.

Kellie tried to keep the discouragement off her face. Although she had insisted on bringing the three pilots together for a pep talk, it was turning into a gripe session, instead. And a gripe session would do nothing to improve the already plummeting morale.

"That's pretty unlikely, Jack," she said, wondering if she trusted her own words. "But we all realized when we took this job that it was an experiment for the first year. If any changes are made, they'll more likely be to strengthen safety measures. And that's only to our advantage."

"If we're not flying safely, I want to know it now," insisted another pilot.

"You know our safety measures, Andy. If you feel there's anything unsafe about our procedures, speak up."

Andy looked at the floor, his voice less challenging when he spoke again. "I'm not so worried, but my wife sure is giving me hell."

For another hour, Kellie tried to counter their pessimism with a fabricated optimism. She defended the hospital's request for a report, insisting that it didn't reflect a lack of confidence in them, even though she wasn't confident of that herself. She pulled every trick she knew to placate them and send them away more upbeat than they had been when the meeting had started. But when it was all over and she sat, drained and alone, on the cot in the apartment, she wasn't sure she had succeeded. Maybe giving them a chance to listen to one another fuss and fume had only exacerbated the problem.

It certainly did the job of dragging me down in the dumps, she thought, wearily running a hand through her curls. *Thank goodness I'm not on duty. After all this depressing talk, I'd go bonkers sitting up here waiting for a call to come in.*

Kellie picked up her purse and jacket, deciding to ask Jack what kind of effect he thought the meeting would have. Jack would tell it to her straight, she knew, and he was on duty tonight, so he would still be around. But when she stuck her head in the office door on her way out, she didn't see him.

"Where's Jack?" she asked Michelle Raft, a nurse who was filling out a follow-up report on a patient.

"He went down to the snack bar for coffee with the rest of the pilots."

Kellie frowned, knowing beyond a doubt that the three men had carried their gripe session to the snack bar. Fitting in as one of the guys had never been a problem for Kellie, but intuition told her she wouldn't be welcome in their little clique right now. They needed a scapegoat for their frustration, and as lead pilot she was the most likely candidate. She could hear Frank and Andy now, discounting all her logical arguments and calling her a mouthpiece for the administration. Especially if Jack reported seeing her at the carnival with Dan.

You need somebody to cheer you up again, she told herself as she headed for the exit, pulling her quilted Oriental jacket on over her skirt and blouse.

With a halfhearted smile, she recalled the way Dan had taken her in hand just days before and showed her a living, breathing reason for believing in what she did, even when things grew discouraging. She wished he was at the hospital tonight to make her feel that positive again. It had been only a temporary shot in the arm, but it had helped her make it through the rest of that day and night.

That's what I need right now, she thought, *something to help me make it through this night. And if Dan's not here, I'll have to do it myself.*

Feeling her spirits lift because of her decision, Kellie wheeled away from the exit and headed for the elevator. She could look in on Amy just as easily without Dan.

Although she sprinted to catch the elevator, the door closed before she could get there. She stood, impatiently tapping her foot for a few moments, then decided to take the stairs.

"Besides, it'll buy you enough calories for ice cream on the way home," she said aloud in the empty stairwell as she took the steps two at a time.

Kellie was already smiling in anticipation when she looked around the door into Amy's room. Her smile faded at the sight of the empty, crisply made bed and the counter space that was free of the flowers, balloons and potted plants that had brightened the room before.

Funny, if they just began therapy a few days ago, Amy would hardly have gone home by now, Kellie thought. But she could see nothing in the room to indicate it was occupied. She wandered toward the nurses' station, sorry now that she had not visited the child earlier so she could have enjoyed her progress more before the girl went home.

"When did Amy go home?" She stopped at the nurses' station.

The two nurses swapped looks before one of them spoke. "She didn't."

Kellie felt a pinprick of apprehension at their closed faces.

"Where is she?" She could see their indecision over what information they should give to a woman they didn't know. "I'm the pilot who brought her in. I came up to talk to her, see how she's doing."

The nurse peered at her. "She's in ICU."

Kellie's blood turned icy at the news that the young patient had returned to the intensive care unit. Amy had been weak when she saw her, but seemed clearly on the way to recovery. "What happened?"

"Infection from internal injuries," the nurse said matter-of-factly. "Then pneumonia set in, her lungs filled with fluid. So we took her back upstairs."

"Will she be all right?" Kellie asked, trembling.

A buzz signaled that a patient was ringing for a nurse. The uniformed woman looked pointedly at the board where a panel of lights would reveal where she was needed. "I hope so, miss, but I really don't know."

She hurried off to see about the patient who had buzzed, and the other nurse excused herself also, clearly too busy for a lengthy conversation. Kellie stood for a few moments, the chill of fear filling her. Amy could die anyway. In spite of getting her the best medical treatment as quickly as possible, she might not leave this hospital alive.

Maybe what I do is *pointless,* Kellie berated herself, heading listlessly for the stairs. *Maybe it's what people say, nothing more than a great public-relations gimmick for big city hospitals.*

As she trudged through the quiet corridors on the ground floor, heading for the exit once again, Kellie started wondering for the first time in years what she would do if she decided to quit flying. Teach others to fly? Or try to find some kind of desk job that wouldn't drive her crazy inside of two years?

While she reviewed her options, she glanced up and down a cross corridor. The hospital was quieter tonight than she had ever seen it, even in the deadly hours between midnight and dawn. Only one other human being, far down the corridor at the back entrance of the pharmacy, was stirring in this part of the building. Kellie suddenly froze.

The tall, thin person coming out of pharmacy hadn't been in hospital whites. He had been dressed in the easy-to-spot tan and green of the helicopter ambulance service. And his mop of thick, salt-and-pepper hair had been equally easy to identify.

Chip? It couldn't have been. Chip was off duty.

Stopping and taking a step backward, Kellie peeked around the corner toward the pharmacy. Taking his own stealthy peek around the corner at the other end of the corridor, the man shoved his hands deeply into his pockets and headed quickly toward the nearest exit.

Chip! What in the world would he be doing here at night?

Unbidden came recollections of the rumors she had overheard more than a month ago in the Medicine Chest.

Drug thefts at Birmingham Memorial. With newfound clarity, Kellie saw Chip's haggard face, his shaking hands. Even Margo's cautious suspicions took on new meaning.

Chip had been leaving the pharmacy by the back door on his own time, on his night off. What that meant, on top of everything else that seemed to be conspiring to destroy air ambulance, Kellie didn't even want to consider.

But she knew, as she quickly left the building, keeping a careful eye out for Chip, that she would have to take action right away on what she had seen. This was one little bit of unpleasantness she couldn't turn her back on.

Tonight, however, it could wait. She spotted Chip far ahead of her and lagged behind. Before she confronted him, she wanted to think very carefully about what she should say. This wasn't the time to lose her cool.

By the time Chip had pulled out of the parking deck and Kellie had reached her beat-up station wagon, her spirits had sunk so low that she even dreaded the drive home alone. She needed someone she could talk to. That usually meant Rachael, but Rachael was out with Elliott tonight.

"Where else would she be, but with Elliott?" she spoke into the darkness as she tuned her radio to a call-in talk show. But the discussion of the latest scandal involving a local beauty queen who had posed for a girlie magazine did nothing to steer Kellie's thoughts away from the reason for her depression.

Depression was so alien to Kellie that she didn't know how to handle it. She never permitted bad thoughts to hang around for long, and now that they were, she didn't know how to get away from them. During the drive home she wrestled with the frustrated demands of the other pilots, with Brian's biting comments when he brought Carrie over a few weeks ago, with her mother's escalating anxiety, even with her own growing misgivings that morale was creating a powder keg at the hospital.

When Kellie pulled up in front of her house, its shadowy windows mocked her, waiting patiently for her to fill the dark rooms with the conflicting feelings and fears that were growing in her, too.

Without even turning the ignition off, Kellie left the dark corners of her house to fill themselves.

KELLIE WASN'T ABLE to admit to herself what was on her mind until she paused in front of the drugstore display. The neighborhood store that was more like an old-time general store—grocery staples and auto supplies shared the shelves with cosmetics and over-the-counter medication—had seemed like the perfect place to wile away a couple of hours. But after a quick cup of coffee with the woman who ran the snack counter, Kellie could sit still no longer.

Restless and impatient with herself, Kellie wandered the store, picking up a tube of toothpaste on sale and a package of neon-colored banana clips she knew Carrie would love for holding back her ponytails.

Then she saw the display. And she knew the reason she had stopped at the drugstore to kill time instead of at the frozen yogurt shop next door.

Without pausing to weigh the advantages of natural versus man-made or ribbed versus ultrasheer, Kellie grabbed a package and crossed her fingers that the silver-haired grandmotherly woman wasn't on the cash register tonight.

Shouldn't I feel nervous, Kellie wondered a few minutes later, *showing up on a man's doorstep unannounced? Or at least a little self-conscious? He could have company—female company, at that. Or he could resent the intrusion.*

For any number of reasons, it didn't seem the smart thing to do. But Kellie couldn't come up with a single reason that fit her image of Dan Brennan. If she found him in the arms of a seductive, half-dressed redhead, it would be a blessing. Because seeing it with her own eyes would be the only way she would believe it. He wasn't the type and she knew it. Unavailable or undesirable go hang. Dan was the exception that proved the rule. Deep in her heart, Kellie knew that.

You're not the type, either, she gibed, reminding herself of the purchase that was now burning a hole in her purse and in her conscience. Nevertheless, her spirits rose a little with each step that brought her closer to Dan's door. Just the prospect of seeing him was pushing her dark mood out of the way.

Is this what it's like to be in love? she wondered as she brought the brass knocker down against the door. She didn't remember it from being in love with Brian, but she was beginning to believe she had been too young then to truly be in love, anyway.

Because this isn't like anything I've ever felt before, she assured herself breathlessly when Dan opened the door.

Kellie's pulse skittered wildly at the slow smile that tilted one corner of his tawny mustache. Blond stubble on the square jaw that was normally smooth added to the rakish look created by the thick blond hair that was overdue for a cut. His midnight-blue T-shirt boasted of a 10-K footrace he had run. But it was his nicely molded torso that drew her attention, not the funky jogger silk-screened onto his chest.

"This is a dream, right?" He slipped an arm around her shoulders and drew her into the room.

"Nope." She snuggled into the curve of his arm, kicking off her shoes, caught up in the heady realization that her appearance at the door needed no preface. His welcome came naturally and without reservation, as if he had been expecting her. Or wishing for her, at the very least. "No dream. Just flesh and blood."

"Mmm." He led her to the couch and leaned so deeply into the cushions that she was almost reclining against his chest. "I believe you're right. There's every indication this is no dream at all."

Kellie snuggled closer, wiggling into a better position to brush her lips against the fair bristles on his jaw. Her hand played along his neck, feeling the thunder of his pulse against her fingertips. "Do all your visitors get such a warm welcome? Suppose I'm here to sell Girl Scout cookies?"

He rolled his head back on the sofa, concentrating on the almost timid exploration of her lips over his neck and face. "I'm buying."

Her laughter was a sultry purr from deep in her chest. "But I haven't even given you my sales pitch, yet."

A low moan told her the journey of her warm fingertips into the new territory of his broad chest excited him as much as it excited her. As her hand splayed over his chest and belly, his muscles tightened involuntarily.

Dan grasped her seeking hand in his and held it fast, then tilted her chin up with his free hand. "Kellie, this is no safer tonight than it was before." He stopped at the flush of color on her cheeks. "Is it?"

"You're not hiding a six-year-old in the closet, are you?" she asked shyly, wondering how to handle the realities of making love without losing the magic.

He smiled, sinking his hand in her tousled curls. "No. But that isn't the only danger you were worried about."

"I've . . . taken care of . . . everything else." Kellie stammered and looked down, knowing that pregnancy was the least of her fears. Was she doing the right thing, or was she getting herself in too deeply, too quickly? Perhaps her decision to book this flight of fancy had been made too hastily. Was a growing love for Dan, and feeling certain he was sincere in caring about her, enough justification for giving in to her desire?

It was the only justification, came the answer from the part of Kellie that was ruled by more than logical decisions—the part that had always insisted she follow her heart.

"Is this why you came tonight? To make love?"

That would be hard to deny, especially since she had made the incriminating last-minute stop at the drugstore. Although the greater need was his closeness, his comfort, his friendship, she knew when she made her decision that the need for his touch would overpower all those simpler needs once they were alone together.

"I came because I needed you," she said simply. "In every way."

Kellie watched his eyes darken and smolder at her words. "And I need you, Kellie."

He released her hand, and it started its meandering trail down his chest again to the hard planes of his belly. Sinking lower still on the couch, Dan moved against her touch.

Kellie raised herself on one elbow, only ceasing her slow strokes long enough to creep beneath his T-shirt. She gasped at the fire in her fingertips as flesh touched flesh. Her control was gone, spirited away on her soaring exhilaration. Playful sensuality now turned to heated urgency, and she lowered her lips to his. His lips opened hungrily; his tongue plunged to taste her, then retreated, then plunged again and quickly left, teasing her to a frenzy.

Without releasing her mouth from his game of sweet torture, Dan pulled her into his arms. He covered the hard contours of his body with her soft curves, urging her long legs to curve around his hips.

Through the sturdy corduroy of her skirt, Kellie felt the hard thrust of his passion throb against her, seeking her heat. Sighing deeply, she writhed against him and deepened their kiss.

Her hips moving over him tempted his hands away from her waist. He sifted through her flowing skirt until he found the firmness of her thighs with each hand. He slid his hands higher to slip beneath the panty hose and flimsy scrap of silk, reveling in the gentle ripple of her muscles.

Bold with the heady knowledge that tonight she would no longer deny their desire, Kellie brought their kiss to a reluctant end. Still astride him, she sat upright, looked down into his smoldering eyes and slowly began to unbutton her blouse.

Dan watched in fascination as she manipulated each button with painstaking deliberateness, revealing nothing until she tossed the blouse aside. Her nipples were taut, dark peaks beneath the champagne-colored silk camisole that was her only cover. He waited for her to pull the camisole over her head and send it sailing to the floor, as well. Instead she drew his broad hand away from her hip and brought it up to her silk-covered breast. Her nipple swelled against his palm.

Aching to pick her up and haul her to his bed, Dan reined himself in, determined to let her carry her seduction as far as she wanted. Slowly, taking care not to break the spell, she stood to slide her skirt over her hips, revealing long, tapering legs. Still standing in the pool of teal-blue corduroy, she spoke for the first time since their lighthearted banter brought fire to their embrace.

"Will you make love with me?"

The simple words, in a husky voice throbbing with vulnerability and passion and pride, cut through him, a sabre of raw need. He knew she was asking for so much more than a joining of their bodies.

"Yes, Kellie. Oh, yes, my love."

Casting aside her silken undergarments, she came to him, her skin glowing softer than any silk. Dan relished the soft roundness of her belly, the swell of her hips, the heavy fullness of her breasts. He started to remove his T-shirt, but she stilled his hands.

"Let me."

Again he surrendered to her seduction. Mesmerized by the light flickering over her agile, golden body, he burned under her pampering touch as she slowly disrobed him. As she revealed each new expanse of flesh, she stopped to taste and kiss. She teased the bend of his arm with her tongue, eliciting a moan at his discovery of the unexpectedly erotic pleasure. She ravaged his broad shoulders with tiny, nibbling kisses. A kiss at his knee, the sensual slither of her tongue up his thigh, filled him with explosive desire.

But when his aroused manhood was uncovered to her touch, she was no longer able to keep the slow, steady pace of her seduction. Caressing him with a tremulous hand, Kellie cried out softly and closed her eyes, oblivious to anything except the powerful evidence of his desire for her and the deep, dark river of desire running through her body in response.

Ready at last to relinquish control, Kellie slipped the drugstore package out of her purse and then followed Dan into the next room. Swiftly pulling back the spread that covered his bed, he pulled her down beside him and took the few moments necessary to assure their protection. Kellie was only dimly aware of the gentle waves that signaled they were on a water bed.

She was, however, vividly aware of the waves of unsatisfied need that consumed her as he began his own slow exploration of every inch of her body.

When Dan at last lowered himself over her, Kellie gasped as the hard power of his maleness melded with her giving softness. He held her, motionless, for a few moments, giving her time to learn the sweetness of his body filling hers. Their eyes caught and held, sharing the wonder of the moment.

She breathed his name, wanting to say more but unable to find the words for the emotional whirlwind taking control of her sensations. But she knew from his eyes that somehow, in her touch or in her look, he felt all of her dizzying reactions.

With sure, slow thrusts, Dan eased Kellie from wondering passion to frenzied turbulence. A whimpering sigh signaled she was at the mercy of her sensations as he swelled inside her, driving himself deeper and deeper. And still she wanted him deeper, so deeply inside her that some part of him would always be there, even when their bodies were no longer one.

She knew before he knew, with some instinct she had never used before, that his next move would catapult them into a world made up only of his warmth filling her completely, and her softness wrapping him in a gentle love he had never before experienced.

And that world, she knew moments later as she lay trembling in the wake of their love, held no easy escape.

She was in for the long haul, no matter how bumpy it grew.

She would worry about whether he felt the same some other time.

CHAPTER TWELVE

"ARE YOU ALWAYS THIS QUIET first thing in the morning?" Dan longed for the sound of her voice to break the quiet of his balcony, just to prove beyond a doubt that she was here. Just to remind him of the sound of her voice when she had breathed his name into the darkness the night before.

Kellie laughed softly, taking her gaze from the autumn-hued hillside beyond his balcony long enough to look him in the eyes. Those deep, soft, telling brown eyes that had mesmerized her soul while his body had practiced magic on her flesh.

"Actually, yes." Their eyes held, each remembering the moment they awoke, snuggled warm and trusting against the other. "I'm as cross as a bear until I've had enough caffeine to wake the entire U.S. Air Force. So I generally keep my mouth shut till I'm civil."

"Sorry. And I'm asking you to face the day without any caffeine." He grinned softly, gesturing to the china pot of herbal tea he had brewed to go with their granola cereal and fruit.

If Kellie had been braver, she would have told him then and there that facing daybreak with his broad, hard body next to hers had been a more effective eye-opener than the stoutest cup of coffee she had ever brewed. His soft caress brushing the curls out of her eyes, his chest hair grazing her breasts, the tantalizing realization that his arousal first thing in the morning was as powerfully hard as it had been when they'd made love the night before. All of it had roused her to instant wakefulness and sent a murmuring hum through her body.

"That's all right. Mom says I should break the habit, anyway. But it's been my only vice for so long, I've hated to give it up."

A half smile crinkled his eyes. "Maybe you should switch to chamomile tea. I could recommend a number of replacement vices for you to consider...."

The invitation in his eyes was strong. But the crisp white shirt and carefully knotted silk tie were stronger statements. The hospital beckoned. In fact, she would have to leave soon, too, to pick up her flight suit and head for Birmingham Memorial. "You'd better finish reading the paper, or we'll both end up with our pink slips."

Dan grinned and turned back to the sports pages, looking up between box scores and weekend football previews to reassure himself that Kellie was still there, sitting across the wrought-iron table, close enough to touch.

Feigning an interest in the front page, Kellie couldn't steal her thoughts away from Dan long enough to read about the latest airline strike. They had talked long into the night, discussing his dilemma over giving up medicine and his anguish over his father's death.

When their passion had risen again, they'd realized Kellie's foresight hadn't covered the possibility of an evening lingering over their lovemaking.

"You only bought *one*? Kellie, they come in packs of twenty-four. Or three, at least. And you bought *one*?" The water bed had undulated with his laughter.

Kellie blushed. "It was a sample. And I...I wasn't sure what to get. So I thought—"

"So you thought you'd just try a sample?"

She traced the edge of his mustache, which tilted up with his crooked grin. "Besides, I didn't want to seem overeager."

"Well, tell me this," he teased, letting his hand linger along the length of her back. "Now that you've tried the sample, do you think you'll come back for more?"

She sighed with pleasure at his touch. "I'm definitely ready to invest in the giant economy pack."

So they had touched and kissed and, when the strain grew too great, pulled back to talk about Brian and becoming a mother and Dan's mixed feelings about leaving his hometown and his family.

"Why did you really come tonight?" he had asked in a moment of silence.

For the first time that evening, Kellie had felt herself holding back. She had needed the comfort of his closeness, but she knew she couldn't risk making him her confidant.

"I found out Amy's had a relapse of some kind." She hadn't liked the chill of isolation creeping around the edges of her heart with her half-truth. "I just ... needed to come to you."

He had pulled her close then and they finally fell asleep, wrapped in each other's arms. As she drifted off, Kellie felt she had never known anyone as deeply as she knew Dan. And no one, she was certain, had ever known her as deeply as Dan knew her.

But what next? she wondered now, sipping at the tea and longing for the swift kick of a cup of strong, black coffee. What they had felt was more than casual. Their hours of intense, probing conversation the night before had been the prelude to much more than an affair from which they could easily walk away.

But if they didn't walk away eventually, then what?

Marriage?

Kellie stared blindly over the top of the paper to the hillside. If they were moving toward marriage, what would that mean to Dan? Would he, too, expect her to stay home and raise their children? Or at the very least, to lock herself into the kind of job that would make her available every night, every weekend?

Maybe that wasn't as unreasonable as she had thought when she'd rebelled at Brian's uncompromising insistence. But maybe it would be no easier now than it had been then.

And if that was the case, would Kellie once again find herself in the tough spot of choosing between living alone and pursuing her career or making a life with someone who insisted on pulling in the reins?

Guiltily Kellie thought back to her recent scare, when she almost lost control of the chopper while flying through the clouds. *Maybe I'm just being selfish,* she told herself. *Maybe part of growing up is accepting the fact that you can't have it all.* Dan had recognized that years ago, she reminded herself, when he gave up medicine to start a family that had never materialized.

Until now. The thought popped in, unwelcome. Frowning, Kellie folded the paper and sat up straighter in her chair. Until he found a ready-made family.

"I hate to do this." Dan's caressing voice broke into her reverie. "But I've gotta run."

She looked up guiltily at the warmth in his voice. "Me, too."

They cleared the table. Still preoccupied with her thoughts, Kellie didn't notice Dan's hesitation as they set their cups and saucers in the sink.

"Kellie, I'd like you to have this." He reached for the lacy African violet on the windowsill. "It's... I'd just like you to have it. My dad always gave Mom violets. He always thought they said something special, and . . . If you like violets, that is. If you don't . . ."

A rush of tenderness tugged at Kellie, watching the square-jawed, broad-shouldered man in the power suit struggle for words. She reached up to press her lips gently to his, then took the tiny potted plant. "Thank you, Dan. That would mean a lot to me."

And it did. It meant he wanted her to know that the night before was the first of many more. Just an hour earlier, that reassurance had been all she'd needed to make the morning perfect. But as she followed Dan out the door to their cars minutes later, Kellie couldn't force away the nagging worry that she hadn't been the main attraction for Dan Brennan. Maybe the real lure had been her daughter. The daughter he had never had. The daughter she might not have much longer.

And if that happened, losing Dan, too, would be more than she could take. Even the freedom to fly couldn't make up for those two losses.

Knowing she already depended on Dan that much scared the wits out of her.

THE IMPACT OF THE WORDS sank in slowly. Jack had quit. Her best pilot had resigned. Effective now. Today. Kellie's first thoughts were of the hassles of advertising for a replacement and interviewing candidates for the job.

But her second thoughts were of hassles of a more serious nature. It would probably take weeks to find a replacement for Jack. Weeks when she would be shorthanded. Weeks when she and Frank and Andy would have to work double shifts to cover Jack's hours. Long hours, long workweeks were always a problem. Pilots who worked too long and grew too tired were more prone to pilot error. And with morale already at the lowest ebb Kellie had ever seen, an added burden like this could easily be the last straw.

Picking up the phone, Kellie dialed Len's office and gave him the news.

"I'll call personnel." He sounded as if he blamed Kellie for the loss. "We'll get the ad out as soon as possible. Do you have any contacts we could tap? The sooner we get somebody in here, the better."

"I'll check around. But most chopper pilots do so well free-lancing that they don't want to give up the freedom for somebody else's schedule."

"One more thing, Kellie." Len stopped her before she hung up but hesitated before he continued. "All things considered, I think you should handle this carefully when you're doing your paperwork, if you know what I mean."

Kellie frowned. Maybe her lack of sleep was catching up with her. She had no idea what Len was getting at. "No, Len, I'm afraid I don't."

She heard his exasperated sigh over the telephone line. "With the FAA breathing down our necks, this might not be the best time for them to get wind of the fact that you're shorthanded. It would probably be wise for you to make that as...unapparent...as possible in your flight logs during the next few weeks."

Shaking her head, Kellie wondered if she could possibly be hearing right. "Are you asking me to falsify the flight logs we send to the FAA every month?"

"Kellie, I'm not asking you to do anything." His voice was tight, one short step from impatient anger. "I'm telling you to exercise your best judgment."

"I can't exercise that *kind*, Len. Do you know what kind of mess we'd be in if—"

"Leave that to me, Kellie. Just remember, I'm expecting you to do your job. It wouldn't do for us to have someone in your position whose judgment we couldn't trust. Do you read me?"

Swallowing hard, Kellie felt a sudden knot in her stomach. "I read you."

Kellie dropped the receiver back into its cradle and stared across the office at the map. Pins topped with tiny red flags marked locations where they had picked up patients in the Birmingham area during the past month. She considered the effectiveness of transferring those pins to a photo bearing the likeness of her boss. Voodoo would probably have no more impact than trying to reason with Len Baldwin.

The man was not only a weasel; she now knew he was dishonest, as well. And he expected her to sacrifice her integrity simply because he ordered her to.

Simply because he threatened your job if you don't, she corrected herself, getting up to pour the coffee she had wanted all morning. Her first whiff of the coffee reminded her of the fragrant aroma of Dan's herbal tea. She smiled, remembering his self-consciousness when she had spotted him squinting at the paper and had forced him to drag out his reading glasses.

How would Dan react if he learned she was falsifying FAA flight logs? Kellie wondered, and realized instantly there was no question how he would react. He would be furious. And rightly so. He would be justified in having her fired.

So, either way, she figured, keeping her job was going to be a pretty precarious balancing act the next few weeks.

Groaning quietly to herself, Kellie wondered what had happened to the gentle euphoria with which she had awakened.

HER FIRST SIGHT of Chip that morning was part two of Kellie's rude awakening. Instantly she remembered what she had managed to shove into the back of her consciousness: Chip's suspicious-looking actions on the way out of the hospital pharmacy the night before.

She had to do something. But what? And why now? she moaned to herself.

What difference could one more crisis possibly make? Kellie thought, reviewing her fears of a custody fight and losing her job and falling in love with a man who would in all probability try to bully her into quitting work so he could fulfill his fantasy of middle-class family life.

You're making yourself crazy, Kellie told herself, jumping up from the desk and grabbing her coat off the rack. A brisk walk around the block would get her adrenaline pumping and help her decide which of her problems to take care of first.

"Chip, I need to get out of here and think. Can you take Jack's resignation letter up to Len's office?" When he looked over at her, she noticed his eyes were bloodshot. It looked as if he had slept no more than she had. But for a different reason, she speculated, wondering just what Chip had taken out of the pharmacy with him the night before.

"Jack's what?" Chip's blank expression suddenly changed to stunned incredulity.

"You heard me." Afraid her suspicions had surfaced in her abrupt answer, Kellie tried a smile. *If he's as out of it as he looks,* she thought, *he won't notice how forced it is.* "We're shorthanded. Have you ever thought of taking up flying?"

Chip rolled his eyes. "Just what we need. Jack's the best we've got. What do we do now?"

"That's what I'd like to think about for a few minutes," Kellie answered, wishing that just once Chip wouldn't take the doomsday approach to everything that happened. "If you'll take care of Jack's letter, I'll see if I can think of any likely candidates."

The early-morning sunshine had disappeared, leaving behind a dreary day punctuated by a biting wind. Kellie huddled into her flight jacket. Her hair flew wildly around her face, and leaves were being vigorously shaken from the trees. The October morning was a taste of the winter that was still months away.

Her worries and frustrations whipped around in Kellie's head as frenziedly as the dry, brown leaves swirled through the air. Brian and Carrie. Len and his darned flight logs. Chip and whatever foolishness he was mixed up in. And most of all, Dan and the tumultuous emotions he had stirred up in her. She shivered, thinking how much simpler all of it would be if she could go back to the peace of mind she had felt when she'd first opened her eyes to Dan's lopsided smile this morning.

If she could just bring herself to trust the feelings that had blossomed between them, she thought, the rest of it would surely fall into place. Finding the courage to stand up to Brian would be so much easier, knowing she had someone like Dan in her corner. Even bucking Len wouldn't seem so intimidating if she could just confide in Dan. But that was out of the question. Just as it was out of the question that she tell him where she had seen Chip the night before.

You were right all along, she told herself. *Getting involved with someone at work is a bad plan.*

And an even worse plan if you start feeling as if you can't function without him, she chided herself. *That's exactly how Brian wanted you to be. And you're not going to give in to that kind of temptation now, just because things are getting a little tough.*

By the time she had rounded the block twice, Kellie had made up her mind. She would do her best in the daily flight logs to disguise the fact that they were pulling double shifts, without actually providing false information. If that didn't satisfy Len, she would face whatever repercussions she had to.

But first, she had to face Chip. Whatever problems he might have, her first obligation was to the air-ambulance service. Chip couldn't be allowed to jeopardize their safety or the safety of their patients. And it was her responsibility to make sure he didn't.

CHIP WOULDN'T sit down. He stood by the table in the flight apartment, fingering the brass frame around the picture of Kellie, Carrie and Rachael. Then paced the room with nervous, halting steps and pretended to study the air-safety precautions poster covering the wall over the cot. One just like it hung in the office downstairs, Kellie knew, but it held his attention as if he'd never seen it before.

He had resisted coming upstairs with Kellie as their shift drew to an end, using weak excuses to avoid her. But Kellie had insisted, knowing she had to deal with this problem right away.

She watched him now, failing miserably in his pretense that nothing was wrong. *Where do you start,* she wondered, *when you have to tell someone you care about that you think they're doing something illegal?*

"Chip, why don't you sit down? This might take a while."

He glanced over at her but didn't meet her gaze. "Better not take long, babycakes. I'm almost off the clock."

Kellie sighed. Getting Chip to open up was probably as big a job as opening up herself. For the first time, she sympathized with what Rachael went through sometimes.

"You've had some kind of problem for quite a while now, and I want to know what it is," Kellie said firmly. "I'm responsible for the safety of this operation, and I'm convinced your problem—whatever it is—may affect our safety."

Chip flattened his palms against the legs of his flight suit. Kellie wondered if his palms were sweaty and wished she could think of some way to make this easier.

"Has Margo been talking to you? She won't stay off my back, and if you're going to start now, too, I—"

"Margo doesn't have to say anything, Chip," she interrupted him sharply. "I have eyes. And I've seen things I don't like. But I'd rather you tell me what's going on than start making accusations."

Chip snatched his flight jacket off the bed and headed for the door. "I'm getting the hell out of here."

"If you won't talk to me about this, Chip, I'll have to tell Len Baldwin what I saw last night."

The words she hadn't wanted to say had instant effect. Chip stopped with his hand on the doorknob and turned back toward her. But he still didn't look at her and, when he spoke, his voice almost quavered with uncertainty.

"I don't know what you're talking about."

"Chip, don't make this harder on both of us." She waited expectantly, but he said nothing. "What were you doing in the pharmacy when you were off duty last night?"

"What are you? The hospital's Mata Hari? Vice President Brennan's best little informant?"

The hostile words were only halfhearted, but they still stung. Especially the crack about Dan. She knew Chip wasn't the only one speculating on her relationship with the new vice president. Would he leave this meeting angry and willing to vent his anger with gossip? Why, Kellie asked herself, was she wasting time on someone who obviously preferred to self-destruct instead of confide in his friends?

Because, she reminded herself, she knew what pressure he was under, with an aging mother to support. And because she knew how good-hearted he was when he wasn't under the influence of whatever demon was plaguing him now. Hadn't he helped Margo's daughter, Carol, study for her college entrance exams? And wasn't he helping Margo look for scholarship money for Carol?

"Don't push me, Chip. I'm your friend. I'd like to help. But I'm also crew chief. And if you'd rather I did this as crew chief, I'll do it that way."

The hand on the doorknob dropped limply to his side. His gray face went white. When Chip finally raised his eyes to hers, she could see the fear and despair. Her heart twisted. He walked over to sit down in the straight-backed chair facing her.

"I'm sorry, Kellie. I thought I could handle this. And it looks like I've let things get way out of hand."

She reached over to place a hand on his arm. "What is it, Chip?"

"It isn't what you think. It isn't drugs. It's..." Chip slumped forward and dropped his face into his hands. "It's my heart. I'm having some kind of problem with my heart. I'm sure it's only a minor problem. I'm sorry it's caused so much trouble."

"Your heart! What kind of problem? What has your doctor said?" Kellie felt her own heart grow cold. If Chip was on the level, it certainly explained how bad he had looked during the past few weeks. But it didn't explain what he was doing sneaking out of the pharmacy.

Chip shook his head and squeezed his eyes shut. "That's just it, Kellie. I haven't been to the doctor. I'm . . . I've been . . . treating myself. I know what medication to take. I thought everything would be fine and no one would have to know. But the medicine doesn't seem to be doing the trick. And Margo knows something is up. I've got the whole thing screwed up."

"You've been treating yourself? Are you crazy? For heart trouble? Chip, you're a nurse. You know better than that!"

He looked up; the defeat in his eyes turned to defiance. "I also know what would happen as soon as this hospital found out I was being treated for heart irregularities. Off the crew I'd go. I'd be shuffling papers somewhere. Len thought I was too old for the flight crew when I first applied. I'd be history, Kellie."

"But, Chip—"

"I've seen what that's like, Kellie, when they put you out to pasture." His hands clenched into fists, white knuckled and trembling. "I saw it happen to my dad when I was a teenager. He died for ten years, one slow day at a time, sitting in front of the TV. And the rest of us— Mother, my sisters, me—died with him. I can't face that, Kellie."

Kellie placed a hand over one rigid fist and pressed. "Chip, that was thirty years ago. It doesn't have to be that way now. Unless you fool around until there's nothing they can do for you."

"That's fine. Then I'll go like that—" he snapped his fingers "—and won't be a bother to anyone. At least Mother won't go through that again."

Kellie remembered how close he and Jane West had seemed at the carnival. And how Mrs. West had chided her son for being such a worrier.

"So you've been stealing from the pharmacy so no one would find out? Chip, how long do you think it'll be before you're caught?"

Chip nodded wearily. "I know. I've been more afraid of that the past few weeks than I have been of going through what my father went through. Kellie, are you going to report me?"

"I'd rather you took care of this yourself. See a doctor. Stop this dumb business of trying to treat yourself. Will you do that?"

Staring at her like a cornered rabbit, Chip raked shaky fingers through his tousled hair. The defiance ebbed slowly out of his dark, bloodshot eyes. "I guess. I don't know, Kellie. I just can't face becoming some kind of invalid."

"Make up your mind, Chip. And let me know by the first of next week. I can't let this drag on. And Chip? Make your peace with Margo. I can't work under these conditions, either. Remember, we're both on your side."

"The first of the week. I promise. I'll let you know. The first of the week." Still he hesitated at the door on his way out. "Kellie, you won't tell anyone about this yet, will you? The higher-ups, I mean? At the carnival, some of us thought you were pretty friendly with...with some of the brass."

The dark flush that rose on her cheeks angered Kellie. But she couldn't be angry at Chip's wariness. "With Dan Brennan. Isn't that what you mean?"

Chip grinned weakly, clearly grateful for anything that took the focus off his problem. "That's it, babycakes. What's the scoop? Are you two hot and heavy?"

In spite of her reluctance to discuss Dan, Kellie was grateful to hear the teasing note return to Chip's voice. "What's an old man like you know about hot and heavy?"

He walked back and gave her a playful nudge on the shoulder. "Plenty. So, 'fess up. I've spilled my guts. Now it's your turn."

"We've been seeing each other. I'm not sure I'd call it hot and heavy." Even as she said the words, Kellie knew that anyone who could have seen her and Dan the night before wouldn't hesitate to call it hot and heavy. But somehow those words weren't the ones she would have chosen. "But whatever personal relationship I have with Dan Brennan ends when we walk into Memorial, Chip."

Chip gazed at her. "No pillow talk about aging nurses who pull stupid stunts, then?"

She blushed again. "No pillow talk, Chip."

THE LIGHTS OF THE CITY twinkled below them as they circled the observation deck at the base of Vulcan, the city's iron statue.

"I haven't done this since I was a kid," Kellie said, leaning back against Dan's chest and into the warm circle of his arms. "I haven't even brought Carrie."

"We'll bring her soon."

Kellie smiled into the darkness, grateful for Dan's ready acceptance of her daughter. She refused to think back to the doubts that had troubled her after breakfast, just as she refused to think of everything that had happened since. Dan's strong arms were a welcome haven, banishing all the unpleasantness in her life.

They were alone in their survey of the sights from the mountaintop overlooking Birmingham. When Dan spoke, the rumble in his chest vibrated through her.

"Do you think Carrie likes me?"

Kellie shifted in his arms to look up at him. She smiled at the need for reassurance that she saw in his eyes. Lifting her face, she planted a gentle kiss on his lips. "Of course she does. Just like her mother, she has impeccable taste in men."

Dan nuzzled her ear, hiding the pleased smile her words brought. "Then you think her mother likes me, too?"

"Mmm-hmm." She closed her eyes to lose herself in his cuddling embrace. Sparks showered through her body when his lips, followed by the soft brush of his mustache, traced her cheekbone to the corner of her mouth.

"Then maybe I could get her mother to come back to my place," he murmured, using the tip of his tongue to tease her lips apart. "The view from my balcony is as good as this. And we could throw a blanket on the floor in front of the fireplace. Just to warm up, you understand."

"I understand," she whispered hoarsely, wanting to leave but hating to stop the coaxing, nibbling half kisses with which he was taunting her.

"But first . . ." Crushing her close to him, Dan covered her mouth with his. His searching kiss made her hunger for the intimacy she knew they would share through the night to come.

When the kiss ended at last and they walked, hand in hand, toward the elevator that would take them back to the wooded park at ground level, Kellie's nagging worries about the events of the day returned. How intimate could they be, she reasoned, when she was hiding so much from the man she was just beginning to love?

CHAPTER THIRTEEN

KELLIE'S HAND TREMBLED so badly she almost dropped the telephone.

Carrie was hurt.

Being trained to handle emergencies had not prepared her for Heather's call to let her know that Carrie was being treated in the emergency room of a nearby hospital.

"I've got to go," she called to Margo as she dashed out of the flight office, thanking her lucky stars Andy was in to cover her shift today so she could finish up the safety report and deliver it to the executive board. If she had been on flight duty, she would have been forced to sit by and wait for word on her daughter. "Carrie's been hurt. Don't know when I'll be back."

"But—"

Kellie didn't wait for the nurse's reply. Within minutes, she was running down the hill to the university Medical Center. Terror chased her the entire two blocks. She hadn't waited for details from Heather when she'd heard that Carrie had fallen from the monkey bars during recess. She fought back sobs, trying to talk herself into calmness as another hospital emergency room came into view.

Her lungs burning from the unaccustomed exertion, Kellie pushed on the automatic doors that didn't open quickly enough to suit her. During the agonizing minutes it took to locate Carrie and Heather, Kellie envisioned the frantic mothers she had seen during her months at Birmingham Memorial. Mothers hearing news so bad Kellie wasn't certain she could handle it herself.

She was shaking all over by the time she was ushered into the examining room. The first thing she saw was the front of Carrie's pink sweatshirt, stained with a few splatters of darker red. But her gasp of fear was cut short by Carrie's beaming face—minus a front tooth, but happy nevertheless.

"Look, Mommy! My tooth came out!" Carrie grinned and poked her tongue through the new gap. "Will the Tooth Fairy come even if it fell out by mistake?"

The tears came now. Not taking her eyes off the wonderful, smiling face of her daughter, Kellie asked, "Is she all right?"

Heather walked over to put an arm around her shoulders. "You poor thing, you've been scared to death. She's going to be fine. Lost a tooth and sprained a wrist, that's all."

"Thank God!" Kellie rushed to the examining table and touched Carrie's face gingerly, not wanting to add to the child's aches and pains with a misplaced hug. "You're sure you're okay, kidlet?"

"Sure," Carrie said matter-of-factly. "The doctor says I have to wear these bandages on my arm, though." She leaned over to whisper in her mother's ear. "But maybe we'll ask Dr. Dan what he thinks."

Unable to restrain herself any longer, Kellie gave Carrie a careful hug, then listened as the young intern filled in her and Heather on caring for Carrie's injuries. As her nerves calmed, Kellie found herself suddenly miffed at the realization that Carrie's school had called her daughter's stepmother and not her.

But as she watched Heather's concern and careful attention to the doctor's instructions, Kellie could no longer feel the resentment she had felt for Heather before the lunch they'd shared. The other woman was doing the best she could in a tough situation—becoming a mother for another woman's daughter, when she would probably prefer starting her own family. Or maybe even doing something else totally unrelated to children and bedtime stories and after-school dance lessons.

"Am I going back to school now?" Carrie asked as the three headed to the lot where Heather was parked. "I want to show everybody where I don't have a tooth now. Lots of kids already have no teeth in the front, and now I've got a hole, too."

"No more school today," Heather said, unlocking the passenger door and helping Carrie buckle up. "The doctors says rest today."

"Aw, Mommy!" Carrie wailed in protest, hating to give up the image of herself as the wounded hero returning to a classroom where she would be the center of attention. "Can't I go to school?"

"You heard Heather. No more school today." Kellie patted the curve of the child's disappointed face again, noting that her hand had not yet stopped its trembling. "But I'll see you right after work. Okay? We've got a big weekend ahead of us, remember? And I've got a surprise tonight."

"What?"

"It wouldn't be a surprise if I told," Kellie said, knowing her daughter would be excited to learn that Dan was having dinner with them. "So you be good and rest this afternoon so you'll enjoy the surprise. Okay?"

"Is it another new puppy?" Carrie asked, remembering when her mother's surprise had been Oscar's arrival nine months earlier.

"No hints." As Heather closed and locked the car door, Kellie turned to the woman who had so much responsibility for her daughter. "Thanks for taking care of her. And thanks for calling."

"I thought the school had called you," Heather explained as they walked to the other side of the sporty compact. "When I got here and realized you weren't here already, I knew something was wrong. I'll call this afternoon and make sure they have your name and numbers on their records."

"Thanks. That would be great." Kellie wasn't sure she would be able to pull herself together enough to work through the day, but she knew it was time to head back and give it her best shot. "About seven-thirty, then?"

"Sure." Heather moved to unlock the car, then stopped. "Kellie, you should know. Brian has an appointment Monday. With an attorney."

Heather didn't have to say more. Kellie knew exactly why Brian was seeing an attorney. And for the second time that day, her pulse accelerated in fear for her child. Brian had threatened to see an attorney before, but never had. It had always been just another threat to hold over her head. Perhaps now the days of threats were over and he had decided it was time to act.

Why now? she wondered as she trudged back up the hill to Birmingham Memorial. What had changed? Images of herself making love with Dan sprang to mind. Don't be paranoid, she chided herself. How could he possibly know? And why would it make a difference if he did? Other images sprang up. Images of Carrie trying to call her late into the night and getting no answer. That might have given Brian all the ammunition he needed to strengthen his case for sole custody.

Dan Brennan might seem to be the answer to her dreams when he took her in his arms and made her feel his love deep in her soul, but nothing—not even that—would make up for the loss if Brian found a way to take her daughter away. She thought of the lonely nights during those six months each year when Carrie lived with her father. The only thing that made them bearable was knowing the next six months would bring Carrie back to her life. She could never stand living without her daughter every day of every year, with only a short weekend reprieve every two weeks.

If Brian meant to make a battle of it, she would have to do whatever it would take to win. Of that Kellie was determined.

SETTLING AT THE DESK with a deli sandwich from the hospital's cafeteria, Kellie went over the report she and Margo had prepared one last time. She was pleased, but still nervous, and not just because she was concerned with how the hospital's executives would receive her plan.

Knowing Dan was one of those executives added to the pressure. Would she be able to keep her mind off the secret memory of his caresses long enough to go over the facts? Would their closeness make it impossible for him to be objective about her report, or would his professional concerns be magnified because of their personal relationship? As Kellie coached herself on the facts so she could make a smooth presentation, she couldn't help but wonder how she and Dan would handle themselves in a situation where they were forced to separate their personal and professional lives. Could they really do it?

She was also nervous about how the group would receive their new safety recommendations. They hadn't asked for them and might not appreciate her being so presumptuous as to make them, anyway. Len, for one, wouldn't be crazy about anything that was going to make his life more complicated. But as she had researched her report, new wrinkles on safety had surfaced from other operations all over the country. And today's audience with the executive board was a much better shot, Kellie figured, for getting her ideas heard than going through the regular channels—which meant going through an unreceptive Len Baldwin.

So give them her new ideas she would, and to heck with the board if they didn't want to hear them. Now if only she didn't have to go alone, but Margo had been adamant about her fears of making a presentation before the board. Kellie was on her own.

At the sound of a clearing throat, Kellie looked up into Chip's uncertain gaze.

"How's Carrie? You scared us to death, running out of here like that."

Smiling an apology that she knew wasn't necessary, Kellie said, "She's fine. Lost a tooth. Sprained a wrist. Thought it was a great lark."

"Figures." Chip fidgeted nervously. "Do you have a couple of minutes?"

Kellie looked over his shoulder at the clock on the wall. "A few. I'm on the firing line in ten minutes. What's on your mind?"

Chip cleared his throat again nervously. "Just wanted you to know... I'm seeing a doctor next week. Called for an appointment today. No more fooling around with this."

Smiling, Kellie stood up and gave him a hug. "I'm so glad. Have you talked to Margo?"

"Yeah. This morning. I feel like a real jerk about the way I've been—"

"Excuse us." They turned toward the cheery voice from the hallway and saw a plump nurse from physical therapy. Beside her, in a wheelchair, was the young hit-and-run patient, Amy. "Amy wanted to come down herself to thank the people who helped save her life."

Kellie felt relief flood through her. So Amy had fought her way back from the pneumonia that had returned her to intensive care. Kellie exchanged a glance with Chip. Getting a look at the positive results of their work might even touch the heart of this card-carrying cynic.

"Amy, we're so glad you came." She moved toward the girl's wheelchair but stopped when the nurse held up her hand.

"I have a surprise," Amy announced, smiling uncertainly and looking up at the nurse, who nodded.

Kellie's heart stopped as she watched the tiny child edge slowly, laboriously out of the chair. At last she stood and, with the steadying hand of the nurse at her elbow, took two halting steps in Kellie's direction.

Breathing heavily but smiling broadly, the youngster looked up into Kellie's eyes, which were covered with a mist of emotion. "Nurse Betty said if I could walk again, I could learn to be a lady pilot like you. See? I can do it now."

With a catch in her throat, Kellie squatted to bring herself to eye level with the youngster. "Amy, that's the nicest thing I could imagine. When you get ready to learn how to fly, you call me and I'll teach you. Okay?"

Amy's eyes widened and she glanced up at her nurse in thrilled surprise. "Wow! Really?"

"Really." Giving the girl a brief hug, Kellie looked up in time to see that even Chip's eyes weren't dry as the nurse helped Amy in her slow, two-step journey back to the wheelchair.

KELLIE'S COLOR WAS HIGH and her heart was racing as she looked into Dan's boardroom mask. She saw no hint in his glance that just last night she had felt his touch along her inner thigh, his lips teasing at her breast. This was business. And, as promised, their personal relationship had no place here.

Pushing all thoughts of last night aside, Kellie started reviewing her report for the bored-looking men and women in their pin-striped suits and stiff-colored shirts. All of them looked as unyieldingly formidable as the dreary portraits of hospital big shots from years past that stared down glumly from the mustard-colored walls.

She told the group how she and Margo had prepared the report and what it contained. She led them in detail through each section of the report, which each person in the room had before him or her.

"We tried to keep it brief and factual. In addition to the report on our safety measures, we've included some charts contrasting our setup with other services across the country. Those charts show pretty graphically that we're a good service, but we're not a first-rate one. But it wouldn't take much to bring us into the league with some of the nation's best air-ambulance groups, and improve our service to our patients while we're at it, which is really the bottom line.

"On the plus side, we have four pilots, and many services across the country operate with three or even two pilots." She stopped to flip through the photocopied report, hoping Len was the only one in the room who knew they were down a pilot. "We operate twelve-hour shifts, and other services ask their pilots to work as long as forty-eight hours in a row."

One of the hospital executives interrupted her. "Are we going overboard on this safety business? If these other hospitals can get by with three pilots and longer shifts, why can't we?"

Unflustered now that she was actually up against the wall, Kellie pointed to the last chart in the report. "Page fourteen is a pretty good argument in favor of our system. It shows the accident rates at various services across the country. And the number of incidents increases dramatically where staffing is lower and shifts are longer. You can see that pattern holding true on this line graph."

She glanced at Dan, hoping for a nod of approval. But his mask remained intact.

"Are you sure you didn't cherry-pick the services you surveyed to get the results you want?" someone else asked.

Wondering if anyone here was on her side, Kellie reached inside herself for an even tone and a calm smile. "As a matter of fact, we did cherry-pick. We called the FAA for the twenty services that had been in operation longest, figuring their records would have the most validity."

Silence greeted her explanation. Kellie began to question the wisdom of bringing up her new ideas here and now. This group seemed anything but receptive. But she knew from experience that anyone was likely to be more receptive than Len Baldwin. It was now or never.

"Now for the areas where we don't measure up. I took the liberty of putting together a few new recommendations based on my discussions with the pilots I interviewed." She was aware of Len stirring uncomfortably on the other side of the table. "Although this report shows we're already doing more than some to assure safety, I did discover a few wrinkles that could make us even better."

Slowly Kellie explained her ideas for cross-training more people in the emergency room, not only to provide backup assistance but to make sure they knew all the hazards of being around helicopters and how to avoid them. She suggested more rigid criteria for approving evening flights, as well as the appointment of a safety-review committee made up of local pilots, airport officials and emergency health care providers.

"And, I suggest we explore with city and county police a cooperative effort to create less chaos at accident scenes." She could tell that her new ideas had riveted the attention of most of the hospital executives, including Len, who looked disgruntled and uneasy. "That's one of our biggest problems right now, but a co-op program with law enforcement and better communication with emergency crews on the site could solve it pretty quickly."

As Kellie wrapped up, a burst of discussion broke around the table.

Len's protests surfaced first. "It seems to me you've gone way beyond what you were asked to do, Ms Adams," he said stiffly. "I'm not sure this group needs your recommendations for changes."

Dan's voice cut in before Kellie could respond. "I thought you were in charge of this report, Len. Didn't you know its content until now?"

Len glared at him, then at Kellie. "I thought the job was in capable hands."

"It appears that a thorough job was done." This assertion from the president smoothed over some of the resentment boiling in Kellie. "Even though you didn't follow through as you should have, Len."

Len squirmed and voiced a few weak protests until he realized the mood around the table was favorable. And when Dan spoke again, praising Kellie and Margo's work, it was clear his vote of confidence was all the group needed to give unanimous approval to the report.

One more load off my mind, Kellie thought as she left the boardroom, switching her thoughts to the quiet dinner at home she had planned for Dan, Carrie and herself.

THE VOICES from the living room warmed Kellie clear to the bottom of her toes. She put the last of the dinner plates into the dishwasher, satisfied that the simple meal of stir-fried shrimp and vegetables had been a hit. It was one of the few nice meals in her repertoire, which leaned to peanut-butter-and-jelly sandwiches for Carrie and a wide range of low-calorie boil-in-bag meals for herself.

But tonight felt special. She wanted to impress Dan with how domestic she could be in spite of her independence. She wanted to see how it felt to come home to a family and settle down to a quiet Friday night like the rest of Middle America.

How it felt was wonderful.

Wonderful to have Dan express appropriate concern over Carrie's sprained wrist. Wonderful to hear Carrie giggling out of control over a game of Old Maid. Wonderful to hear the corresponding laugh of the man who had it in his power to bring Kellie almost to tears with the emotion in his touch. Wonderful to know she'd be able to tuck her daughter in and come back downstairs to the arms of someone who could make everything seem right.

Kellie felt like hugging herself as she dished up bowls of fresh fruit for dessert, hers and Dan's laced with Amaretto, and carried them out to the living room.

"And then, I got to hold up my sign with the number four on it—'' Carrie paused for dramatic effect as she recounted once more the tale of her success at the recent school program "—and we all sang a song about counting to ten. And I didn't forget a single word.''

"I'll bet your mom was so proud of you," Dan said, glancing up as Kellie paused at the door.

"She said I was the best one there," Carrie admitted. "I wish you could have seen it, too."

"So do I." Dan tugged on her braid. "Maybe I can make it to your dance recital."

The youngster's face lit up. "Yeah! Mommy, when will that be?"

"Not until spring, I'm afraid. You've just started your lessons, remember?" She held up the tray of fruit to counteract Carrie's long face. "Okay, sports fans, who's ready for dessert?"

"Ice cream?" Carrie's tales of success onstage were as quickly forgotten as the abandoned card game.

"Strawberries and blueberries and grapes," Kellie said, settling down next to Dan as closely as seemed proper.

"Can I eat it with one tooth gone? Maybe I should have ice cream, instead."

"You'll be fine." Kellie smiled at her daughter's con game. "You ate shrimp for dinner with no trouble. Remember?"

"Oh, yeah."

Holding his bowl in one hand for a moment, Dan squeezed her knee with the other. "You were great today. Or did I say that already?"

"You said that already," Kellie admitted, smiling at the approval in his voice and going soft at the warmth in his touch. "But it sounds good. What a stone-faced group! I couldn't even tell if they were listening, much less approving of anything I said."

"They knew you must be on track when they saw how nervous you were making Len," Dan said, and both knew there was more truth to his remark than not. "The crazy part of it is, everybody was so worked up over why the FAA wanted the report. And the answer may be that the FAA just wanted to appear on top of the situation. I talked to a buddy in Washington today, and he said the FAA's under a lot of pressure now. This may be their way of looking effective without actually having to do any work."

"Bureaucrats!" Kellie shook her head, stunned to think the report she had labored over might simply be government game playing. "Does that mean Margo and I did all that work for nothing?"

"Not at all. You've got the hospital administration more solidly behind you now. And the new safety measures you recommended will be a real plus."

The doorbell suddenly chimed, and Carrie jumped up to answer it. Rachael and Elliott came in, dressed to kill. Rachael, her face glowing, sat with Elliott perched next to her on the arm of the chair.

"Where are you guys headed tonight?" Kellie asked after they turned down her offer of dessert.

They exchanged glances, then Rachael's smile broadened. "Out to dinner. Then dancing. We're celebrating."

"I don't suppose you'd like to let us in on the reason for your celebration, would you?" Kellie felt her spirits take off even higher as she guessed what was behind her sister's big grin.

Rachael swallowed hard, tears glistening in her eyes. "We're going to get married." Her tears spilled over as

Kellie jumped up to hug her and Carrie started squealing in delight. "Oh, gosh, I didn't expect to act like this."

"That's wonderful!" Kellie enthused, not wanting to release her sister from her bear hug. "I'm so excited. Did you tell Mom yet? Tell me all about it."

While Dan gave his congratulations and Carrie wore herself out jumping up and down, Rachael told her they planned an April wedding.

"We didn't tell the folks yet, because I wanted you to be the first." Rachael sniffled, pulling a tissue out of her evening bag. "I want you to be my maid of honor. And—" she turned in the direction of Carrie's gleeful clapping "—we want Carrie to be the flower girl."

"Can I, Mommy? Can I?" Carrie's eyes were big and pleading until her mother nodded.

Dan watched the scene quietly. He had been through it too many times as nothing more than an interested bystander, with his brother, with cousins, with friends. And with each year that passed, it grew harder for him to stand by, smiling with equanimity while he nursed the emptiness in himself.

As his eyes roamed the room and landed on Kellie, bright eyed and smiling, Dan decided then and there that he wouldn't be on the outside anymore. Kellie was the one. She was tough and tender and had the courage of her convictions. And he loved her.

They might not have ironed out all their differences yet. And doing so might not be easy—his gut reaction was that she still held back too much, still resisted letting him get too close. But it *would* work. He would make damned sure of that.

With a sly grin, he wondered what would happen if he added an announcement of his own to the bedlam. Kellie would kill him, for starters. But once this madhouse had cleared out and he had her all to himself...

"Oops!" Elliott looked at his watch in the middle of the discussion over whether Aunt Helen could come down from Kentucky to play the organ or whether they should ask Rachael's college roommate. "We've got to get a move on if we're going to make our dinner reservations."

Kellie stood to see them to the door. "Looks like we finished stripping the woodwork just in time. I'm about to lose my most dependable laborer."

Rachael playfully tested Elliott's biceps. "I don't know. Maybe you've just increased the size of your crew."

"Just in time for the wallpaper, too."

"Now don't tell Mom," Rachael admonished as they moved toward the door after another round of hugs. "I'll call her tomorrow."

"Would I steal your thunder?" Kellie waved from the porch as Rachael walked down the sidewalk, hand in hand with Elliott.

As soon as she closed the door behind her, Kellie's gaze caught Dan's. His eyes had the dreamy glaze of someone looking into the future. His smile was hopeful.

Could it be that seeing Rachael and Elliott so happy had put ideas into his head? she wondered, hit by a moment of unease. Surely not. Their relationship was still too new. They hardly knew each other.

She pushed aside the memories of how deeply they had touched each other in the past two days. That wasn't enough to make—she couldn't voice the *M* word, even in her thoughts—a commitment work. Was it?

"Okay, kidlet, it's time to get you ready for bed," she announced, giving Carrie a pat on the seat.

"Oh, Mo-o-om."

"I know it's been a big night. But by the time you have a bath, it's going to be past your bedtime," Kellie said, stacking their fruit bowls for the trip into the kitchen. "And you have a big day tomorrow, Carrie. Say good night to Dan and scoot."

When Kellie came back from the kitchen, Carrie's halfhearted good-night had turned into a series of giggles. Kellie didn't know what magic he worked on long-faced children, but she felt some of the warmth seeping through the cowardice that had settled around her heart. Hadn't she been thinking how nice it felt to be at home, just the three of them?

But if she was faced with the reality of a decision about their future together, Kellie knew her avoidance technique would take over. She had to focus her energy on other things, she thought, remembering Heather's somber warning that Brian planned to see an attorney on Monday. She didn't have time or emotion to spare on making her relationship with Dan work. It might be heartbreaking, but she could afford to lose Dan. But losing Carrie would be the end of her life.

Besides, she told herself as she remembered Chip's problems and the carefully worded flight logs Len had demanded, *there's too much between you and Dan. Too much you're keeping from him. Too much you* have *to keep from him.*

"Okay, sport, it's time to march." She couldn't help but smile as Carrie looked to Dan for help.

"Better do what the lady says," he told her, winking. "And don't forget what we talked about."

"I'll be down in a few minutes," Kellie told Dan, uncertain now that she should try to revive the intimacy of the past few days. Maybe it would be better to keep her distance and send Dan home early.

Dan was watching a baseball play-off game on television, his brawny frame sprawled on the couch, when she came back downstairs. Just looking at him, thinking of the ways they had touched and the feelings he had sparked in her, took her breath away.

"What inning?" she asked as she sat beside him on the couch.

"Bottom of the fifth, two to one, Baltimore. Two outs, nobody on base, and the count is one and one."

She laughed at his thorough rundown. "What are you, the official scoreboard?"

Her laughter was hollow and he heard it instantly. He turned away from the crack of the bat against the ball coming from the television set.

"Yes," he said, reaching over to pull her close and wrap her in a tender embrace. "And you look like you're two runs down at the bottom of the ninth. What's wrong?"

Kellie snuggled into the deliciously familiar warmth of his well-muscled arms, her breasts pressing against his chest. Her misgivings began to evaporate.

"Nothing's wrong," she whispered, brushing her lips over the strong set of his jaw.

Dan didn't believe her, but her soft body insinuating itself so alluringly against his was impossible to ignore. Bending his head to capture her lips in a kiss, he slid his hand under her loose cotton sweater, along her midriff and up to one perfect breast. The tip responded instantly to his touch, hardening beneath its lace covering to a tiny bud pressing into his palm.

Sighing, Kellie arched closer. Her desire began a slow simmer in answer to his seeking, stroking hand at her breast and the hot demand of his tongue as he deepened their kiss. After a moment she began her own loving exploration, running her hands over his broad shoulders, then trailing a teasing finger to the hollow at his throat, where tiny golden curls were soft against her fingers. Kellie longed to follow that softness along the broadness of his chest and down his flat belly.

Kellie moaned a breathless protest when he ended their kiss and stopped the gentle massage of her breast. Dan dipped his head lower, trailing moist kisses along her neck and shoulder while the hand that had warmed her skin deftly uncovered her breast. She whispered his name, urging him on as his lips circled closer to the dark, swollen peak. She felt her simmering passion break into a steaming, bubbling boil as he covered her nipple with a damp kiss, teasing her with tongue and teeth and lips.

Feeling her quiver at his touch and the aching evidence of his own growing need, Dan gradually reversed the circling kisses that had brought him to her breast, lowering her sweater as he retreated to safer kisses against her shoulder and neck.

"As I recall, we have a light sleeper upstairs," he explained huskily when her green eyes turned to him in confusion.

Kellie smiled sheepishly. Her voice was heavy with desire when she spoke. "Actually she's just like her mother. She sleeps like a log."

Dan grinned crookedly, unable to stop himself from lightly stroking her breast on the way to a caress of the full flare of her hips. "I suspected as much," he said, closing his eyes as he savored the subtle motion of her curves against his hand. "I also suspect you still don't want to run any risks with her in the house."

With a heavy sigh, Kellie buried her face in the crook of his neck, continuing to revel in the bold caress that said every inch of her flesh was his to love, his to please. "You're right."

He turned her chin up so their eyes could meet. "Let's do something about that. Marry me, Kellie, and make an honest stepdad out of me."

She reached up to cover his lips with a long, tapered finger. She didn't want reality to intrude upon the moment again. Things felt too right, too tied-up-in-bows perfect at this moment to let the real world in. "Don't. It's too soon."

He kissed her, letting the soft pressure of his lips remind her that what was between them was too strong to be ignored.

"I love you, Kellie. And I believe you love me." His honey-brown eyes spoke volumes as they roamed her heart-shaped face. "It's not too soon for us to know that. And if we know it, we ought to do something about it."

Her throat constricted as she fought unwelcome tears. How could his words fill her with so much peaceful ecstasy and so much uncertainty at the same time? She wanted to pass his words off lightly, to turn them into a moment of flippancy followed by another dreamlike kiss. But there was no denying him the declaration he deserved to hear. There was no clipping the wings of the emotions that filled her to bursting. "I do love you, Dan. I do."

His hand was soft against her cheek, his eyes warm as he compelled her to hear him out. "Then marry me."

She stiffened, wishing for a side door that would let her exit this moment with her happiness intact. If only he wouldn't push her. "Now isn't . . . it's not the right time, Dan. We can't talk about this now."

Dan fought her withdrawal, reaching out to take her hand in his. "Why not?"

"We just can't," she insisted, pulling away and refusing to look at him.

"That's not good enough, Kellie." His frustration grew. Why was she shutting him out? And now of all times? "I love you, Kellie. I want to marry you. And you refuse to even discuss it. You have to tell me why."

Kellie jumped up from the couch and turned to face him. He knew instantly from the look on her face that he had gone one step too far.

"You keep trying to tell me what I have to do!" she fumed, her fists tightening at her sides. "I don't have to do anything. And certainly not because you say I do. Until you can handle things between us without trying to bully me, I don't see that we have anything else to talk about."

Dan sat for a moment in stunned silence, then stood. "If asking you to open up to me is bullying you, maybe we don't have the kind of relationship I thought we did."

Even as he said it, he knew it wasn't so. And he waited for her to deny it, for her flash of anger to dissipate into remorse. But the rigid look in her eyes held. She was stubbornly determined not to talk with him about whatever was troubling her tonight.

"I'll go now."

Even after he said the words, he stood in the middle of the room, waiting for her to say something, to retract her words, to reach out and make things all right again. When she didn't, when she remained rigid and close faced beside the couch, he headed for the door.

She watched him leave, every bit of the frustration and disappointment that had burst out of her as unreasonable anger dissolving as she peeked through the shades. He hadn't been a bully, and she knew it. He stood for several minutes looking back at the house before he got into his car. But she couldn't go after him.

It was better this way.

CHAPTER FOURTEEN

KELLIE AVERTED HER EYES from the reflection in the full-length antique mirror as she smoothed Carrie's hair into a braid.

Carrie couldn't keep herself or her mouth still as they readied themselves for her best friend's birthday party at a local skating rink. The six-year-old babbled nonstop about what kind of dress she would wear for Rachael's wedding, vowing that she would be an even better flower girl than she had been for her dad's wedding.

Dashing from those topics to her excitement about the day ahead, Carrie was oblivious to her mother's swollen eyes and the dark circles beneath them. She didn't notice the unenthusiastic monosyllables that were her mother's answers to everything she said. For that, Kellie was grateful.

But everything else had her in a darned foul mood.

The final, soul-searching look from Dan's soft brown eyes had reduced her to a sniveling crybaby before she had made it up the stairs the night before. Just when she wanted to be furious with him for trying to force her into decisions she didn't feel ready to make, he melted her heart with a look that said he was hurting, too.

Well, it's his own darned fault, Kellie told herself as belligerently as she could manage, snapping a rubber band into place at the end of Carrie's golden braid.

"Go get me the ribbons off the dresser, kidlet," she said dully, remembering how hard she had battled the night before to keep herself from picking up the phone and calling Dan. *He's brought this on himself,* she had declared, tears trickling down her cheeks while she crawled beneath the quilt.

Trying to blame Dan hadn't saved her from tossing and turning all night or reaching to the wicker bedside table for tissue after tissue to whisk away the tears. Trying to blame him hadn't stopped her from remembering how easy things had seemed the last time she simply told Dan everything she was thinking. Hadn't he been understanding once she finally gave up being so stubborn about the Tennessee crash? And hadn't she felt a tremendous burden lifted off her shoulders once they talked?

Trying to blame him hadn't stopped Kellie from needing the comfort of his body close to hers during the night, either. After only two nights of sleeping close to him, of accepting his protective warmth, Kellie found herself unable to sleep in the cavernous emptiness of her bed.

"Mommy, your new flower's dying. It's all droopy and sad." When Carrie brought the ribbons to her, she pointed to the African violet Dan had given Kellie just days ago. Its leaves were, indeed, hanging limply, and one of the fading pink blossoms had fallen onto the cluttered dresser.

That figures, Kellie thought. *It's lasting about as long as this so-called love of ours.*

"You're right, sweetheart," she said listlessly, tying the bright lavender ribbons at the base of Carrie's braid, where they might stay in place half the morning, if she was lucky. "All set."

Carrie pirouetted in front of the mirror to show off her new jeans and sweater, woven with ribbons that matched the ones in her hair. Before she turned to head down-stairs, she stopped and looked once again at the violet.

"Maybe if you water it, it won't be droopy anymore. That's what Heather does. She says they just want some attention to stay pretty."

"That's a good idea, Carrie. I'll try it."

As her daughter dashed down the stairs to feed Oscar before they left, Kellie doubted that such simple tactics could save the plant. Listlessly she filled the toothpaste glass from the bathroom with tap water and poured it into the dry soil, thinking it was no more likely to revive the plant than it could revive her relationship with Dan. No matter how much she wanted him, she had to realize that there was no future in another relationship like the one she'd had with Brian. Someone to make her decisions for her was not what she needed.

Kellie dashed on lipstick, then backed off to look at herself in the bulky sweater and slim jeans, wondering if they made her look pudgy. In the past few days, she hadn't felt pudgy, just voluptuous. It had been easy, with Dan's appreciative eyes following her everywhere. Today she felt like a blimp.

"Maybe a jacket." She pulled out an off-white quilted jacket that was long and loose enough to cover her hips. But when she put it on and looked in the mirror, she felt like a white elephant. Before she could yank it off and hang it back in the closet, the phone on her nightstand jangled at her.

"I love you, Kellie," he said, the moment she picked up the receiver.

Instinctively, without thinking, she smiled.

"I'm sorry about last night."

Kellie didn't like the way his voice washed over her in spite of herself. Just like Brian, he seemed able to walk all over her. *What's wrong with me?* she asked herself impatiently.

"Listen, I'm on my way out," she said, hating herself for the abruptness in her voice even before she finished. But suddenly, all she could think of was the new schedule she had posted in flight headquarters the day before, the one that meant she and the other pilots would be working too many hours with too little time off. And Dan Brennan was the last person she wanted hanging around to find out about that. Even if she managed to keep him at arm's length personally, he was still in the driver's seat at Birmingham Memorial. "Maybe we can talk about this later."

He said nothing for a moment. She could almost see the furrow deepening in his forehead. "That's always your answer, Kellie. When do we get to 'later'? If what you mean is 'never,' why don't you have the guts to come right out and say so?"

The harsh words were like a blow to the stomach. Kellie's throat contracted and she squeezed her eyes shut. *I will not cry again,* she vowed.

"If you want it your way or not at all, that's fine with me." She forced the words out, straining to sound normal. *He will not hear me cry.*

"Kellie, that's not the point! All I want is the chance to talk. And you're so damned bullheaded you won't even talk to me!"

How can I? she wanted to scream. *I can't tell you about Chip. I can't tell you about Len.* And her biggest fear—Brian's threat of seeking custody—she couldn't even bring herself to put into thoughts this morning.

"I have to go now, Dan. Maybe later we can—"

"I doubt it. Not until you're ready to let somebody in, Kellie. Goodbye."

GOODBYE. THE WORD echoed in her heart all week, and she didn't have the nerve to do anything about it.

Goodbye. It had sounded so final. It *was* so final, she insisted to herself. He meant it. And she should be glad.

But she couldn't be glad. She couldn't even accept that it was final. In a secret place in her heart, she allowed herself the fantasy that once all the problems keeping them apart were settled, she would call him. Once she had found the solutions, she would explain everything. And once again, he would sweep her up in his arms and say he loved her and everything would be all right. He might even ask her to marry him. Although she wouldn't blame him if he never brought the subject up again.

But Kellie refused to let herself think about it. And she refused to let herself think beyond her perfect fantasy to what might happen if he wasn't so forgiving. If he wasn't able to forget how easily, how swiftly, she had shut him out of her life.

It's not like that, she protested to herself as the circles under her eyes grew darker. *There's no other way to handle it,* she told herself each day as she placed futile calls to every helicopter pilot she knew, looking for someone who wanted to fill her job vacancy. As twelve-hour shifts stretched into eighteen and twenty-four and the signs of stress and exhaustion among the pilots mounted, she remembered how important it was to keep her distance from Dan. As she struggled over the daily flight logs, she speculated how long it would take Len to decide she needed to do more to disguise the fact that they were short staffed.

If only she could find a pilot, she could go straight to Dan and . . .

Then Chip would pass her desk and Kellie would remember that more than a fourth pilot lay between Dan and her. There was Chip, who avoided her eyes and crept in and out of the flight office so quietly she couldn't help but wonder if he had changed his mind about seeing the doctor. If anyone at the hospital found out what Chip had been up to, it would be a serious black mark against the air-ambulance service.

There was Margo, whose nagging had changed to suspicious surveillance, at least when it came to Chip. For her nagging, she had found a new target.

"Listen, I didn't much like the idea of you getting so tight with the brass," the outspoken nurse had chided. "I was glad you decided to call it off. But if I have to put up with this long face much longer, I'm going to ship you off to college with Carol in the fall."

"Does that mean the scholarship came through?" Kellie studiously avoided any reaction to the main point of Margo's preaching.

"Yes, as a matter of fact, it does. Thanks to Chip. I wouldn't have known where to turn if it hadn't been for him." Margo folded her arms across her chest. "But don't try changing the subject on me, girl. I want to know what you plan to do about Dan Brennan. I heard he was a hatchet man, and I'd say he's done a pretty good job on you."

Kellie frowned. Even in her present state of mind, she couldn't let Margo think that way about Dan. "We were wrong about him, Margo. When it comes to running Memorial, he's one of the good ones. But I don't plan to 'do' anything about him. Except forget about him."

And then there was Brian. And his attorney. His threat to disrupt her life.

But Kellie used her long hours and her other worries as the perfect shield to avoid thinking about a court battle over Carrie. The prospect was more frightening even than the thought of losing her job. She avoided it completely,

almost grateful for the distraction of work-related hassles.

As she hung up the telephone from yet another fruit-
less discussion with a friend at the airport who stayed in
touch with most of the city's chopper pilots, Kellie rum-
maged through the desk drawer for a bottle of aspirin.
With her friend's information that free-lance flying for
corporate clients had boomed with the opening of the
airport's newest runway, the steady throb in Kellie's tem-
ples had exploded into a jackhammer of a headache.

How long could Frank, Andy and she continue flying
safely without the backup of a fourth pilot? Fresh in her
mind were the safety charts from other services around the
country whose pilots worked longer hours with less time
off. As the pilots' time on duty increased, so did the rate
of accidents.

Finding the aspirin bottle in the back of the drawer,
Kellie reached for her coffee cup and swallowed a couple
of the pills. She looked up in time to see Chip stick his
head around the door, then back away.

"Come on in, Chip," she called out, hoping she could
find out something without pressing him.

He stepped back to the doorway, shaking his head.
"No, that's okay. I was just . . . just looking for Margo."

Kellie looked at him skeptically. That seemed unlikely,
in light of the continued tension between them. "Sit
down. I won't bite."

Chip stared at the chair. He hesitated for a few moments, then walked into the office and lowered himself
into the upholstered swivel chair across the desk from
Kellie. "Well, maybe just a few minutes. I can find Margo
later."

His entire body slumped when he sat, like a puppet
whose strings had been snipped. When he spoke, his voice

was weak and breathless. "I have...been a little... tired."

Tempted to ask him when his doctor's appointment was scheduled, Kellie bit back the words and watched him. All the color had drained from his face, and his eyes slowly closed. He looked worse than ever. She wondered, suddenly, if he had conned her with his story about his heart and his father. Could he really be hooked on some kind of drugs, after all?

Before she could decide how to open another conversation with him, Chip's body started a slow slide out of the chair. Kellie watched in horror as he slipped onto the floor.

"Chip!" She jumped from her chair and bounded around the desk. Jostling his shoulder brought no response. "Chip!"

Whatever was wrong with him, it had suddenly gone from bad to worse. Sprinting out the door, Kellie ran toward the emergency room and grabbed the first nurse she saw. "I need help! Chip. He collapsed!"

"A GAME OF TENNIS will do you a lot more good than finishing up those reports tonight," Anna Robinson admonished Dan in her sternest mothering tone. "You look like you died last week and somebody forgot to tell you."

"Thanks." Dan knew she was right but didn't want to hear about it. "The last thing I need tonight is to have you wipe me out on the tennis court."

Anna smiled, retrieving her briefcase from the library table beside his office door. "If that's all that's holding you back, I promise to let you win."

Dan chuckled, the closest he'd come to a laugh all week. "Thanks a lot. I'm not sure my ego's strong enough to take you, Anna."

"Brennan, you've got ego to spare. See you tomorrow." Before she closed the door behind her, Anna turned back to face him. "But . . . Brennan? You better take care of what's buggin' you. This old lady knows what she's talking about."

"I'll keep that in mind, Anna."

How could he do anything but keep it in mind? he asked himself wryly as Anna closed the door on the outside world. He'd hidden behind that door most of the week. But it hadn't enabled him to hide from his anguish over Kellie.

Kellie. She filled his mind, his heart, every waking hour. He went over every minute of their time together, including the night his proposal had infuriated her so much that she had thrown him out and refused to talk to him.

Damn the woman! Since when did a marriage proposal make a woman mad?

As tempted as he had been to call her again, to go down to flight headquarters to see her, Dan had resisted. But it had taken every bit of willpower he possessed. This time, she would have to come to him.

When hell freezes over, he thought bitterly, trying to turn his attention back to the flight logs Len Baldwin had passed on today for his signature before they went on record at the hospital and with the FAA. Dan's signature wasn't part of the normal routine. But until he was certain the FAA was finished giving them the eagle eye, he intended to make sure Birmingham Memorial had dotted every *i* and crossed every *t* on everything it submitted.

As Dan pored over the reports, struggling not to be distracted by the fact that Kellie had prepared every word he was reading, the number of corrections in the logs started to trouble him. On virtually every flight, something had been whited out and retyped—the pilot's name, especially, although sometimes flight times had been changed. Dan wondered if Kellie, who had signed every log, was really that sloppy in her bookkeeping; it didn't add up with how seriously she appeared to take the flight service.

Scratching his head, Dan was about ready to initial the logs and put them in his Out basket for his secretary to route. Then he noticed something that bothered him even more than the number of changes.

The changes had been made with a different typewriter from the one used originally to make out the logs.

Dumbfounded at the implication of his discovery, Dan examined every correction. They were all in a slightly different typeface. Just a shade larger. The letters were rounder and more modern.

Why would Kellie do that? Pushing his chair back and pacing to the other side of the room, Dan tried to make sense of his discovery. Were there two typewriters in flight headquarters? And if there were, why would so many changes be necessary?

Dan held one of the logs up to the light, straining to read what had been whited out. But he could tell nothing.

Stopping in the middle of his office, Dan shook his head. It made about as much sense as everything else about Kellie Adams, he thought. But like everything else he didn't understand, this gnawed at him.

About this, he told himself, *I have a right to demand answers.* Dan grabbed up a fistful of the reports and shoved them into his briefcase. *She's not going to put me off on this.*

KELLIE STOPPED on her front porch—jacket under one arm, tote bag slipping off one shoulder, purse under the other arm—to fish the mail out of the box before she went into the house.

"Thanks for the help," Rachael called as she let herself into her side of the house. "Are you sure you don't mind the antebellum look?"

Kellie forced a grin as she started losing her grip on everything she carried while in search of her house key. "I'll look great in flounces and festoons. Women my size need a little something extra to give them a fuller look."

Rachael wrinkled her face in sympathy and came over to catch Kellie's jacket and purse before they fell. "Oh, sis. Maybe I should go with something sleeker, something more modern. If you're not going to feel good—"

"It's *your* wedding," Kellie repeated the reminder she had used at least six times during their two-hour visit to a nearby bridal boutique. "You're the one who has to be happy about it. Not me. Besides, Carrie will love being a junior Scarlett O'Hara."

Rachael gnawed her lower lip as Kellie backed in her door. "But are you sure peach is the right color for your dresses? Maybe—"

"Rach. Stop." It was all Kellie could do to keep from growling at her wavering sister. "We've had this conversation too many times already this evening. You're going to love everything. Trust me. It's going to be a beautiful wedding. It will be the envy of all your friends. But not if you keep changing your mind and wait too late to order the gowns."

Rachael took a deep breath and smiled apologetically. "Right. Thanks again, sis."

Kellie's enthusiasm died as soon as she was safely locked in her own living room. Keeping her spirits up while Rachael debated the pros and cons of every single style of wedding grown available in the free world had taken more acting ability than she had known she possessed. But going for the Academy Award had taken its toll.

She let her armload of bundles drop onto the trunk table beside the now-thriving African violet. As soon as she'd watered it and brought it downstairs, where she remembered to care for it, the plant had perked up and had begun mocking her with a message she didn't care to decipher.

Before she could turn away from the cheerily blooming plant and slump into the papasan chair, she thought of Chip.

The doctors hadn't been able to tell her a thing when she'd left for the day. In the back of her mind, while she oohed and aahed over lace and beadwork and square-cut necklines and dropped waists, Kellie had let the guilt eat away at her. What if Chip died or was permanently disabled? What if, in all the scrutiny over his illness, someone put two and two together and figured out that he had been the one responsible for pilfering the drugs from the hospital pharmacy?

You'd have to share some of the responsibility, she told herself as she dialed Margo's number. *You knew what was going on and didn't do anything about it.*

But I was trying to do the right thing, she excused herself as Margo's phone rang.

But maybe you didn't, her guilty conscience warned.

"Margo, what's the latest on Chip?" she asked briskly when her friend answered.

"That darned fool," Margo said crossly. "Scared the devil out of all of us. And for what? A virus. The fool man has a virus!"

Kellie instantly recognized her friend's irritation for what it was—relief.

"What do you mean, a virus?" Kellie had seen the viruses that Carrie brought home from school and day care, but she had never heard of one that would make a grown man pass out.

"A viral infection surrounding his heart," Margo explained. "Mimics the symptoms of a heart attack, which is what the darned fool was treating himself for. But instead of getting himself well, he just kept getting worse because he was treating the wrong problem. I tell you, I'm ready to snatch that man bald headed, all the headaches he's given us lately. And then passin' out in the office, worryin' me sick!"

Kellie laughed, as relieved as Margo that something, at least, seemed to have a happy ending in sight.

"So what happens now? Is there permanent damage? Will he get better?"

Some of the edge disappeared from Margo's voice, which Kellie knew meant there was a downside to the outcome of Chip's story. "The docs aren't sure yet. They've done some tests and they'll know by tomorrow if there's permanent damage. The darned fool waited so long, there could be. And even if there's no permanent damage, he's gonna be laid up for quite a while. Now how does he expect us to stay in the air with him layin' up on his butt for a month?"

"That we can work out, Margo. Listen, thanks for the news. See you in the morning."

Drawing a deep breath, Kellie headed back to the softness of the papasan chair and started sorting through the mail. Electric bill. A magazine subscription offer. Bank statement. And an envelope from Parker, Myers and Dilworth, Attorneys at Law.

Kellie's blood froze at the discreetly simple lettering of the law firm's name. Parker, Myers and Dilworth. The masterminds behind the destruction of her life. It had to be. The people who wanted to take her child away from her. Her first impulse was to throw the letter away, to deny she had ever received it.

That won't work, she told herself. All feeling died as she stared at the crisp parchment envelope, printed in a very corporate, very distinguished gray. Every clock in the house, the hum of every appliance might just as well have stopped. In fact, the entire world might have ceased turning while she stared at the envelope with the news she wanted desperately to ignore.

Slowly, taking undue care not to tear the envelope, she opened it. "Dear Ms Adams... regarding custody of minor child Carolyn Ruth Adams... due to serious considerations regarding your suitability...seeking sole custody of said minor child... your cooperation in reaching out-of-court settlement... stability and lack of disruption in home life of said minor... your legal counsel to contact this office... Regards."

Said minor child. The smiling face of said minor child swam in Kellie's mind. Giddy and giggling and trusting the world to return the love she had always given so freely. Kellie couldn't bear the thought of dragging Carrie through a court fight between her parents. Between the two people who were supposed to be committed to protecting her.

For the moment, Kellie was too numb to be angry. Too frightened to move. Too stunned to cry.

She sat for what seemed like hours. At first, all she could do was relive some of the precious moments in Carrie's life. The day she was born, with no hair and a wrinkled pink face that even Ellen Carpenter hadn't been able to pronounce as beautiful. The day she spoke her first word, which everyone at first had thought was "Da" for

"Daddy" and had turned out to be "dog" for the gentle, aging collie who had become the infant's self-appointed protector and nanny. Her first birthday, when Carrie had been more interested in practicing her newest trick—pulling the tablecloth off the table—than in opening her presents. Learning the alphabet. Kindergarten. And the first day of school, which Kellie had experienced only secondhand because her daughter was with her father that month.

And now he was asking her to give it all up.

It was too much to ask. Especially after she had been so willing to share custody, to make sure he wasn't shut out of his daughter's life. But what could she do? Hadn't Brian won every time they'd had a confrontation? How could she hope to win this time? How could she even hope to enter the battle without permanently scarring her little girl?

An attorney. You'll have to get an attorney, she told herself. *You have to decide what to do. If you fight this, Carrie loses. If you don't fight it, you lose Carrie. You have to decide. But how?*

Kellie almost jumped out of her skin when the doorbell rang. She sat staring at the door, unable to decide whether to get up and answer it or not. There was no one she wanted to see. She couldn't imagine being able to act normal with anyone.

The doorbell rang. And rang. And rang. When she realized whoever it was didn't plan to go away, Kellie dragged herself out of the round chair and opened the door.

Her first impulse when she saw Dan was to throw herself into his arms and cry and tell him about Brian and the custody suit and absorb his strength and take comfort from his warmth and find the answers in his arms.

Then she recognized the papers he was pulling from his briefcase and noticed the rigid harshness in his face.

"Dan, I can't go into this now," she said tiredly, knowing there was no way she could make sense of flight logs right now. Flight logs didn't matter. Helicopter ambulances didn't matter and the FAA didn't matter. Even Chip, who might have done himself serious harm with his stubbornness, didn't matter. Only Carrie mattered. "We'll have to talk about it later, maybe tomorrow or—"

"Wrong." His voice echoed off the walls with unquestionable authority. "I let you put me off about everything else. But this won't wait. I want to know who's been changing these reports and why. And I want to know now."

CHAPTER FIFTEEN

SHE HAD BEEN sabotaged. Kellie knew it the moment she looked at the flight logs Dan handed her. Someone had altered her flight logs. And had done a darned sloppy job of it.

"Who did this?" she blurted out angrily and immediately regretted it. Figuring out who was responsible didn't take a Sherlock Holmes. Len Baldwin and his secretary were the only ones who saw the flight logs after Kellie completed them.

But how in the world can I tell Dan that? I can't just go around pointing fingers at my boss, she told herself, fury battling with despair to rule her mood. *How could that weasel put me in such a predicament? And how can I possibly defend myself?*

"I hoped you could tell me that." Dan loosened the knot in his tie, a harried expression on his face. "Who had the opportunity to tamper with the logs after you signed them?"

Kellie opened her mouth, then snapped it shut. Distractedly twisting the garnet ring on her finger, she debated with herself over her reply.

"Do you think I did it?" she challenged him, suddenly wondering why he had automatically come to her for answers.

Dan hesitated. "You certainly had the opportunity. But why would you bother? It doesn't add up. What I do figure is that you know who else could have done it. And why."

Wishing for a brilliant excuse that would let her put Dan off until she had a chance to think through the repercussions of her response, Kellie felt her hands begin to shake. *Why now? Why in heaven's name now, when everything else is falling apart on me, too?*

Dan's hands firmly gripping her shoulders forced Kellie to look into his honey-brown eyes. They were as unyielding as the set of his jaw. "You have to trust me sometime, Kellie. Whatever this is all about, don't you know by now that you can trust me?"

She didn't have to search his face—or her heart—for more than a moment to find the answer. Of course she knew. Dan had never been anything but honest with her. He had always gone out of his way to be supportive. And open. And giving. All the things she hadn't been able to be for him in return.

Remorse filled her heart at the realization that Dan had remained steadfastly loyal to her in spite of her childish resistance to his attempts to become part of her life. No matter what the outcome, it seemed to Kellie that she owed him the truth.

"It was Len. It had to be Len or his secretary." She held her breath, wondering if he would believe her. Wondering if he could serve as a buffer between Len and her when Len discovered she had betrayed him. Her knees suddenly joined her hands in becoming unsteady.

"I thought so," he said grimly. "But why?"

"It's a long story," she said, wondering if her wobbly knees could hold her up much longer. "Can we sit down first?"

"Are you okay?" Dan asked when they sat down on the couch.

Kellie nodded unconvincingly. Even her stomach felt shaky. "I guess I'm just hungry. Things got so busy at work today, I forgot lunch. And I haven't had dinner yet."

Shaking his head, Dan got up and headed toward the kitchen. "I don't care what you say, sometimes you *do* need somebody to take care of you."

He looked through the refrigerator, rolling his eyes at the near-empty shelves. A tub of diet margarine. Diet soft drinks. A jar of taco sauce and a head of lettuce that had turned a shade of unappealing brown. He grabbed the carton of orange juice, found a glass in the dish drainer and filled it with juice.

"Drink this," he said, sitting back down beside her on the sofa. "Then talk."

His tone of voice softened what would have sounded like an order and made Kellie's blood boil at any other time. She was shaking so hard she had to hold the glass with both hands. She drank every drop of the juice before she set the glass down on the trunk, where the envelope winked malevolently at her.

She turned away from the envelope, for once grateful that Dan had come in and taken control. She felt a little better already, with the juice calming her nervous stomach.

"Talk?" she said uncertainly.

"Talk."

And she did. Hesitantly at first. But once the story started, it poured out. Beginning with Len's obvious nervousness over the FAA report and continuing through his paranoid insistence that she cover up the pilot's resignation, Kellie outlined her boss's actions during the past several weeks.

"And now, with Chip out, too, I don't know what other dumb stunts Len's going to want me to pull," she said wearily, wishing she could sag against Dan's chest and let him comfort her.

"'With Chip out'? What's wrong with Chip?"

Kellie screwed up her face into a grimace. *What a big mouth,* she thought. Then, deciding she was in so far she might as well spill everything, she told him about Chip's foolhardy gamble with his health, his stealing drugs from the hospital pharmacy and his collapse earlier in the day.

"My God, you've been under a lot of stress," he said, clasping one of her hands in his and pressing it. "Is Chip going to be okay?"

"They don't know yet. They should have the test results tomorrow." Tomorrow. Tomorrow could go from bad to worse, with falsified flight logs and Chip's escapades in danger of being revealed. Her role in either situation could land her in the unemployment line. Which would play right into Brian's hands. The tears that hadn't come when she'd opened the attorney's letter tightened her throat now. "I don't know what to do about all this."

"Is there something else?" He inched closer to her and lifted her chin so he could look into her eyes. "What else is wrong, Kellie?"

"Do you think I'll lose my job?" She fought to keep her voice steady. "If Len finds out I've told you this, he'll send me packing. He as much as told me so when he told me to change the logs."

"Don't worry about Len," he said softly. "I'll take care of him. Just do me a favor and find yourself a pilot in a hurry. It'll be my pleasure to handle Len for you."

For once, she was glad to hear a man say he would handle something for her. If anyone could right that situation, it was Dan. Feeling even that much of the burden slip off her shoulders brought tears closer to the surface.

"Are you worried about Chip?" he asked, his voice still concerned.

Kellie knew she was doing a miserable job of hiding her emotions. She nodded to avoid revealing the quaver in her voice, but the tears spilled anyway.

Murmuring words of consolation, Dan pulled her to his chest. "Tell me the rest, Kellie."

Sobbing in earnest now, Kellie reached for the letter. Showing it to Dan, she wiped her tears on the paper towel Dan had brought from the kitchen with her juice.

"Is he crazy!" Dan tossed the letter onto the table and squeezed her closer, running a comforting hand over her unruly curls. "Doesn't he realize what this will do to Carrie? He must be nuts!"

Half crying, half laughing to have someone so vocally and so unquestionably on her side, Kellie slipped her arms around his waist. "But what can I do? If I fight back, it's not good for Carrie. If I don't . . ."

"Giving Carrie to him full-time isn't good for her, either," Dan said forcefully. "What does your lawyer say?"

Kellie let out a long, shuddering breath and tried to bring her tears under control. His chest felt so good against her cheek. His arms around her felt so safe. And the confidence in his voice gave her back the confidence that had been shattered when she opened the letter. "I don't have a lawyer. This just came tonight."

"Where does this SOB live?" Standing decisively and pulling her up with him, he looked into her eyes. "I'll go see him tonight and tell him what he can do with his legal mumbo jumbo."

Dan's determination to solve this problem for her brought a small smile to her lips. With Dan behind her, she felt somehow that finding a solution wouldn't be as tough as she'd thought.

"You can't do that, Dan," she said softly as he blotted the dampness from her cheeks. "Carrie will be there, and I don't want her upset by all this. Besides, it's my problem and—"

"Don't try to shut me out again, Kellie Adams," he warned. "I won't have it."

Kellie wanted to cry again, realizing for the first time how Dan must have felt at her refusal to share what she was thinking with him. What could he have thought, except that she didn't care enough? She reached up to press the side of his face with her palm.

"I won't. I think I'm going to need you to keep my confidence up," she admitted, pleased with the pleasure in his eyes. "But I don't think you can fight this battle for me. If you take care of Len, I'll take care of Brian."

"It's a deal."

Lowering his lips to her face, he kissed away the last traces of her tears. His mustache was soft against her cheek. The cold numbness Kellie had felt earlier in the evening melted away completely as his lips then sought hers. They were moist, warm, and his tongue parted her lips with a gentleness that promised to soothe the anguish she felt.

While his mouth explored, Dan cradled her head in his hands, gently massaging her tension away and replacing it with longing. Kellie let her hands drift down his back, savoring the muscles along his shoulders and both sides of his spine. Without worrying about the boldness of her actions, she slid her hands along the smooth cotton of his dress shirt to the soft wool of his slacks. A sigh rose in his throat, and she felt the first stirrings of passion as she caressed the hard contours of his buttocks.

She pressed her hips to his, urging the hard thrust of his erection against the softness of her belly. He writhed against her, leaving her awash with heat, moist with readiness. Sneaking her hand beneath his belted waistband, she played at the small of his back, enjoying the pulsing against her belly.

Aware that Kellie's need for comfort had changed to desire, Dan deepened their kiss and let his hands stray along her slender neck and inside her blouse until he could cup a breast in his palm. Her nipple was a bud of desire, warm and taut.

Pulling her lips from his, she let her hand slip to the front of his slacks and whispered, "Have you ever made love in a papasan chair?"

He looked at the huge, round cushion of the wicker chair as she slowly removed his belt and unzipped his pants. "Never."

Kellie smiled, her lids heavy with passion as his erection, now released from its confinement, thrust proudly and impatiently at her. She pushed him toward the chair and made him sit, then slipped out of her clothes. "Neither have I. But I'll bet we can figure it out."

With one knee on either side of his waist, Kellie gently lowered herself so that they barely touched, her damp softness teasing over his seeking hardness the way her tongue played over his lips. Slowly unbuttoning his shirt, her hands roamed the soft hair on his sharply defined chest. His nipples were button hard against her palms. She quivered inside at the sense of power his arousal gave her.

When he could no longer stand her teasing body moving slowly above him, Dan sheathed himself for protection and drew her down to him. He slipped into her easily, slowly, her steady sighs changing to deeper and deeper moans the farther he sank into her heated softness. He couldn't take his eyes off her as she started the undulations that quickened as her passion peaked. Eyes closed, cheeks flushed, breasts swaying gently, she called out to him.

Smiling as Kellie lost herself in passion, Dan felt the sweet pressure as her muscles tightened around him, urging him to join her. But he held back, waiting for her climax to subside. She leaned closer to him, her cries subsiding to tiny whimpers of pleasure as he caressed the taut tip of her breast with his tongue. The damp, swirling touch brought her once again to the slow undulations that built in intensity, that drove him finally to explode within her.

They lay in the chair, Kellie still astride his spent body, her breasts heavy against his damp chest. When she tried to stir, he held her still.

"But I'm heavy," she whispered against his ear.

"Oh, no," he whispered back. "You're perfect right where you are."

KELLIE WAS LOST in a fog of exhilarating memories the next morning when the phone rang.

"Kellie, glad I caught you," boomed the voice on the other end. "I'm heading out for two weeks and was afraid I'd miss you. I've got a prospect for you."

The voice of her old pal from the airport brought her to instant attention, almost making her forget the pleasure that still hummed through her body. Almost, but not quite. The glow would be with her for quite a while, of that Kellie was certain. "A pilot?"

"Yeah. He's young, but he's got good army experience. I flew with him yesterday after I talked to you, and he looks good at the stick,'' Art said. ''He just found out his wife's expecting their first kid, and he's thinking about something a little steadier than this free-lance flying.''

''When can he come down to talk?'' Kellie grinned, thinking she was almost desperate enough to hire the fellow without even looking at him. If Art trusted him, he must be okay. She just wanted everything back to normal. Well, almost everything. Some things were definitely better than they used to be....

''YOU LOOK HAPPY. What's up?'' Margo asked as she came into the office.

''I've got a hot prospect and he's coming in this afternoon,'' Kellie said. ''I just wish we could speed up the bureaucracy around here. You know how long it takes them to finish all the paperwork in personnel and offer someone a job.''

Margo smiled slyly. ''Why don't you call Dan? If you've got the inside track to the executive offices, why not use it?''

''I might just do that,'' she said with a smile, not timid for once about being up-front about her relationship with Dan. Besides, Dan had urged her to fill the job as soon as possible. ''He really is one of the good guys, you know.''

The nurse shrugged, but her smile reassured Kellie. Margo's smile wasn't the kind that could be turned on and off at will—if she smiled, she meant it. ''That's the scuttlebutt. And I guess you're proof. You've been looking so long you're hardly going to settle for second best now.''

Kellie thought for a moment about how long and how adamantly she had believed in her unavailable or undesirable philosophy, marveling that she had finally found the exception that proved the rule.

"How's Chip?" she asked, feeling the need to change conversations before she told Margo more than she was ready to reveal about her relationship with Dan. "Have you been up to see him this morning?"

"We got good news and bad news," Margo said, propping an elbow on a straight-backed chair. "Good news is, no permanent damage. Bad news is, if Chip tries to come back to work within the next four weeks, the doc's gonna string 'im up by his toes."

Some of Kellie's high spirits ebbed. "A month?"

"At least. He can drive his mother crazy, for a change."

"What do we do until Chip can drag his old, grumpy self back to work?"

"I've got a couple of nurses in mind who could be trained pretty quickly," Margo said. "This might be the perfect time to get started with your idea for cross-training everyone who works in emergency."

"Good plan. Let's work out the details on that right after lunch. I'll take it to Dan when I tell him about this pilot and see if he can help us with that, too."

"Great. I'll go talk to the head nurse in emergency right now and let her know what's going on."

Things are falling in place at last, Kellie thought, closing her eyes for a moment to enjoy the inner peace she had felt all morning. She felt strong. She felt whole. She felt loved. And although she felt far from perfect, she even felt good that she had learned so much about her shortcomings in the past few days.

Only one thing remained that she didn't feel happy about. With a passing frown and a deep sigh, she picked up the phone to dial Brian's office.

Last night, safe in the crook of Dan's arm, with one hand tangled in the thick softness of his hair and the other resting on his thigh, she had talked at length about her fears for Carrie and how she should handle the threat from her ex-husband. When she at last fell asleep, her back curled warmly against the refuge of Dan's chest, it had been with the calm reassurance that she could handle Brian.

Today, with the telephone against her ear, her courage began to wane. Brian's receptionist answered. Kellie listened to the echoing silence after she was put on hold. Her heart started to thump. She knew exactly how she wanted to handle Brian. But if her bluff didn't work, then what?

When her ex-husband came on the line, Kellie's mouth went dry. "Brian, I'm coming by tonight to talk about Carrie. Does seven-thirty suit you?"

"I don't think that's such a good idea, Kellie. Why don't you just have your attorney call mine and—"

"This is our daughter we're talking about, not a piece of real estate," she interrupted, the words as hard-nosed as they were evenhanded. "I'll be there at seven-thirty. Why don't you see if Carrie can play with one of her friends in the neighborhood? I don't think she needs to hear this."

"My attorney says—"

"Brian, I don't give a damn what your attorney says. If you care about your daughter, be there."

And with that, she hung up. Her heart was thundering, but she felt the exhilaration of someone who had just passed the competition with the finish line in sight.

WHEN KELLIE WALKED into Dan's outer office that afternoon, his secretary was nowhere to be seen. She stuck her head into his private office, but it was empty, also. Grabbing a pad from his desk and a pen from his drawer, she leaned over to leave a message. But before she finished the first sentence of her note, a typed memo on the top of the stack on his desk caught her eye.

It was about Chip.

The memo, from Dan to the hospital president, started by outlining the information about Chip's collapse in flight headquarters and concerns that his health problems might be too serious to permit him to fly again. But it was the first words in the second paragraph that enraged Kellie.

In addition, speculation exists that Nurse West's illness is linked to the rash of thefts in Pharmacy. The medication that has disappeared on a regular basis . . .

Kellie looked up at movement across the room. Dan had come in and, smiling in her direction, tossed his jacket onto the couch. Balling up the note she had started, Kellie stalked around the corner of his desk, the rest of the memo unread.

"Kellie, good news! The FAA was so impressed with your report they've asked you to serve on a national safety panel. I'm recommending today that you—"

She cut into his cheerful greeting, not even registering his words, the betrayal she felt spilling out in her disappointed tone. "You used me. But it won't happen again."

Dashing out of the room, she ignored his worried voice calling after her. If he planned to use the information she had passed on to him in confidence because of her love for him and her need for someone to confide in, she didn't need his excuses. He caught up with her at the elevator.

"Kellie, what the hell are you talking about?" His fingers cut into her shoulders.

"Leave me alone!" She wrenched out of his hold and headed for the staircase.

Obviously at a loss for words, Dan followed and watched as she dashed recklessly down the stairs.

"I saw the memo about Chip! How could you do that to me?" she called out as she ran.

No wonder he didn't make any excuses. There aren't any, Kellie raged to herself as she burst into flight headquarters. *You can't make excuses for that kind of deceit.*

BACK IN HIS OFFICE, Dan saw on the top of his desk the memo his secretary had typed before she left for lunch. For whatever reason, Kellie had been in his office and spotted it.

Dan cursed his luck that the memo had been on top. But if she had read it, why was she so furious? Dan shook his head in bewilderment.

Once again, Len Baldwin had been—even if only inadvertently—the cause of another rift between Kellie and himself. Shortly after Dan had confronted the weak-willed administrator with the altered flight logs and listened to his stumbling explanations, Len had appeared in Dan's office to insist that Chip West was no longer physically able to handle the stress of the air-ambulance job. He had even alluded to a possible connection between Chip's illness and the missing drugs. He had just come, he had said smugly, from the president's office, where he had said the same thing.

Trusting Kellie's judgment that Chip had learned his lesson, Dan had hoped to salvage Chip's job by putting his recommendations in the official memo—which Kellie had apparently been too impatient to read to the end. Stressing that a hospital was the last institution that should make snap judgments about a person's career based on health problems, Dan concluded by pointing out that Len had no substantial evidence—in fact, not even any circumstantial evidence—to link Chip to the drug thefts. The memo went on to say:

In conclusion, I recommend that we monitor Nurse West's physical condition and trust the judgment of his physician regarding his return to work in the air-ambulance service.

As far as his possible connection to a recent rash of drug thefts at the hospital, any attempts to link him without substantial evidence could result in justifiable legal action on the part of the employee.

That, along with my verbal report on Len's handling of the flight logs, should take care of that, Dan thought, satisfied that Len Baldwin's position at Birmingham Memorial was too precarious now for him to do much more damage. He would be lucky to hold on to his own job, much less get anyone fired.

But that didn't help Dan straighten things out with Kellie. Picking up the phone, he dialed flight headquarters and was relieved when Kellie answered.

"Kellie, could you calm down long enough to tell me what's wrong?"

"I am calm," she bit back. "And you should know what's wrong. You're using information I gave you in confidence to try to ruin Chip's career. Dan, how could you?"

"Kellie, you don't know what you're talking about," he said, trying to hold on to his patience. "Let me bring you the memo so you can read the whole—"

"I read enough to see what you're up to. Is that the way you've built your career, Dan? If it is, you'll have to find yourself another patsy."

The line went dead.

Dan dropped into his chair and wondered what his next move should be. If he had learned one thing about Kellie Adams, it was that her temper fizzled about as quickly as it flared. But the drawl that surfaced when she flared up didn't seem quite as entrancing as it had seemed before.

To hell with her moonlight and magnolias voice, he thought. He was damned if he planned to put up with a woman who was suspicious of his every move.

On the other hand, he was damned if he knew how to get along without her anymore....

CHAPTER SIXTEEN

STARING AT BRIAN over his coffee table felt to Kellie like staring down the barrel of a rifle.

If I can just keep from exploding, everything may turn out all right. But my track record on explosions isn't very good today, she reminded herself.

As Kellie had driven to her meeting with her ex-husband, she couldn't still the nagging suspicion that she hadn't been quite fair with Dan. Again. He was right—she hadn't read the entire memo. Maybe she had missed something.

And hadn't she missed something he'd said about the FAA? Good news, for a change? Good news that she might, just might, have been too pigheaded to listen to?

Meeting Brian's eyes with her most unyielding glare, Kellie forced her problems with Dan onto a back burner. Brian had to be dealt with and, right now, the whole situation felt almost surreal. Heather poured coffee from a graceful china pot in a vain attempt to pretend they were gathered for a sane, civil discussion. The living room was spotless, as picture perfect as a furniture-store display room. Soft music from an easy-listening station incongruously set the mood.

The setting was middle-class suburbia, but the script called for guerrilla warfare. And Kellie had begun to fear that she hadn't come armed with enough ammunition.

"Before you get started, Kellie, I think you ought to know that I've thought this through very carefully," Brian said, casually stirring a packet of artificial sweetener into his coffee to demonstrate how in control he was.

Kellie had seen the tactic too many times not to know what he was up to. She thought, fleetingly, how nice it was to deal with Dan, for whom every action wasn't part of a carefully calculated plan.

At least she'd thought so, until this afternoon.

Brian looked up and smiled, his eyes devoid of animosity or concern. "I don't think—and Bernie doesn't either—that we'll have much trouble in court. Bernie's my attorney. And he said your dangerous job and your lack of a stable home life won't look good to a judge."

Kellie counted to ten, amazed that Brian seemed less concerned with how a custody fight would affect Carrie than anyone else she had talked to about it. Heather had mentioned the effect on Carrie the first time she brought up Brian's intentions. Even Dan had zeroed in on that as the main issue.

Forget Dan, she told herself, although it was hard to do so when she remembered that it was Dan's support that had given her the strength to fight back.

"You've thought this through carefully?" Kellie asked, matching Brian's measured calm with a coolness that was at odds with her emotional turmoil. "Have you thought about how it will affect Carrie?"

"Well, of course I have." His coffee cup stopped on its way to his lips. "She'll be much better off with us."

Kellie had never noticed before how carefully he avoided looking her straight in the eye. *Not like Dan,* she thought. "Why?"

Brian stared at her, openmouthed, as if such a question had never occurred to him. "What do you mean, why? She just will, that's all."

"If you've thought this through, I'm sure you have some very good reasons," Kellie prodded, all the while never moving from her relaxed posture in the low-slung modern chair. "What factors, what advantages, can you bring to Carrie's life that will offset the disruptive effects of a custody battle?"

For the first time in her life, Kellie saw Brian grow disconcerted. He shifted uncomfortably and looked to Heather for support. His new wife smiled blandly—a carbon copy of Brian's innocuous smile—and sipped at her coffee. Kellie had to work hard to squelch the smile that was rising on her lips. It was working! For once in her life, she was keeping her temper under control. And it was working!

If only I had known that earlier today, she thought. *I might have listened to what Dan was trying to tell me.* She cringed inside, growing more certain that once again she had jumped to a conclusion and treated Dan unfairly.

"This won't be disruptive for Carrie," Brian said, his cup clattering to rest in his saucer. "This is between you and me. It doesn't . . . that is, in the long run it'll be better for her."

"I'm still waiting for you to tell me how."

"Because . . . because she'll have a full-time mother." Kellie noticed the belligerence creeping into his tone.

"She has a full-time mother now, Brian. And a full-time father. And the added benefit of a full-time stepmother." Kellie smiled at Heather, who hid a grin behind her coffee cup. "I'd be interested to know why you think she would be better off being separated from her birth mother except for two weekends a month. I never thought it would be good for her to keep her away from her father. I always thought she needed both her parents. The child counselor we met with during the divorce agreed. That's why we came to this shared custody agreement."

The words were delivered in the same tone of voice Brian had used on her too many times.

Brian's usual self-assurance was disintegrating slowly, but he sat up straighter on the couch and leaned forward intently. "But your job is dangerous."

"I'm glad you brought that up." She smiled again. The calm she faked moments ago was now genuinely taking control of her nerves. She wished Dan was here to see her; he would be proud. And astonished. "I recently put together a safety report for the FAA and the statistics are simply fascinating. Do you know how many people are killed every year in Birmingham driving to and from work in rush-hour traffic?"

She waited calmly for the answer she knew wouldn't be forthcoming.

"Dammit, Kellie, you're being ridiculous," he snapped, lines of tension showing around the rigid set of his mouth.

"Don't worry. Most people don't know." Kellie's voice was soothing. She couldn't believe how calm she felt. "But if I were you, I wouldn't count on using that argument in court. You'll just look foolish."

"If you've come here to change my mind about this, you might as well leave now." His voice wasn't nearly as convincing as the words.

As he started in on another dissertation about his attorney's confidence in their case against her, Kellie couldn't help but compare Brian with Dan. How she had ever decided they were alike, she couldn't imagine. Brian tried to get his way through intimidation; Dan tried logic and persuasion. Brian pouted when he didn't get his way, lapsing into the whining complaints of a little boy; Dan backed down with a smile. Brian's tactics had always been sneaky and underhanded; Dan, she suddenly realized, had never done anything even remotely sneaky or underhanded. Until today. And if she had been willing to listen, she might have heard a logical explanation for the memo she saw on his desk.

Come to think of it, Dan had never even questioned finding her at his desk reading his private correspondence. Unlike her, he refused to jump to conclusions. He refused to lose his head. And he had refused to give up on her.

That, she realized, might have changed. He had proposed and she had turned him down, angrily and with no explanation. He had offered his support and once again she had turned on him in anger.

If there was any backing down to do, Kellie decided, she would have to be the one doing it this time.

"I'm not leaving," she said as Brian finished the speech he and his attorney had no doubt carefully scripted, "until you understand that what you are doing will hurt our daughter."

"Now wait a—"

"No, you wait a minute." She stopped him cold, her calm smile now turned to calm determination. "You may be so selfish you don't realize how something like this will affect Carrie, but I'm not. Any authority you check will tell you that one of the worst traumas a child can go through is a custody fight. I won't put our daughter through that, and I don't intend to let you, either. You're going to drop this custody suit idea. Now."

"But—"

"And if you don't, I'll bring in the best authorities I can find in this country to testify to the damage you've perpetrated against your own daughter. At the least, you'll look petty and foolish. At the worst, you'll look like someone who has no business making any kind of judgments about raising a child."

"That's ridic—"

"And when they've given me full-time, permanent custody, I'll stick you for so much child support you'll be eating pork and beans every night."

Kellie felt like Humphrey Bogart giving an ultimatum to Peter Lorre. And it was fun watching Brian squirm.

"I can't believe..." He turned in confusion to Heather, not knowing how to handle a Kellie he had never seen before. "Heather, don't you think... I mean, we've thought this through carefully. It's the right thing to do, isn't it?"

Heather reached out to place a gentle hand on his arm. "Actually I think Kellie may be right. Right now, Carrie feels safe and sure of both parents. This would confuse her and scare her, it seems to me."

Brian's brow wrinkled in dismay. "But don't you want my little girl?"

"Of course I do," Heather assured him in the comforting tone one would use with a child on the verge of hysteria. "But I think we stand a good chance of losing her love if we try to keep her away from her mother, Brian. You don't want to risk losing her love, do you?"

Brian threw up his hands and jumped up from the couch. "I don't believe this! All I want is my little girl."

He stared from one woman to the other, as if challenging them to deny the unselfishness of his motives.

"And all I want," Kellie said, "is what is best for my little girl."

For the moment, Brian stood speechless, stumped by her statement. Then he plunged in. "Then give her the stability of a home with a mother and a father," Brian countered.

Kellie looked at him and back at Heather, who was sitting tensely on the edge of the couch. Although Brian's mouth fell open at his ex-wife's next words, no one was more surprised than Kellie.

"I think you're absolutely right, Brian. You'll be glad to know that I'm planning to be married soon. In fact, I'm going to propose as soon as I leave here."

KELLIE SAT in the car, afraid to move. She watched Dan smashing tennis balls against the practice wall with unrestrained force under the lights that kept the evening darkness at bay. Each ball that flew back at him seemed to increase the anger and frustration he directed into every swing.

Although she had left Brian's house buoyed by her ex-husband's shocked reaction to her announcement and his resigned capitulation on the custody suit, seeing Dan like this had her rooted to the car seat.

Her brash statement that she planned to marry had seemed to come out of nowhere. But as she drove to Dan's condo, smiling and excited, Kellie realized the thought had been in the back of her mind all day. Her high-handed refusal to discuss Dan's proposal had been so unfair and so unkind that it would be asking too much to expect him to propose again. If marriage was to come up again, it would have to be her doing.

And she definitely wanted marriage to come up again. Being forced into a close-up comparison of Dan and Brian had also forced her to acknowledge that the two men were nothing alike. Her own insecurities about men had trapped her into that dumb notion, she decided. In fact, no two men could be more different.

But the rest is up to you. And if you can stampede Brian Adams, you can certainly stand up to Dan Brennan.

But as she killed the engine and got out of the car, she wasn't so sure. She walked toward the tennis courts slowly, her apprehension growing with each step. What in the world would she say? How could she possibly expect civil treatment after the way she had treated him? What if he told her to take a hike? Never to darken his door again?

Kellie almost smiled, trying but unable to imagine Dan acting as explosive and unreasonable as she so often acted.

When she walked onto the court, he glanced in her direction. Recognizing her, he let the returning ball whiz past him. Sweat dripped off his forehead, in spite of the evening chill. His damp T-shirt clung to his chest, molding itself to the powerful muscles, which heaved now with his ragged breathing. Every muscle in his body seemed poised, quivering on the edge of action.

Kellie's mouth went dry. She wanted to press herself against his hard slickness, to feel the tautness of his just-worked sinews. She wanted to capture his salty taste with her lips....

She couldn't read his face. Was that a twitch at one side of his mustache, the beginning of a smile he wasn't yet willing to release? In the shadows at the corner of the court, she couldn't tell. But it was her serve and, smile or no, she had to take the first swing.

"I was wrong, wasn't I?"

He looked at her, unmoving. Was that it? The elusive smile? No, perhaps not. He walked over to the towel he had tossed to the edge of the practice court, blotted the perspiration from his face, draped the towel around his neck and came to stand in front of her.

"Who told you?"

Kellie's heart pounded as furiously as if she had been the one madly chasing tennis balls. If it had been a smile, it had probably only been in anticipation of telling her off. "Nobody. I just figured it out."

He pulled the edge of the towel up to stop the perspiration that still rolled off his forehead, then crossed his arms in front of his chest. "What did you figure out?"

Did he sound angry? She couldn't tell. Trying vainly to dampen her lips with her cottony tongue, she looked into his eyes and pleaded for compassion. "That you're not a sneak. That you wouldn't do that to anyone, much less me." She paused and took a deep breath. Her mouth was so dry her words were sticking in her throat. "That I love you."

"You love me and I'm not a sneak." The grin almost broke out for sure that time. She was positive of it. "How romantic."

She reached out, hesitantly, and touched his forearm with the tip of her finger. It was rigid with his exertion, the blond hairs curled in tight, damp ringlets. He didn't pull away from her touch, and she started to breathe a little easier.

"I thought it was." She tried a little smile.

"Do you want to know the whole story?"

She shook her head. "Not now. It doesn't matter. You can tell me later, if you want to. Right now... right now, I have to tell you one more thing I figured out."

"What's that?"

"I want you to marry me." When he didn't say anything right away, or change expressions, Kellie almost panicked. *What now?* she wondered. *Is this where you*

*pop the ring out? Get down on your knees? Declare un-
dying devotion? Or pick up what's left of your pride and
slink away?* "I . . . I wondered if you'd still consider mar-
rying me."

In one swift move, Dan pulled the towel from around
his neck with both hands and, swinging it over her head,
used it to pull her close to him. This close, there was no
denying the hint of the half smile curling the edge of his
mustache. This close, there was no misunderstanding the
soft light in his brown eyes as he drank her in. This close,
there was no mistaking the melting warmth surging
through her as she pressed her softness against his hardness.

"Does this mean you'll never jump to conclusions
again?" he asked, feigning gruffness as his face inched
closer and closer to hers.

"I doubt it," she admitted softly.

"Does this mean you'll always be even tempered and
understanding?" His lips were close, his breath warm and
sweet against her face.

"I doubt that, too."

His half grin deepened, chiseling the dimple deeply into
his cheek.

"Good. I like a volatile woman."

His lips closing over hers stopped the laughter bubbling up from inside her as she knew with certainty, once
and for all, that she and Dan could handle whatever turbulence their life together might bring. In his arms were
all the safe landings she could ever want or need.

Harlequin Superromance®

COMING NEXT MONTH

Have You Ever Wondered If You Could Write A Harlequin Novel?

Here's great news—Harlequin is offering a series of cassette tapes to help you do just that. Written by Harlequin editors, these tapes give practical advice on how to make your characters—and your story—come alive. There's a tape for each contemporary romance series Harlequin publishes.

Mail order only

All sales final

Harlequin Presents...

CAROLE MORTIMER

Award of Excellence

elusive as the unicorn

*When Eve Eden discovered that Adam
Gardener, successful art entrepreneur, was
searching for the legendary English artist, The
Unicorn, she nervously shied away. The Unicorn's
true identity hit too close to home....*

*Besides, Eve was rattled by Adam's
mesmerizing presence, especially in the light
of the ridiculous coincidence of their names—
and his determination to take advantage of it!
But Eve was already engaged to marry her
longtime friend, Paul.*

*Yet Eve found herself troubled by the different
choices Adam and Paul presented. If only the
answer to her dilemma didn't keep eluding her....*

HP1258-1

HARLEQUIN
American Romance®

Live the

Rocky Mountain Magic

Become a part of the magical events at The Stanley Hotel
in the Colorado Rockies, and be sure to catch its final act
in April 1990 with #337 RETURN TO SUMMER by Emma
Merritt.

Three women friends touched by magic find love in a
very special way, the way of enchantment. Hayley Austin
was gifted with a magic apple that gave her three wishes
in BEST WISHES (#329). Nicki Chandler was visited by
psychic visions in SIGHT UNSEEN (#333). Now travel into
the past with Kate Douglas as she meets her soul mate in
RETURN TO SUMMER #337.

ROCKY MOUNTAIN MAGIC—All it takes is an open heart.